CHALLENGERS
OF THE REALM

WHEN GREATNESS CALLS

For My Children:

May you find the courage to answer when greatness calls your name. May you discover that true strength comes not from standing alone, but from the bonds you forge with those who believe in you. And may you always remember the light within you shines brightest when shared with others.

With all my love and faith in the heroes you're becoming,

Dad

CHALLENGERS
OF THE REALM

WHEN GREATNESS CALLS

HUNTER FOWLER

Challengers Of The Realm: When Greatness Calls by Hunter Fowler
Copyright © 2025 by Hunter Fowler
All Rights Reserved.
ISBN: 978-1-59755-844-0

Published by: ADVANTAGE BOOKS™
                     Orlando, FL, www.advbookstore.com

Library of Congress Catalog Number: 2025944019	
Name:	Fowler, Hunter., Author
Title:	*Challengers Of The Realm: When Greatness Calls*
	Hunter Fowler
	Advantage Books, 2025
Identifiers:	Paperback : 9781597558440
	eBook: 9781597558518
Subjects: Books ›	Fiction

Cover Art by: Ted Anthony

First Printing: September 2025
25 26 27 28 29 30   10 9 8 7 6 5 4 3 2 1

Prologue

In the ancient times,

Long before the pages of history were written, the people who would come to be known as the Ileydrians lived dispersed across the land. This existence, simple yet full of the raw beauty of life, was forever altered by a momentous encounter that would shape the destiny of their world.

It was the Ildini who first beheld The Everlight — a being of such power and majesty that his very presence defied comprehension. His power transcended the known laws of the universe, an essence imbued with a force that could shape the fabric of reality itself.

The Everlight, in his wisdom, offered the Ildini a pact of unprecedented generosity. In exchange for their pledge to serve as guardians of the land and to uphold the virtues of selflessness and humility. The Everlight would grant them the knowledge and power to thrive beyond the constraints of their former existence. Embracing this covenant, the Ildini were elevated from their tribal origins to become the stewards of a new era.

The Kingdom of Ileydria was founded, a realm where the Ildini, transformed by their pact, rose to prominence. They became the architects of a society that celebrates the arts, fostered a culture of wisdom, and sought to embody the principles bestowed upon them by The Everlight. The kingdom flourished, and the Ildini enjoyed blessings that were once beyond imagination — gifts of intellect, physical prowess, and lifespans that spanned centuries, barring the misfortunes of war or disease.

Central to the prosperity of Ileydria was the discovery of Incada, a luminescent stone seeded by The Everlight across the realm. This miraculous mineral, glowing with an ethereal, bluish light, became the cornerstone of Ileydrian advancement. When mined and refined every seven years under the guidance of The Everlight, Incada revealed its true potential — enhancing the natural abilities of those wielding it, imbuing objects with extraordinary properties, transforming the environment itself.

The stewardship of Incada and the wisdom imparted by The Everlight gave rise to four distinct guilds, each integral to the kingdom's fabric. These were The Envoys, soldiers, fighters, and athletes whose bravery protected the realm. As well, The Originators, innovators, inventors, and entrepreneurs who pushed the boundaries of technology, marketplace, and craftsmanship. Also, The Weavers, artists and storytellers who captured the essence of the world and inspired all who surround them. And The Bringers, scholars, strategists, and mystics who seek to understand the mysteries and partner with The Everlight to see the fullness of his plans.

However, the golden age of Ileydria was not to last. Ambition and jealousy took root in the heart of Lord Belaran, one of the Ildini, who believed himself more deserving of leadership than the first king. Betraying the ideals of The Everlight, he raised an army, The Obsidian Shade, and plunged the kingdom into darkness. His rule, marked by greed and the relentless exploitation of Incada, led to the creation of Incadise, a corrupted form of the stone that brought power at a terrible cost. With an ominous yellow glow, extended exposure to this substance results in the loss of one's sanity.

Cloaked in the shadows of his once-glorious capital, the dethroned king found solace in the unlikeliest of places — a humble bladesmith's forge. It was there, amidst the sparks of the anvil and the warmth of the hearth, that he fell deeply in love with the bladesmith's daughter, a woman of unmatched spirit and grace. Their love, a beacon in the darkness of his exile, was a secret shared between heartbeats, hidden from the prying eyes of the city that had forsaken its king. They eloped, their union sealed in the quietude of the night, absent the father's blessing. This clandestine marriage, however, was not to remain unchallenged. There was a confrontation borne of the bladesmith's fury and the king's desperate plea for understanding culminated in tragedy. The king, in a twist of fate, was accidentally struck down, leaving behind an unfulfilled love and a legacy in jeopardy. In an act of desperation, the bladesmith quickly swept the whole tragedy under the rug, and forced his daughter to give her newborn son, the rightful heir, up for adoption.

The news of the king's demise, veiled in whispers and shadows, reached the ears of two factions, each bound by a singular obsession. That was to find the heir who would unlock the power of The Everlight's greatest gift, the Sentinel. The Servants of The Everlight, true to their vow, had already wrestled the chest containing the mystical armor from the clutches of the Obsidian Shade. Yet, the key to unleashing its power was not a simple lock, but the blood of the king's lineage. Meanwhile, Lord Belaran, ever cunning and ruthless, sought the heir for his own ends, dreaming of dominion unchallenged by the light.

In the underbelly of a kingdom now shadowed by tyranny, Duriel, the orphaned heir, grew amidst hardship and neglect, his royal blood a secret veiled by the mundane. The boys' home, a place of desolation and despair, became the crucible in which his resolve was forged. Unbeknownst to him, the blood of the king coursed through his veins, a latent promise of redemption for Ileydria. His days were marked by struggle, each moment a lesson in survival, as he navigated the treacherous waters of a society that had forgotten the meaning of justice.

Fate, however, is a tapestry woven with threads of both chance and destiny. It was through a series of serendipitous encounters that Duriel's path crossed with the Servants of The Everlight. Recognizing the mark of the king on a pendant hanging from his neck, they unveiled the truth of his birthright. United by purpose and driven by the will to restore the light to Ileydria, they devised a plan. The ensuing struggle was fraught with peril, a testament to the resilience of those who dared to challenge the darkness.

The culmination of their endeavors saw the downfall of Lord Belaran, the near extermination of the Obsidian Shade, and the reclamation of the throne by Duriel, the rightful heir. His coronation was not merely a ceremony of ascension but a renewal of the covenant between what was left of the Ildini and The Everlight. Under his rule, Ileydria was reborn, a kingdom revitalized by the strength of its people and the wisdom of its king. Once more, the halls of the palace echoed with the promise of peace, and the land thrived under the guiding light of The Everlight, a beacon of hope for generations to come.

A millennium has passed since the crowning of Duriel, marking an era where the Kingdom of Ileydria flourished, its foundations strengthened by unity, creativity, and an enlightened bond with The Everlight. At this point, new technologies are being developed daily, and the overlapping of the traditions of old and the innovations of the new consume conversation for the average Ileydrian. But, for all the advancements, The Everlight's power is still beyond compare, and even the modern advancements are mostly due to new ways of using the power of Incada.

Now, the mantle of leadership rests upon King Ryune, Duriel's grandson, who began his rule at the age of 50, and now serves in his 170th year as

King. The lineage of the King, and several of his advisors are the last living Ildini. Ryune's reign is characterized by a profound connection to his people, and the ancestral wisdom of The Everlight. Early in his kingship, Ryune embarked on a years-long pilgrimage across the breadth of Ileydria. Disguised among his subjects, he sought to understand their lives, aspirations, and the fabric of the society over which he ruled. This journey unveiled a troubling insight: amidst the splendor and progress, Ileydria had grown complacent, its people distant from the challenges and trials that had once honed their spirit and resolve.

Disturbed by this revelation, Ryune pondered deeply on the tales of old, particularly those of the Sentinel — a legendary armor bestowed by The Everlight, which had safeguarded the realm through generations. Reflecting on his grandfather Duriel's teachings, Ryune sought counsel with The Everlight, yearning for a path that would reawaken the kingdom's vigor without leaning on the crutch of concentrated power.

In a profound encounter, The Everlight heeded Ryune's earnest plea, imparting a vision of unity and shared responsibility. His instructions were clear, Ryune was to bring the Sentinel before the Originators. With a drop of his own blood, and the work of their hands, The Sentinel was dismantled into 400 shards, each infused with a fragment of its original power. These shards were then researched and placed into weapons, armor, and trinkets as their uses became clear. Sentinel Shard items were then distributed among the most deserving members of the four guilds, who swore above all else their loyalty to The Everlight's will.

The dispersal of the Sentinel's power served as a catalyst for Ryune's next endeavor. He convened the leaders of the guilds. Together, they forged a strategy that would see the guilds collaborate and challenge one another. This initiative aimed to uncover latent strengths, expose weaknesses, foster innovation, and fortify the kingdom against complacency, ensuring that Ileydria would continue to thrive, not just in wealth and knowledge, but in spirit and resilience.

From this crucible of leadership and vision, Ryune instituted Challengers of The Realm, a celebration of unity, strength, and the pursuit of excellence. This event, transcending mere competition, became an annual holiday, a time when the entire kingdom pauses to engage in festivities that test their mettle, showcase their talents, and honor the legacy of The Everlight. It is more than a tournament; it is a declaration that the heart of Ileydria beats strong.

1

The Call of The Guilds

The sun crept over the horizon, bathing the stone towers of Ileydria in hues of pale gold and lavender. Morning mist curled around the grand guild hall, where the echo of footsteps mingled with the low hum of conversation. Recruits streamed through the massive archways like a flood, clad in the crisp gray uniforms marked with vibrant green accents — symbols of both growth and untested potential.

The air felt electrified with excitement. The ancient corridors, adorned with banners of the four guilds, seemed to hum with history as the new class pressed forward. Some whispered words of encouragement to each other. Others moved in silence; their focus narrowed on the challenge ahead.

Liam Valoria stood among them, his stride steady, purposeful. The crest of his lineage, stitched in silver thread across his cloak, caught the morning light. His keen amber eyes scanned the hall, not with curiosity, but with a quiet certainty — as if he already belonged here.

The burnished leather of his boots scraped against the stone as he moved, broad shoulders square beneath his tunic. He adjusted the sword at his hip, fingers flexing instinctively against the hilt.

Another step closer to proving himself. Another step toward becoming more than just a name.

A familiar voice broke through the crowd.

"Trying not to break anything before we've even started, Liam?"

Nysara Thandor emerged from the throng, a half-smirk playing on her lips. Auburn hair, wild but expertly tied back, caught the sunlight like a flame. A complex gadget — no doubt one of her own creations — rested on her wrist, glowing faintly with an Incada charge.

Liam mirrored her grin. "I thought you were too busy tinkering with toys to show up on time."

Nysara rolled her eyes. "Gadgets. Not toys." She tapped the device on her wrist. "I finished this last night. It's a stabilized pulse regulator, if you must know. Might come in handy when someone decides to stop relying on brute force."

"Brute force works just fine," Liam shot back, though his smirk faded slightly. "So long as you know how to use it."

Nysara was about to respond when a third voice joined them — quieter, softer, but no less striking.

"I'm fairly certain brute force and clever engineering are both going to be less useful than staying calm and not embarrassing ourselves."

Alarion Cyrus stepped closer, dark hair loose around his face, a finely crafted violin strapped across his back. His long fingers traced a thoughtful rhythm against his side, as if playing invisible notes.

"I can't believe I'm saying this," Nysara said, brow raised, "but Alarion makes a decent point."

Liam snorted. "You both sound nervous."

"I am nervous," Alarion replied, tone low. "It's not every day you join a guild where you either rise — or get left behind."

Before Liam could counter, a fourth figure approached. Celeste Osman moved with the practiced grace of someone who never wasted energy. Her posture was perfect, her uniform pristine. Everything from her polished boots to the gleaming Incada pendant at her collar exuded precision and control.

"If you're quite done trading quips," she said, voice calm but cool, "you might want to focus. We're here to become champions, not entertain each other."

Liam bristled, his jaw tightening. "You act like we're already in the middle of a war."

Celeste's brown eyes narrowed. "We're always preparing for one."

The tension stretched, unspoken words filling the space between them, until Nysara broke the silence with a forced cough. "Okay. So...maybe we focus on not getting kicked out on day one?"

A hush rippled across the hall as the massive iron bells above the central tower began to toll. The sound echoed through the guild hall, carrying weight and history with every strike. Conversations ceased. Recruits turned as one, eyes drawn toward the raised platform where the four guild leaders stood in formal array.

At the forefront stood General Alexander, his yellow Envoy cloak draped over armor polished to look brand-new. He radiated authority, his tone measured as he began to speak.

"Recruits of Ileydria. Today marks the beginning of your trial. Not merely to test skill, but to forge your hearts and minds. The guilds do not merely accept. They shape. They demand."

His eyes swept the hall, resting on no one yet commanding the attention of all.

"To those who seek the Envoys," he continued, voice unwavering, "you must embody courage. Discipline. We are not a shield, but a force. You will stand where others falter."

Beside him, Bella of the Originators stepped forward, her blue uniform embroidered with silver circuitry patterns. Her piercing eyes sparkled with a different kind of fire — curiosity and intellect.

"To the innovators, the builders — those who dare to create," Bella said. "You will learn that true progress demands more than ideas. It demands mastery. It demands failure. And rising again."

Ava of the Weavers, dressed in deep crimson, a household name across the entire Kingdom, lifted her voice next. Her words flowed with warmth yet held undeniable gravity.

"We, the Weavers, are storytellers, artists, and visionaries. But make no mistake — art is power. To inspire. To heal. To shape the heart of this kingdom."

Finally, Arch-Bringer Roland stepped forward, stoic and mysterious as a cloak of white and gold billowed behind him.

"And to those who would call themselves Bringers," his tone was quieter but no less powerful, "your strength will not be measured in battle, but in wisdom. It is easy to break an enemy. Harder still to keep the peace."

The hall remained silent as Roland's gaze lingered, not at the crowd but beyond them — as if seeing something deeper. Something farther.

"Remember this," Alexander added. "The Challengers of the Realm Tournament is not just tradition. It is our legacy. A testament to our unity, our resilience — and our promise never to repeat the darkness of our past."

Liam felt a knot tighten in his chest. Not fear — but something heavier. The weight of history pressing on his shoulders.

The silence broke with a thunderous cheer as the ceremony concluded. The recruits were dismissed to the assessment chambers, the first test of the day already looming.

As the crowd shifted, Liam caught Nysara's eye.

"No pressure, right?" he said with a half-smile.

Nysara smirked. "Sure. Just centuries of tradition watching your every move."

Alarion sighed. "At least we're in this together."

Celeste, already moving toward the next hall, called back over her shoulder.

"If you can keep up."

The crowd had barely begun to disperse from the grand hall when guild leaders gathered near the base of the stage, the echoes of Alexander's speech still hanging like a cloud in the vast space. The last of the recruits filtered out, a blend of excitement and tension as they made their way toward the assessment grounds.

Alexander, arms crossed over his broad chest, watched the departing throng with the quiet intensity of a soldier accustomed to measuring the weight of a moment. "You can see it already," he said, voice low but commanding. "Most of them believe this will be a test they can pass with skill alone. They think they know who they are."

Roland nodded, his intense, calculating glance following the recruits as well. "Because, for most, they've been told who they are their entire lives. Family expectations. Guild legacies. It's not their fault. They've been prepared for this path since they were children."

"They're not wrong to be confident," Ava added softly, adjusting the cuffs of her embroidered sleeves. "The way most are trained — by the time they reach this point, most are well suited to their chosen guild. They already show talent in the arts we require."

Bella gave a wry smile, her arms folded as she leaned back against a stone pillar. "Talent's only the starting line. Comfort is a liability." She tilted her head toward the doors where the last of the recruits had vanished. "They need to understand their confidence doesn't mean they're ready. We're not testing skills today. We're testing how they react when it fails them."

Ava arched her brow. "And we wonder why half of them leave the assessments believing they've been rejected."

Alexander's expression hardened. "Because they assume it's a pass or fail. But they're wrong. This is the first lesson, whether they realize it or not. How do they handle being pushed past their limits? Do they retreat? Lash out? Adapt? It tells us more about their character than any demonstration of skill ever could."

Roland's expression turned thoughtful, tone quieter but no less firm. "We push them to the breaking point because the world will do far worse. The question is never 'Are you ready?' It's 'Who are you when you're not?' That is what we need to see."

Bella nodded, her grin sharpening. "Exactly. When the devices fail. When the expression falters. When the blade isn't enough. That's where the real training starts."

Ava glanced toward the balcony where the banners of each guild hung, swaying gently in the high-arch space. "And yet, most of them will still end up where they expect. We're not here to uproot destinies today. Just to test if they're prepared to live up to them."

Roland countered, "Most… but not all."

Alexander gave a curt nod. "No. Not all." His voice dropped lower, steel lacing the words. "Every guild needs more than specialists. It needs leaders. The kind who can fail and rise anyway."

Ava grinned, ever cheerful. "Let's hope they're ready for the fall, then."

"Hope?" Bella smirked as she pushed off the pillar. "No. Let's see how they fight their way through it."

With that, the leaders turned, each making their way toward the observation chambers where the tests were already beginning, each tailored to expose far more than technical skill.

The assessment grounds stretched beyond the main hall, divided into four sprawling chambers, each tailored to the philosophy of its guild. The Envoy chamber was a brutal test of endurance and combat instincts — measured not just by strength, but by how long one could hold their ground under mounting pressure. The Bringer chamber, by contrast, was a test of perception and problem-solving, where recruits were confronted with puzzles and tactical scenarios meant to disorient and confuse. For the Weavers, the trial was a performance under scrutiny, requiring emotional resonance and creative control through their craft. The Originators' domain was filled with shifting mechanical challenges, devices intentionally rigged to malfunction, testing how recruits adapted when their tools betrayed them. Each trial was designed to push recruits beyond their skill — forcing them to confront failure, not as a test of defeat, but as a measure of resilience.

The trials hit harder than Liam had expected.

His skill, sharpened through years of training, had been undeniable — but it hadn't been enough. The obstacles weren't just physical. The examiners had pressed him in ways he hadn't prepared for, exploiting his need to push forward, his refusal to slow down. For every opponent he outmatched, another had drawn out the fight, stretching him past his endurance. He'd felt the burn in his muscles, the strain of every breath. And then he slipped. A single misstep, his foot sliding out from under him.

He could still hear the judge's calm words: "You rely too much on power without precision, Liam Valoria."

Now, leaning against one of the marble columns in a quiet alcove of the guild hall, he found himself replaying that moment again and again.

The ache in his limbs was nothing compared to the sting of doubt gnawing at his mind.

"What if I'm not as ready as I thought? What if I can't meet everyone's expectations?"

He exhaled slowly, eyes drifting to his friends.

Nysara sat on the stone bench nearby, arms crossed tightly, her gear strewn in front of her as if she'd been rechecking it for the hundredth time. She hadn't said much since the trials ended, her usual easy grin replaced by a furrowed brow.

Finally, she spoke...softer than usual. "It felt...different today. Like every choice mattered too much." Her fingers fiddled with the edge of her jacket as she stared at the ground. "The puzzles were brutal. Not hard, just...layered. I kept thinking, one mistake, and that's it. It felt like they were waiting for me to crack."

Liam nodded. "Yeah. Same." His voice was quieter than he meant it to be. "I kept pushing harder, thinking I'd wear them down, but it just — it wasn't enough. They knew how to break my rhythm. Had me doubting myself."

Alarion sat a little farther off, his violin resting across his lap, his fingers trailing absently over the strings. For a long moment, he said nothing. Then, without looking up, he murmured, "It wasn't just you."

Both Liam and Nysara glanced his way.

Alarion's voice remained quiet, but there was an uncharacteristic sharpness beneath it. "I was supposed to perform. Create. But the judges — they kept asking for more. More depth. More control. As if music could just be...calculated." His hands tightened on the violin. "The more they asked, the harder it was to play at all. Like I was trying to prove I deserved to be there instead of just being there."

Liam exchanged a look with Nysara.

It was strange — he'd always assumed Alarion had this effortless talent. But now? He sounded as shaken as the rest of them.

A shadow shifted near the doorway. Celeste had been standing there, arms folded, listening.

She stepped forward, calm tone but clipped. "I failed today."

Liam blinked. "What?"

Celeste's expression didn't change. "The strategy trial. I miscalculated a defensive maneuver — too rigid. The scenario adapted, and I didn't." She exhaled. "I kept thinking I had it under control, but the test didn't care how much I'd planned. It forced me to adjust, and I...hesitated. For too long."

Silence settled over them.

The weight of the trials pressed heavier now — shifting from individual failures to a collective truth.

They all had cracks.

Liam finally broke the silence. "You know...I thought we were supposed to prove ourselves today. Show them why we belonged."

Nysara shook her head, the spark slowly returning to her voice. "Maybe. Or maybe they wanted to see what we'd do when things didn't go our way."

Alarion's fingers brushed the strings again, softer now, a faint melody drifting into the air. "Or who we'd turn to when we couldn't fix it alone."

Celeste met his look, then gave a small, thoughtful nod.

For a moment, none of them spoke — they just sat in the quiet hum of the guild hall, each pondering the trails and what was to come.

Then, from the far end of the hall, General Alexander's voice rang out.

"Training begins at first light. Prepare yourselves."

The finality of it struck like the toll of a bell.

Liam watched the sun begin its descent beyond the high windows, painting the sky in streaks of amber and violet.

He wasn't sure if he felt ready.

But he knew he wasn't alone.

The next morning arrived with the pale blush of dawn creeping through the narrow windows of Nysara's quarters. She didn't sleep much.

Lying awake beneath the rough linens of the recruit's cot, her mind churned, replaying the trials over and over. The puzzles. The pressure. The mistakes she'd made.

"What if I'm not good enough?"

The thought hit harder than she wanted to admit.

With a quick breath, she pushed it aside, throwing back the blanket and rising. Today was another test. A different one. She had no intention of failing twice.

Her hands moved with practiced efficiency as she adjusted the straps of her gear, securing the modified gauntlet she'd recharged the night before. The hum of Incada energy flickered faintly beneath her touch, a quiet reassurance.

The mess hall buzzed with the steady clamor of early morning activity — clattering plates, the low rumble of conversation, the scent of freshly baked bread mingling with herbal teas. Recruits from every guild were spread across long wooden tables, some laughing, others poring over half-eaten meals with exhausted stares. The tension of the previous day's trials hadn't yet faded; it showed in the hunched shoulders and quiet exchanges, a reminder they were still being measured.

At a corner table near the arched window, Liam sat with his arms folded, a half-eaten plate of food pushed aside. His gaze drifted out over the crowd, though his mind seemed elsewhere. Across from him, Celeste methodically stirred her tea, her posture as straight as ever but her expression unusually thoughtful. Alarion, perched at the edge of his seat, tuned the strings of his violin absently, the soft hum of a note vibrating just beneath the noise of the room.

Nysara spotted them from the entrance and made her way over, balancing a tray with one hand and slinging her gear pack off her shoulder with the other.

"Morning," she greeted, sliding into the seat next to Liam with a teasing grin. "You all look chipper."

Alarion exhaled a quiet laugh. "Or we're just functioning on the illusion of rest. Half the Weavers' bunkhouse was up playing music past midnight." He strummed a few experimental chords. "Poetry readings, impromptu duets… it was inspiring. Exhausting. But inspiring."

Liam blinked, finally looking up. "Wait — so you voluntarily stayed up all-night? After that test?"

Alarion shrugged. "I was trying to sleep, but when someone pulls out an instrument at two in the morning, what choice do you have?"

Celeste finally spoke. "I didn't sleep much either."

The others turned toward her in mild surprise, and she hesitated before continuing, pressing her fingertips lightly to the rim of her cup. "I had...a dream. About The Everlight." She shook her head, as though trying to find the right words. "I was fighting. Every time I planned a move, I'd hear this voice — Not yours… Mine. Over and over. Every strategy I relied on, it shut down. It was frustrating. But —" her brow furrowed in thought "— I think...He was trying to teach me something. To challenge how I see control. I'm not sure I've figured it out yet."

Silence settled briefly around the table. Liam tilted his head, a rare softness in his expression. "That's...intense."

Celeste nodded, her focus distant. "Yes. But not in a bad way. I think I needed it."

Nysara, who'd been quietly nibbling a slice of bread, set it down. "Well, I'm jealous. You had deep revelations, and Alarion got a concert. I just stared at the ceiling for three hours thinking about how close I was to messing up that puzzle." She ran a hand through her hair, tone dropping. "I kept second-guessing myself...like every move I made was another chance to fail."

Alarion gave her a gentle nudge with his elbow. "But you didn't. And it's not like the test was meant to be easy."

Liam snorted, finally shaking off his brooding silence. "You're all overthinking it. Me? I hit the pillow and was out like a light. Woke up, good as new." He stretched with exaggerated confidence, then added under his breath, "Though I'm pretty sure my legs are still recovering."

Celeste arched her brow. "So, you were too tired to worry?"

"Exactly," Liam replied, grinning. "You should try it sometime."

Their laughter rippled softly through the tension, a much-needed break from the weight that had followed them since the assessment. For the first time since arriving, the shared strain of the trials felt like something they could face together rather than bear alone.

Nysara leaned back, her arms crossed. "So...does anyone know what we're actually doing today? Or is this another find out the hard way situation?"

Liam gestured toward the bulletin board near the door, where a fresh poster hung. "General studies. Group session. Whole cohort. And guess who's teaching it?"

Alarion followed his glance, squinting to read the finely scripted name at the bottom of the announcement. His face paled slightly. "Captain Sunniva?"

Celeste's expression shifted instantly — shoulders squaring, lips pressing into a thin line. "I've read about her. Battle tactician. Heads up core recruit training for all the guilds at this point."

Liam grinned. "Yeah, and they say she's brutal. Breaks her recruits down so hard they can barely stand by the end of the week." He paused, eyes narrowing playfully toward Alarion. "Think you'll survive that one, music boy?"

Alarion sighed, tucking his violin away. "Let's just say I hope she isn't the type who confiscates instruments."

Nysara cracked a grin but looked back at Celeste, who hadn't joined the teasing. "Hey! You, okay?"

Celeste blinked, then nodded, though her expression remained guarded. "I'm fine. Just...thinking."

Liam leaned forward, with a voice covered in sarcasm. "Oh, the great Celeste is worried, huh?"

"Not worried," she corrected, her manner calm but firm. "Prepared. Sunniva doesn't tolerate mistakes. She tests strategy and adaptability, not just technical skill. If we get through this first class with our dignity intact, I'll consider it a win."

Liam's smirk returned. "Good thing we're fast learners, right?"

Alarion nodded, rising from his seat and strapping his violin case to his back. "Well, no use stalling. Let's go see if Sunniva lives up to her reputation."

Liam gave one last dramatic stretch before standing. "Bet you five she tries to make us run drills before breakfast tomorrow."

Nysara smirked. "I'll take that bet. Double if it's during breakfast."

They left the mess hall together, the nervous energy still there but now the excitement for what was soon to come to the front of their minds.

2

Legacy and Valor

The sun barely crested the stone walls of the guild complex as Liam Valoria and his companions entered the grand lecture hall for their first session of general studies. Morning light filtered through tall, arched windows, painting streaks of pale gold across the polished floors. Rows of wooden desks filled the room, their surfaces worn smooth by generations of recruits who had passed through this very hall.

Liam dropped into a seat near the center of the room, leaning back just far enough to make the chair creak. His sword belt rested against the desk's edge, the silver-threaded crest of his family catching the light as he stretched his legs out beneath the table.

"Okay, real talk," he said, speech breaking the quiet hum of conversation as the rest of the class settled in. "Did anyone else get the feeling General Alexander could recite that speech blindfolded? I mean, I get it — 'honor, legacy, duty' — but it was like...the fifth time he's rehearsed it this week."

Alarion, already halfway tuned out while tightening the strings on the violin resting in his lap, smirked. "You think that was rehearsed? Ava's was worse. The whole 'art weaving the heart of the realm's thing? Pretty sure she's memorized her lines for life."

Nysara, seated on the other side of Liam, snorted. "Please. Bella's the real gem. Did you catch how she said 'exploration' six times? Half the Originators haven't seen sunlight since they learned to hold a wrench. 'Explore the inside of your toolbox' doesn't count." She shot Liam a sideways grin and jabbed him lightly with her elbow.

Liam chuckled, but before he could chime in, Celeste — sitting ramrod straight a few seats away — closed her notebook with a *snap*.

"This isn't a performance," she said coolly, her brown eyes narrowing. "The guild leaders have earned their authority through years of service. Their words weren't just speeches — they were lessons. Maybe you should actually *listen* instead of treating it like some tavern story."

Liam raised an eyebrow, lips curling into a half-smirk. "Yes, *Instructor Osman*. Should I take notes too? Maybe sketch the banners while I'm at it — oh, wait! Should I kneel before the lectern just to show proper respect?" His voice dripped with sarcasm as he leaned forward, wiggling his fingers as if preparing to take exaggerated notes.

Celeste's glare focused, her jaw tightening — but before she could retort, the door to the lecture hall swung open.

Captain Sunniva entered.

The shift in the room was instant.

Her presence hit like a blade drawn from its scabbard — cold, sharp, demanding attention. She moved with the measured precision of someone who expected discipline, her grey captain's cloak trimmed with gold cords, fastened perfectly at the shoulder. A streak of pale silver ran through her blonde braided hair, but her face was ageless, hard as if carved from stone.

Silence fell, broken only by the faint creak of leather as Sunniva folded her arms behind her back, surveying the room with the stillness of a predator.

Her eyes landed on Liam.

"Valoria."

Liam stiffened, fighting the sudden tension coiling in his chest.

"When I learned you were under my instruction," Sunniva continued, her words like frost on steel, "I expected better. Leadership isn't about bravado. It isn't about heritage. It is about respect — respect for the role you've been entrusted with and for those who paved the way before you."

Sunniva's words pressed down on Liam like a lead weight, heavier than the steel crest embroidered on his chest.

"Respect. Legacy. Bravado."

The words echoed, striking somewhere far deeper than the lecture hall.

In his mind, the stone walls of the hall blurred and shifted, replaced by the grandeur of the Valoria estate. Tall windows cast fractured light through stained glass, painting the polished marble floors with hues of crimson and gold. The air was thick with the scent of old parchment and oiled steel. Portraits lined the walls — paintings of ancestors in full Envoy regalia, their expressions stern, ever watchful.

And at the center of it all stood his father.

Lord Dorian Valoria was as commanding as the house he ruled. Broad-shouldered, with streaks of gray beginning to cut through his once jet-black hair, he seemed as immovable as the stone foundation beneath them. His speech was as measured as it was unyielding.

"You are a Valoria, Liam."

The words struck not like encouragement but a verdict.

"It is not merely a name," his father continued, pacing slowly in front of the hearth, the flames dancing behind him. "It is a standard — one you will carry whether you succeed or fail. Our bloodline does not stumble. We *lead*. Do you understand?"

Young Liam nodded stiffly, though his fingers tightened around the wooden practice sword in his hand. The weight felt awkward now, heavy not from its size but from the invisible expectations wrapped around it.

The morning had started with playful energy. He had been sparring with his older cousin earlier — less a lesson, more an excuse to turn training into a game. They'd dueled across the lawn, laughter echoing, the imaginary clash of heroes from the tales he loved in his mind.

But his father had been watching.

Always watching.

"Enough," Dorian snapped suddenly, and Liam startled, the practice blade slipping from his fingers to clatter against the marble floor.

"This is not a game!" His father's voice was sharp but not raised. It didn't need to be. "You train not for amusement but to bring *honor* to this house. Every strike…every step…every breath must be taken with the weight of those who came before you. A Valoria wields a blade with *purpose*, not…theatrics."

The words stung worse than any blow.

Liam clenched his fists with head bowed, wanting to explain — I *was trying. I just wanted to have fun while learning.* But the words never came.

Fun wasn't the point.

He knew that now.

But standing there beneath his father's unyielding authority, a single rebellious thought had sparked in his heart — one that had never quite left him.

If I can't win their respect by skill alone...then I'll make them see me another way.

I'll be unforgettable.

A sharp nudge to his side jolted Liam from the memory. Alarion.

Captain Sunniva's focus remained locked on him, her intense blue eyes expectant.

Had she asked him something?

Liam blinked, his pulse kicking up as he scrambled to piece together the last thing she'd said. His jaw tightened as heat rose to his face.

"I can handle this," he snapped, delivery harsher than intended as he shot a glare toward Alarion. The words hung heavier than he'd meant, the frustration from his own lapse bleeding into his tone.

Alarion raised his hands in surrender, lips parting as if to speak but deciding better of it.

Sunniva's brow lifted ever so slightly, but she didn't comment on the exchange. Instead, she addressed the room with the same cutting precision she had when she first entered.

"You're not here to impress me. You're here to prepare." Her eyes swept across the entire class, focusing on no one and yet making everyone feel as if she spoke directly to them.

"Half effort leads to half results. In this room, you are not just artists, inventors, soldiers, or strategists. You are recruits in the heart of Ileydria's legacy. The Challengers of the Realm will not care how gifted you were when you arrived — only how much you were willing to become."

The silence that followed was absolute.

Then, with a clipped nod, she dismissed them. "Training rotations begin this afternoon. Return to your guild halls and prepare. Dismissed."

The sound of chairs scraping echoed through the hall as the recruits gathered their things. Hushed conversations rippled through the space. Liam remained seated a beat longer, jaw still tight, hands flexing against the worn wood of the desk.

He could feel Sunniva's words lingering like the ache after a sparring match.

She's right.

And yet, her words stung more than they should have.

The walk from the lecture hall to the Envoy training grounds was quiet, deep reflection coating every measured step Liam took.

The guild complex mirrored the contradictions of Ileydria itself — rooted in history yet undeniably moving forward.

Towering stone archways and weathered statues lined the corridors, their craftsmanship ancient but maintained with care. Streaks of pale blue light pulsed softly from fixtures set into the walls — lanterns powered not by flame but by slivers of processed Incada encased in crystalline cells. The light pulsed in slow, steady rhythms, a quiet beat of energy sustaining the space.

Beyond the guild halls, the city unfolded in layers. Closer to the heart of the complex, the architecture remained much the same — ornate stone towers, sweeping staircases, and vaulted ceilings that had stood for centuries. Yet as Liam crossed one of the main courtyards, he caught sight of the newer districts rising in the distance.

Steel-framed structures climbed higher than the old towers, their glass-paneled walls reflecting the midmorning sun. Veins of Incada cells were embedded in the city's infrastructure — energy coils mounted discreetly beneath streetlamps, their pale blue glow visible even in daylight. Some of the newer buildings pulsed with that same light, infused panels laced with Incada channels that powered entire blocks with a single charge.

The streets beyond the guild grounds buzzed with life. Merchant stalls lined the walkways, some simple wooden carts, others equipped with Originator-crafted devices — mechanical scales and price displays powered by cells the size of a coin. The scent of fresh bread mingled with the tang of burning coal from a nearby forge, where a smith adjusted the charge on his hammer before bringing it down with a bright flash against glowing steel.

Liam's gaze lingered on the sight, caught somewhere between admiration and curiosity. The power of the Incada was no longer reserved for the elite wielders of sentinel weapons — it had become part of everyday life, a resource harnessed as much for innovation as it was for defense.

And yet, the deeper he walked into the heart of the Envoy grounds, the more the focus shifted.

Discipline. Strength. Legacy.

Those values still define the Envoy training halls.

Liam exhaled, rolling his shoulders as he approached the arched stone entrance. The past and the future seemed to press against each other here — but this was where he belonged.

Where he was *expected* to belong.

Yet for all the tension between tradition and progress, it never seemed to fracture the kingdom. As different as the guilds were, as varied as the tools and ideals they embraced, there was a unity that persisted — an invisible thread woven through it all.

The Everlight.

That had to be the answer.

Not as a force to be wielded, but as something *greater* — the source behind the power, the balance holding all of it together.

Liam's thoughts drifted back to a journey from his childhood — the only time he had left the capital. His father had called it a "lesson in perspective." To Liam, it had felt more like being paraded through the kingdom under the constant weight of expectation.

What had stayed with him, though, were the cities themselves.

Some were sprawling hubs of progress, where massive Originator forges filled entire districts with the rhythmic clang of hammers and the hiss of steam. Incada cells fueled everything — mechanical lifts, barrier gates, even the lamps lining the streets. In those places, the air seemed charged with restless energy, a constant hum of motion and invention.

Yet just beyond those industrial heartlands were towns that seemed untouched by time — quaint villages where stone bridges arched over narrow rivers and the people moved at a pace that felt...older. Craftsmen wove intricate tapestries by hand, and farmers still tilled the soil with tools that looked as though they belonged to another age entirely.

And binding it all together was The Everlight's influence.

Despite the shifting faces of progress, the kingdom's foundation had never fractured. The ancient sentinel shards, remnants of a time before the now common advancements in Incada technology, still shaped the heart of Ileydria. Objects from eras long past had been infused with modern Incada energy. There were shields capable of projecting translucent force barriers large enough to cover entire squads, cloaks woven with ethereal strands that shimmered like captured starlight, and blades, both ancient and reforged, that never dulled.

It was a kingdom suspended between ages.

A place where history and innovation refused to erase one another.

That same balance echoed in the space before him as he crossed the threshold into the Envoy training center.

The vast chamber unfolded in layers — sunlight filtering through towering arched windows, catching the banners of the guild hung high above. Rows of worn stone pillars flanked the perimeter, their carved edges bearing the marks of generations who had passed through these very halls.

The scent of steel and oiled leather clung to the air.

To Liam's left, a training array filled with weapons both old and new awaited the recruits. The swords were forged in a style centuries old. Their edges gleamed with a telltale blue sheen, each blade carefully reinforced with an Incada core — enough to withstand the demands of modern battle without drawing too deeply on its charge. Next to the racks of blades and shields, javelins and bows stood ready, their construction simple but deadly.

Further down the line, more contemporary equipment caught his eye. Firearms — sleek and unfamiliar — sat mounted at precision training stations, their magazines marked with small Incada cells pulsing faintly. While the Sentinel Shards still served as the pinnacle of individual combat, Liam knew not every Envoy would be granted the honor of wielding one. These modern weapons, though less extraordinary, were powerful in their own right.

The entire room buzzed with controlled intensity.

Groups of recruits were already engaged in drills — at one station, a formation of Envoy trainees practiced the seamless shift between shield defense and counterattack, the rhythmic clash of steel punctuating their movements. Elsewhere, pairs sparred with weighted staffs under the watchful eye of a senior instructor.

On the far side of the hall, a circle of trainees worked through disarming techniques, wooden training blades clashing as they exchanged fluid, precise strikes. The instructor, a grizzled veteran with greying hair, moved among them, offering quiet corrections with the ease of someone who had done this a thousand times before.

Liam took it all in — the mix of old and new, discipline and invention. Tradition sharpening the edge of progress.

And at the center of it all stood Commander Elise.

She waited near the sparring platforms, arms crossed, a pillar of unwavering authority. Sunlight caught the edges of her armor, its plated sections reinforced with Incada channels embedded along the seams. Her dreadlocks were pulled back tightly, and a longsword rested sheathed at her side — one of the Shards, though it pulsed with none of its fabled power now.

Even standing still, she radiated control.

Liam felt the weight of the training ahead settle fully now. The spectacle of the hall no longer mattered.

This wasn't a place for grandeur.

It was a forge.

And he was about to be tested.

"Today, we focus on the phalanx formation," Commander Elise's voice rang out, steady as the steel she wore. "This is not just a defensive maneuver. It is unity. It is discipline. The strength of this formation lies not in the shield you hold, but in the warrior beside you. Fail to uphold your part, and you do not fail alone — you endanger everyone in your line."

The room had fallen utterly silent.

Elise paced slowly along the front ranks, her keen eyes sweeping over the gathered recruits. Each step echoed with authority, her presence commanding but not unkind.

"The phalanx has protected Ileydria for generations because it is more than a tactic. It is a mindset. Anticipate your opponent. Adapt. Hold the line. And above all —" Her look intensified, locking briefly on Liam as she drew her longsword from its sheath, the polished steel catching the light.

"— protect each other."

She stepped back; the blade leveled at her side with effortless precision.

"Let's begin."

The recruits scrambled into position, shields locking together with a low, synchronized *clank*. The line of reinforced barriers formed a near-perfect wall, each interlocking edge designed to cover the weaknesses of the warrior next to them. Liam adjusted his grip, pressing his shoulder against the recruit beside him, the worn steel of his shield cool against his forearm.

A beat of silence.

Then Elise struck.

Her first blow collided with the formation like a thunderclap. The impact rippled through the line, shields shuddering under the force. Dust billowed up from the stone floor as her blade connected again — precise, relentless, yet restrained. Each strike felt heavier than the last, as if she were testing not only their defenses but their will to endure.

Liam gritted his teeth, absorbing the shock through his frame. His arm ached already, his stance faltering for half a breath before he realigned his weight.

Again.

And again.

The rhythmic clashes blurred together, the force of her attacks steadily increasing. Elise was holding back — Liam could tell — but even so, it felt like trying to stop the tide.

A sharp vibration traveled through the line as another recruit lost footing, his shield dipping just enough for a glancing blow to break through. The force sent the trainee staggering back, the line buckling slightly.

She's going to break us.

The thought struck hard. Sweat dripped down Liam's brow, his muscles burning from the strain.

And yet...she wasn't using the shard. Not really.

He had seen her blade — one of the Sentinel Shards, unmistakable — yet it remained inert, no pulse of Incada energy, no shimmering force rippling from its core. This was skill, not power.

And they were still struggling to hold her back.

If she's this strong without the shard activated..., what would it be like in a real battle?

A cry of pain snapped his attention back to the line. Another recruit faltered, a crack forming in the shield wall. Liam saw it — felt it — the exact moment the formation weakened further.

And then he saw the gap.

A flicker of an opening as Elise shifted her stance.

Now.

Driven by sheer instinct, Liam surged forward, breaking from the line. He felt the rush of adrenaline as he pivoted out of formation, raising his blade in a bold counter strike aimed at her exposed side.

His blade never landed.

Elise moved faster than he could track.

A quick twist of her body, the fluid grace of a warrior born from decades of mastery. Her sword swept beneath his guard, hooking his shield arm aside. In a single, fluid motion, she pivoted, knocked his legs from beneath him, and slammed him to the ground.

Liam hit the stone floor hard, the impact rattling his bones.

Before he could react, the point of Elise's sword hovered just above his chest. The silence that followed felt louder than the clash of steel moments earlier.

His heart pounded. The world narrowed to her standing above him.

Elise held the blade steadily, her voice calm but cutting.

"You broke formation."

Liam swallowed, his pride stinging almost as much as his ribs.

He braced himself for the reprimand he knew was coming.

Instead of the scolding Liam expected, Commander Elise lowered her blade and extended her hand.

"Valoria." Her words, though still commanding, softened slightly. "Your courage is noted. But courage alone is not enough. The battlefield demands more than boldness — it requires restraint and awareness. Wisdom to know when to strike and when to stand firm."

Liam hesitated before taking her hand, the ache in his ribs flaring as she helped him back to his feet.

Her eyes remained level, unwavering as she addressed him — not just as a recruit, but as someone capable of more. "The strength of the phalanx lies not in the individual, but in the bond between every shield. When you broke formation, you didn't just risk yourself — you risked your entire unit."

Liam swallowed hard, nodding. The sting of failure was deep, but there was no mockery in her tone — only expectation.

"I understand, Commander. I acted impulsively. It won't happen again."

Elise held his attention for a beat longer, weighing his words. Then, with a curt nod, she stepped back.

"See that it doesn't. Leadership is not charging ahead simply because you *can*. It's knowing when to lead...and when to trust those around you to hold the line. The greatest leaders understand the value of both."

Liam exhaled, tension beginning to ease from his shoulders. "Yes, Commander."

A beat passed. Then, his lips quirked into a lopsided grin, the flicker of his usual confidence returning. "So... while I've got you here — think I could try that sword of yours? Always wondered what using a Sentinel Shard felt like."

A few nearby recruits exchanged surprised glances, but Elise didn't so much as blink.

She raised a brow, her expression shifting to something between mild disbelief and warning.

"Do you enjoy seizures?"

Liam blinked. "Uh...what?"

Elise's delivery grew sharper, the lesson clearly not over.

"Untrained hands on a Sentinel Shard can lead to...unpleasant results. Your nervous system wasn't built to handle raw Incada energy without preparation. There's a reason we train before bonding with them."

The humor drained from Liam's face.

Her voice remained even but dropped in volume, quiet enough now that the surrounding recruits instinctively strained to hear.

"You've read the history, I assume? King Duriel wielded the Sentinel Armor when he struck down Belaran's corruption. The armor was whole then — one artifact, bound entirely to the king's will. And when the armor was not with the first king…" Her eyes narrowed. "The kingdom *burned* in his absence."

The weight of the words settled differently this time.

"The Everlight itself guided King Ryune to divide the armor, not because it was too powerful — but because it was too *centralized.* One life, no matter how righteous, cannot bear the entire weight of a kingdom's defense. Because the first king was caught without The Sentinel when Belaran betrayed him, the Kingdom burned for years. And so, the armor was broken. Four hundred Sentinel Shards, reforged and entrusted not to kings, but to those with the strength — and discipline — to wield them."

She lifted the blade slightly, angling it so the light caught the shard bound to the pommel by the same leather strap that wrapped the sword's grip. A steady silver glow coursed beneath the metal's surface.

"This blade is not merely metal infused with Incada — it carries a fragment of the sentinel armor. The shards do not yield their strength lightly. Without proper attunement, they resist. They reject. A body unprepared for their strain could be shattered in moments. Do you understand, Valoria?"

Liam nodded, throat tight as he shifted his weight.

"Good," Elise continued, drawing herself back to full height. "The Sentinel Shards were not divided to make them safer. They were divided so that the burden of defending this realm would never again fall to a single set of shoulders. It is the duty of *every* guild member who wields them now. Do not mistake power for privilege."

Liam swallowed, the earlier smugness completely gone. "Yes, Commander."

Elise let the silence linger just long enough for the point to settle before finally raising her voice to the rest of the recruits.

"Class dismissed."

As weapons were returned to the racks and boots echoed against the stone floor, Liam caught fragments of hushed conversations trailing behind him.

"Did he seriously ask to hold a *Shard?*"

"I heard the last untrained recruit who touched one was in the infirmary for a week."

Liam kept his head down, the weight of the exchange pressing heavier than before.

But beneath the sting of embarrassment, another thought endured.

Not just a lesson.

A challenge.

And he *would* be ready.

Later, as the last of the recruits filtered out of the general studies hall, Liam remained behind with Nysara, Alarion, and Celeste, their desks pulled close in the quiet hall. Sunlight filtered through the tall windows, casting long, pale streaks across the polished stone floors.

Liam leaned back in his chair, arms crossed over his chest, the tension from the morning still hanging on his speech. "I *thought* I saw an opening. We were barely holding together, and she just kept pressing us harder. I mean, what was I supposed to do? Stand there and *wait* for her to break the line completely?"

Alarion, resting his violin case on the desk, offered a half-smile. "So... you thought the best solution was to throw yourself in front of her blade alone?"

Liam's scowl deepened. "I wasn't just throwing myself —"

Alarion raised a hand. "No, no, I get it. Very heroic." He gestured with a flourish. "'Valoria the Bold, standing against impossible odds!'"

Liam groaned. "That's *not* what happened."

"I heard she had you on the floor faster than you could blink," Nysara cut in, arms crossed, a smirk tugging at her lips. "Is it true she didn't even *activate* her shard? Because if you lost to her *at full power*, I'd at least understand."

Liam groaned, rubbing his temples. "That's not the point. And *yes*, she didn't even activate it. It was skill, not — ugh, you're missing the point."

Celeste, who had been silently listening while tidying her notes, finally chimed in, arching a brow. "Actually, the point seems pretty clear. You abandoned your position during a coordinated defense exercise. If I didn't know better, I'd say you were *trying* to make an example of yourself."

Liam blinked. "It wasn't —"

Nysara leaned in, a voice full of mock seriousness. "Oh, I get it now. The great Liam Valoria, *breaker of formations*, thought he'd show off a little, huh? Sweep in, save the day, dramatic finish — too bad you forgot the part where you're supposed to *win*."

Alarion gave an exaggerated sigh, resting his hand on his chest. "A tragic tale. Truly."

Liam groaned, slumping lower in his chair. "Why do I even talk to you people?"

Celeste's expression didn't soften, though the corners of her mouth twitched. "Because we're right."

Liam shot her a glare but didn't argue.

After a beat, his response dropped back into something quieter. "It's just…confusing. Every lesson feels like it contradicts the last. *Be bold. Stay in line. Lead. Hold your ground.* Which one is it? How am I supposed to figure out the difference when it *counts*?"

The teasing faded.

Alarion shifted, his usual grin giving way to something more thoughtful. "Maybe…that's the whole point. Maybe they're not asking us to follow one rule forever. They're trying to see if we can figure out when to follow instinct and when to trust the people next to us."

Liam blinked. He hadn't thought of it that way before.

"Or," Celeste added with a faint smirk, "you could just try listening instead of assuming you're the hero of every scenario."

Liam threw up his hands. "And *there* it is."

"Hey, you said it, not me," she replied, flipping a page in her notebook with a too-innocent smile.

As Liam opened his mouth to retort, he noticed Nysara had gone strangely quiet. Her head had dipped forward slightly, arms still crossed but her breathing even.

"…Nysara?"

Nothing.

He waved a hand in front of her face. "You're kidding me, right? Were you seriously asleep just now? You were awake *thirty seconds ago*!"

Nysara jolted awake with a quick inhale, blinking rapidly. "Huh? No! I was *resting my eyes.*"

Alarion snorted. "Yeah, sure you were."

Nysara groaned, rubbing her temples before offering a sheepish grin. "Look, you'll get used to it, okay? I'm either going *full speed* or passing out where I sit. No in-between."

Liam blinked, shaking his head. "That's...weirdly impressive. And also concerning."

"I'm fine!" she insisted. "Anyway, what I was *trying* to say before I drifted off —"

The sharp voice of Captain Sunniva cut through the hall, her words carrying effortlessly across the stone.

"Recruits. On your feet. Report to the mess hall, now!"

The four of them exchanged glances, the playful energy dissipating as Sunniva's words echoed in their ears.

Liam adjusted his sword belt, glancing once more toward his friends before they all rose to leave.

The teasing was done — for now.

But the lesson lingered.

Hunter Fowler

3

Forged In Innovation

The midday sun cast a warm glow over the guild complex as Nysara Thandor walked alongside Liam, Alarion, and Celeste toward the mess hall. The rhythm of their steps filled the brief silences between conversations.

She had barely begun recounting her morning when the swell of recruits thickened around them, the crowd shifting as lunch hour reached its peak.

"You wouldn't believe the day I had," she started, her green eyes brightening despite the press of bodies. "You guys kept me talking so long I nearly missed my first session. I practically sprinted across the whole guild complex to get there on time."

Liam raised a brow, clearly ready to tease. "Let me get this straight — you were late? Did you break a law of nature or something?"

Nysara shot him a glare, though the corner of her mouth twitched. "Well, I did say you kept talking and holding me up…"

Alarion chuckled under his breath, while Celeste shook her head with a sigh.

"Just tell the story, already," Celeste said, tucking her notebook under her arm. "Or are you planning to build suspense until we're already eating?"

Nysara grinned but didn't argue. "Fine. So, I'm practically flying through the halls, barely avoiding the second year's practicing spell projection drills — when I finally make it to the Originators' training center…"

Earlier that day...

Nysara's pulse thrummed in her ears as she raced through the stone corridors, the strap of her satchel digging into her shoulder.

"Don't be late on the first day. Don't be late."

The southernmost corner of the guild complex finally came into view, where the towering structure of the Originators' training center loomed. It stood in striking contrast to the older guild halls — a blend of polished stone and reinforced steel, the arched windows inlaid with thin threads of glowing Incada cells. Soft pulses of energy traced the edges of the glass, a steady pulse of power coursing through the building itself.

She slowed, catching her breath as she reached the entrance, but the tension coiling in her chest didn't ease. This was it — the moment she'd been waiting for.

A chance to prove she belonged.

A chance to prove herself worthy.

She swallowed hard, squared her shoulders, and stepped inside.

The interior was alive with motion and sound. The rhythmic hiss of steam vents mingled with the hum of power conduits. Machinery clicked and whirred from every direction — automated presses shaping metal components, mechanical arms adjusting the tension on delicate copper coils. The scent of oiled gears, scorched metal, and faint traces of heated Incada filled the air, a fusion of industry and innovation.

Nysara barely noticed the noise, her attention caught by a figure at a nearby workstation. Hadassah the Mender.

The legendary innovator was hunched over a long-barreled firearm unlike anything Nysara had ever seen. Thin copper channels etched along the weapon's frame pulsed faintly with blue light, a sign of low Incada charge. A cylindrical chamber, cracked open at the base, revealed a depleted Incada cell, the gemstone core dull and lifeless. Sparks danced as Hadassah adjusted a minuscule filament near the trigger assembly, each motion precise, surgical.

Nysara hesitated, torn between awe and anxiety.

Focus. You're already late.

Clearing her throat, she stepped forward and tapped Hadassah gently on the shoulder. "Excuse me, Hadassah? I'm Nysara Thandor — a new recruit. Could you tell me where I should be reporting?"

Hadassah blinked, as if pulled from deep concentration. Her keen eyes swept over Nysara, assessing her with a mix of curiosity and mild impatience before her eyes softened slightly.

"Forge room. Left at the second junction. You can't miss it," she replied, voice calm but clipped as she returned her focus to the weapon.

Relief bloomed in Nysara's chest. "Thank you."

Hadassah had already turned back to her work, muttering under her breath as she replaced the spent cell with a fresh one, its vibrant blue core flaring to life.

" — Bella really should be here to guide these recruits herself."

The words stung.

Nysara swallowed hard and turned away before the flush could rise to her cheeks.

But as she stepped through the next corridor and into the forge room, her breath caught.

It was magnificent.

Massive boilers lined the walls, their metal casings humming with the transfer of heat into suspended Incada cores, each one housed in a crystalline cell pulsing with faint blue light. Copper conduits veined the ceiling, feeding energy to the various workstations, where Originators — some clad in soot-streaked aprons, others in crisp uniforms — were immersed in their projects.

Some hovered over drafting tables, sketching complex schematics. Others tinkered with half-built constructs; the air tinged with the scent of heated metal and scorched circuitry. A wheeled automaton no larger than a house cat scurried along the far wall, projecting diagrams onto a glass panel while a group of recruits debated calculations.

And at the heart of it all was the sound — the constant hum of creativity, the forge itself breathing life into ideas.

It was near the heart of the forge, amid the rhythmic pulse of tools against metal and the hum of charged Incada, that Nysara first encountered Cobus Akiva.

The foreman's presence was impossible to miss. Broad-shouldered and clad in ornate golden armor trimmed with deep violet, he stood with the calm authority of someone who had earned his place through both skill and wisdom. His armor, though regal, bore subtle scuffs and marks of use, a reminder that even leaders of the Originators weren't strangers to hard work. A matching violet cloak draped from his shoulders, fastened at the collar by a simple clasp. The turquoise accents along his gauntlets and chestplate pulsed faintly, traces of Incada energy woven into the design, though restrained.

Cobus' face was marked with quiet confidence, his dark eyes focused and discerning beneath a golden half-helm that left his face exposed. Faint scars traced his cheek, subtle but not hidden, and his expression carried both a weight of experience and the expectation of excellence.

When he spoke, his voice carried over the din of the forge — calm, but firm enough that the room seemed to quiet on instinct.

"Recruits," Cobus's words cut through the hum of the forge, powerful yet even. "You stand in the heart of the Originators. This hall exists to advance not just our craft but the strength of all Ileydria. Precision. Control. Innovation. These are not just words here — they're the foundation of our work."

His eyes stopped on each of them in turn, intense but not unkind.

"Today, your task is simple — supply distribution. These crates," he gestured to the neatly stacked containers along the wall, "contain components essential to the work being done. Your job is to ensure they reach their designated stations. It may feel mundane, but understanding the flow of a forge is critical. Interrupt it, and nothing functions as it should."

Straightforward enough.

Nysara nodded and stepped forward, claiming a crate with both hands. The weight surprised her — dense, but manageable.

"This is fine," she whispered under her breath, adjusting her grip. "Simple deliveries. No problem."

Yet, as she moved deeper into the forge, the enormity of the space unfolded around her.

The sound alone was enough to make her chest tighten — the rhythmic pounding of hammers on steel, the hiss of steam, the steady thrum of Incada-powered mechanisms. Great glass channels lined the upper walls, glowing faintly with processed Incada fluid that pulsed as it powered the entire facility. Massive boilers along the far end hissed softly, their surfaces glowing from the heat radiating within.

Nysara stared for a moment too long.

"This place is...incredible."

The first delivery took her to a nearby workstation where two second-year apprentices were bent over a gauntlet etched with Incada circuitry, their expressions tense with concentration.

"I told you the discharge ports were misaligned —" "Yeah, and I told you it's a containment leak. Look at the draw pattern."

Nysara set the crate beside them carefully. The taller of the two barely noticed, giving her a quick, "Thanks," before returning to the debate.

Her gaze caught on the gauntlet as she turned away — its design was sleek, but the Incada channels didn't seem to pulse evenly. She paused for a second, half-wanting to ask about the problem.

But Cobus's instructions echoed in her mind.

"Focus. Just the deliveries."

The next stop was a complex frame structure near the forge's center, where a mechanical construct — its arm half-assembled — stood rigid, cables snaking from its joints. A smith worked beside it, carefully fitting a stabilizer coil into the shoulder mount.

Nysara recognized the part she had just delivered — the coil was faintly humming with Incada charge.

"That's a stabilizer core! Wait, are they...reinforcing the entire frame with active dampeners? How much power would it need for — "

A sharp clang from another station startled her out of the thought.

Stay focused.

The deliveries continued, her route weaving between workstations where components both ancient and modern blended seamlessly.

At one station, a smith carefully etched Incada channels into a longsword, the thin lines glowing faintly with every delicate pass of his engraving tool.

At another, a device resembling a half-built crossbow lay disassembled, its pieces organized with meticulous care. A small vial of liquid Incada sat beside it, the fluid rippling slightly as though reacting to the energy already present in the weapon's frame.

By the time she reached her fifth station, her initial nervousness had begun to ease.

"This isn't so bad. I'm already halfway done, and there are no disasters yet."

But she was distracted.

Her eyes kept drifting — curiosity constantly tugging her attention from the task.

That was when it happened.

Turning away from a delivery table, her focus caught on a set of miniature turbines being tested at a nearby station — delicate, precise components spinning in perfect synchronization.

"Are those micro-turbines? I didn't think anyone had stabilized."

Her boot caught against something solid.

The crate shifted.

The weight tipped — too fast. With a sharp yelp, Nysara stumbled forward. The contents of her crate tumbled loose, clattering against the stone floor in a chaotic cascade. Gears, seals, small coils — scattering in every direction.

The noise was loud enough to break the rhythm of the forge's work.

Silence rippled out around her.

Heads turned. The clang of hammers slowed.

Nysara froze, heat rushing to her face as she dropped to her knees, scrambling to collect the scattered components.

The clang of metal against stone echoed in her ears, louder than it should have been.

Scattered components lay sprawled across the floor — precision-crafted gears, delicate seals, tiny Incada coils — each one a painful reminder of her mistake.

A mistake everyone had just seen.

The heat in her face deepened, and the forge blurred slightly as her vision dropped to the floor, hands trembling as she reached for the fallen parts.

Not again...

The hum of the forge faded, the present slipping from her grasp.

She was back there.

The school workshop was smaller than the grand forge hall, but to her younger self, it had felt just as overwhelming. Rows of tools meticulously arranged on the walls; shelves stocked with half-assembled projects. It had been her favorite place — until that day.

The principal's voice echoed in her mind, stern but measured. "You've shown promise, Nysara. I'm challenging you — and a few others — to create a functioning pulverizer by the week's end. Precision. Execution. The finer details matter. Let's see what you can do."

A pulverizer. Standard equipment for refining raw Incada stone into usable form — breaking it down to a fine, reactive dust without losing potency.

She had worked tirelessly, spending hours after classes sketching and resketching the design, fine-tuning every detail she could think of. Calculations had filled her notebooks. The assembly process had been careful, precise — or so she thought.

When the presentation day arrived, she felt unstoppable.

But as she fed the test stones into the machine, something was wrong. The pulverizer churned with a low, uneven whine. The stones were ground, but instead of reducing to fine powder, fragments remained — too large to be properly processed.

Her heart had sunk.

The principal had studied the results, arms crossed, his face unreadable.

"You have the right idea, Nysara. But look closer. Your output is compromised because your refinement chamber is misaligned — half the stone isn't even reaching the primary grind cycle."

She wanted to argue. Wanted to explain how much effort she'd put into the design. But his next words had silenced her.

"You have potential. But you're not careful enough. Precision and thoroughness. If you try hard enough, you may come to realize it."

No praise. No acknowledgment of the work she'd almost got right. Just...a reminder of how far she'd fallen short.

Now, as she knelt on the forge floor, those same words echoed louder than the murmurs around her.

"Not careful enough."

"Not precise enough."

Her chest tightened as she fumbled with a loose coil, her pulse pounding in her ears.

Then — a pair of hands reached down beside her, scooping up a handful of scattered components.

"Relax, kid. Happens to everyone."

Nysara blinked, the present rushing back into focus.

A senior engineer with oil-streaked gloves gave her a crooked grin, holding out a few of the parts she'd dropped. "Seriously. I trip over stuff all the time. Someone should really clean up around here."

The casual humor caught her off guard — and just like that, the knot in her stomach loosened.

A small, reluctant laugh escaped her. "Yeah...maybe."

Together, they finished gathering the supplies.

Her hands had steadied.

By the time the last of the supplies had been delivered, Nysara's arms were aching, the scent of ash and faint traces of Incada residue clung on her sleeves. Her attention shifted as the recruits gathered once more near the central platform where Foreman Cobus Akiva stood waiting.

His stance was as solid as ever, arms folded, but there was something almost playful in the curve of his grin as he surveyed the group.

"Not bad," he said, nodding in approval. "You've gotten a glimpse of the heart of our craft today — of what it takes to keep this forge running. Now, it's time to see if you can create, not just assist."

The room quieted, focus drawn completely to him.

"Here in the forge, we are measured by more than how well we follow instructions. We shape the future with our own hands. So, your first true challenge as Originators begins now."

Nysara straightened, her fingers curling at her side as she hung on his words.

"You and your fellow recruits will be tasked with designing and constructing a functional Incada Cell," Cobus continued. His voice was calm but carried the unmistakable weight of expectation. "Not just a copy of what already exists. You are innovators. Push the limits. Improve the design. The tools we forge here power everything — the workshops, the defenses, the city itself. If you can learn to create and improve the core of our craft, you will understand what it means to be an Originator."

His eyes swept over the recruits, pausing long enough to make sure his words were truly sinking in.

"Creativity, resourcefulness, and practical application. These will be tested today. You will work in teams. Impress me."

The words hung, their simplicity making them feel heavier, somehow.

An Incada Cell? Nysara swallowed, her mind racing. Designing one from scratch was no small feat, let alone improving the design. "Cells power the entire kingdom...If we could create a better one, imagine what that could mean."

But it wasn't just about the challenge. It was an opportunity. The chance to prove she belonged here.

Cobus clapped his hands once, breaking the thoughtful silence. "Get to it."

As the recruits began to break into groups, the energy of the room shifted — nervous chatter blending with the clang of tools and the hum of nearby machinery.

Nysara paused for a moment, watching as clusters began forming across the hall. Some recruits were already discussing designs, speech animated, while others hesitated at the edges, unsure where to begin.

She took a measured breath. "This is my chance. I can't let one mistake define the day."

Gathering her courage, she made her way toward a quieter corner where a small group of recruits was beginning to gather, ready to take the next step.

Nysara stood at the edge of the small group, arms loosely crossed as ideas began bouncing back and forth. The pressure of her earlier mishap clung stubbornly, keeping her silent while the others debated.

A tall recruit with ink-stained hands scratched his chin. "We could try altering the shape — like hexagonal cells for better stacking efficiency?"

Another shook his head. "Stacking doesn't improve energy flow. The core design has already been optimized for balance. That's why the cells haven't changed much in years."

"Right," the first mumbled, deflating. "I guess there's a reason for that..."

Nysara shifted her weight, biting her lip. The same words echoed in her mind. Haven't changed in years...There has to be something we're missing.

She could feel the heat rising in her chest — the same restless energy she'd felt back in school when they'd told her "The design is fine as it is."

No. She hadn't come this far to stay quiet.

Clearing her throat, she spoke up, delivery wavering at first. "What if...we tried something different with the internal structure? Not just the shape but how the energy moves inside the cell."

The group turned to her.

"I mean — " Her voice steadied as the thought solidified. "When was the last time we improved how cells function instead of just redesigning the casing? What if we built a rotating core? Something that cycles the energy, constantly keeping the Incada flow active instead of static?"

A few skeptical glances flickered her way.

"Wouldn't that just burn through the charge faster?" someone asked.

Another added with a shrug, "There could be a good reason it hasn't been done before...maybe we've already hit the limit."

"Limit?" Nysara's arms dropped to her sides. Her brow furrowed, frustration bubbling up. "No way. That's the same mindset that's kept half the cells in circulation unchanged for decades! Just because it works doesn't mean it can't be better."

The words spilled out faster than she meant, her passion overwhelming as she continued, "What if the rotation maintained stability? Kept the Incada flow more efficient? Look — spinning energy fields are already used in surge dampeners and grav compensators, right? It's not impossible. If we could get the core to cycle instead of storing in bursts — "

"Hold on, hold on," the ink-stained recruit interrupted, waving a hand. "You're saying...like a constant recharge loop? How would you keep the energy from bleeding off during the spin?"

Another recruit chimed in, catching the spark. "Back home, I helped design an irrigation wheel that kept water moving through a filter — same concept, right? Maybe we could create a controlled spin with shielding to regulate the flow?"

Nysara nodded, momentum building. "Exactly! But if we're talking increased output, we need to reinforce the casing. Maybe sacrifice some capacity for durability — like the reinforced cells they use in those infrastructure lights near the guild gates?"

"I saw those too!" another added, excitement catching on. "The shielding system balances charge loss with durability. We could layer that into the design."

The ideas tumbled out faster now, recruits building off each other in rapid succession. The tension from before dissolved, replaced by a rising pulse of collaboration.

Nysara felt her earlier self-doubt fade as the group rallied around the concept. They were brainstorming, adapting, building on one another's strengths.

"This...this is what it means to be an Originator."

By the time their ideas began settling, a working concept had taken shape — a rotating Incada Cell with a dynamic energy cycling core, reinforced by layered shielding to prevent destabilization. It was ambitious, untested, and far from perfect — but it was theirs.

And Nysara couldn't help but feel...proud.

The planning session had left Nysara and her team with a surge of confidence as they reconvened with Foreman Akiva, their rotating Incada Cell concept fully formed. The air in the forge still hummed with residual energy, but their small circle felt suspended in a charged stillness, the weight of the moment pressing on each of them.

Cobus stood at the center, arms crossed as he observed the recruits expectantly. His keen eyes, usually sharp with critique, now held a glimmer of curiosity.

Nysara took a calm breath before stepping forward, clutching the schematics in both hands. "We've developed a new Incada Cell design," she began, voice controlled though her pulse hammered beneath it. "It uses a rotating chamber to maintain continuous energy flow instead of static storage. Based on our calculations, this could...potentially, triple the capacity of a standard cell while minimizing energy loss."

Silence.

Cobus's head tilted, his brow furrowing as he processed her words. Then, with a shift of his stance, his expression cracked — not into skepticism, but into rare, genuine surprise.

"Triple the capacity?" His reply softened, as if testing the idea aloud. "And the structural integrity? How are you preventing overcharge strain?"

One of her teammates chimed in, her manner a little more hesitant. "We're working on a reinforced casing design. Layered shielding, similar to the infrastructure barriers in the northern quarter. It should reduce instability as the rotation increases."

Cobus nodded slowly, his thoughtful glance returning to Nysara. For a heartbeat, she worried he was searching for flaws. Then his face broke into a wide grin, the expression both approving and eager.

"That's impressive work," he said at last. "Ambitious, but grounded. Exactly what we expect from Originators." His grin maintained for just a moment longer before his expression sobered. "This is something Bella needs to see."

At the mention of the Mastermind, Nysara felt her chest tighten. Bella — the brilliant, enigmatic leader who had practically reshaped modern Incada engineering — was known for both her genius and her high standards. Presenting an unfinished design to her felt...suddenly, overwhelming.

Cobus must have noticed her hesitation, because his voice softened just slightly. "Trust me. Bella values ideas like this. She's been waiting for something groundbreaking — this could be it. She'll see the potential."

Nysara gave a hesitant nod, her teammates offering quiet encouragement behind her.

"It was really Nysara's idea to begin with," one of them added, nudging her shoulder. "She led the whole project."

Nysara's cheeks flushed, but there was no time to dwell on it. Cobus was already gesturing for them to follow, leading them out of the forge and into the corridor beyond.

The walk toward Bella's office felt longer than it should have, the echoes of their footsteps oddly loud against the polished stone floor. Nysara's heart pounded harder with every step, the excitement of their achievement tangled now with the weight of expectation.

What if the calculations were wrong? What if they'd overlooked something?

Cobus didn't slow.

They reached the door, slightly ajar, and he rapped his knuckles against the wood. No response.

Frowning, Cobus pushed it open.

Bella was slumped over her desk, face pressed into a pile of papers, a small pool of drool seeping into the edges of a half-sketched schematic. The room itself was chaos — piles of notes and half-finished contraptions cluttered every available surface. Incada cells, some fully charged, and others cracked open for analysis, lay scattered among the mess.

Cobus cleared his throat. Loudly.

Bella stirred, blinking blearily as she jerked upright, wiping her face with her sleeve and smearing ink across her cheek in the process. "I — uh — wasn't sleeping," she muttered, eyes still unfocused. "I was...contemplating rotational output ratios...very complex. Important work."

Nysara's team stood frozen, half in awe, half uncertain whether they should even be here.

Cobus, unfazed, crossed his arms. "Bella, you need to see this. Now."

Bella blinked again, shaking off the last of her exhaustion as her focus on the group intensified.

"Right," she said, brushing the papers aside with renewed focus. "Let's see it. What have you got for me?"

Undeterred, Nysara and her team launched into their explanation, laying out the rotating Incada Cell design in full detail. Nysara took the lead, describing the dynamic storage chamber, the reinforced casing concept, and the potential for greater energy capacity compared to the standard cells.

As the words flowed, Bella's earlier exhaustion seemed to dissolve. She leaned forward, eyes narrowing with focus, her fingers drumming lightly on the edge of her desk as she processed each point.

"Increased capacity without structural compromise...more efficient energy flow...You do realize what this means, don't you?" Bella's speech had shifted, no longer groggy but sharp with understanding. "If this works, it could change how we harness Incada entirely — greater capacity, reduced drain..."

Her words trailed off as she stared past them, already racing ahead in her own mind. Then, just as quickly, her brows knit together.

"But how do you know the rotation won't destabilize the cell's energy retention? Increased capacity means nothing if the movement ends up consuming as much power as it generates."

Nysara froze. The excitement she'd felt moments earlier drained like water through her fingertips.

"I — " Her voice faltered, fingers curling at her sides. "I didn't...we haven't tested for that yet. I'm sorry. I should've —"

Bella's head snapped up.

"Sorry?"

Before Nysara could stammer out another word, Bella was on her feet, moving so fast she nearly knocked over her chair. She crossed the room in three quick strides, seizing Nysara's shoulders with both hands.

"Problems aren't for quitting! They're for solving!" Bella's eyes were alight now, her earlier fatigue fully replaced by raw energy. "You're onto something real here — something worth figuring out. The fact you haven't solved every angle yet means there's more to discover, not that you've failed."

Nysara blinked, words catching in her throat as the weight of Bella's reaction sank in. She hadn't dismissed the idea. She hadn't even criticized it.

She believed in it.

In her.

By now, Bella was vibrating with enthusiasm, pacing the room as her mind raced. "We need a dedicated workspace for this — yes, a full project station. I'll have the western lab cleared out, and I'll make sure it's stocked with everything you need. Materials, tools, stabilized Incada. This is too important to delay."

Cobus nodded approvingly from the doorway, arms crossed. "I told you she'd like it."

Bella shot him a glance. "Like it? Cobus, if they can crack this design, it'll redefine power storage efficiency across the entire guild. Maybe beyond."

Nysara felt her heart lift again, the initial sting of uncertainty eclipsed by Bella's unrestrained excitement.

As they were dismissed, her team filed out first, their voices bubbling with quiet excitement. Nysara stood for a moment longer, glancing back at the chaotic desk, the discarded notes — reminders of Bella's own relentless work.

"Thank you," she said quietly.

Bella gave her a tired but genuine smile. "Don't thank me yet. Go prove you're right."

Walking back toward the general studies hall, the tension that had gripped Nysara's chest all morning finally began to ease. Her mind replayed every moment — the stumble in the forge, Cobus's encouragement, Bella's energy, the rush of collaboration with her teammates.

She had doubted herself — again. And yet, here she was. Not just contributing. Leading.

Today, she had done more than present an idea. She had begun to step into the Originator she'd always dreamed of becoming.

And for the first time, she wasn't just hoping she belonged here.

She knew it.

"Wait, wait — hold on." Liam's words broke in, eyes widening with disbelief as he interrupted Nysara's story. "You met the guild leader on your first day and impressed her? Seriously?"

Nysara blinked, caught off guard by his reaction. She gave a modest shrug, though her grin betrayed her pride. "I mean… yeah, I guess. It sounds more impressive when you say it like that."

Alarion let out a low whistle, crossing his arms with an exaggerated shake of his head. "Unbelievable. We've been here for what, a day? And you're already making history. Way to raise the bar for the rest of us."

Nysara laughed, the tension of the morning finally lifting. "I didn't *plan* it! Now come on — I'm starving, and if we don't hurry, we'll be stuck in line behind half the complex."

Celeste arched a brow, her lips curling into a smirk. "Oh, clearly. Wouldn't want our resident prodigy to wait for her food like the rest of us common folk."

Liam grinned. "Yeah, I bet by next week they'll be naming workshops after her. 'Nysara's Hall of Wonders' has a nice ring to it."

Nysara rolled her eyes, but the warmth in her chest remained as their laughter carried down the corridor.

They turned the corner, expecting the usual chaos of the mess hall — the clatter of dishes, the low hum of conversation, the scent of freshly baked bread —

But instead, the hall was silent.

The group came to a quick halt, the sudden shift in atmosphere as jarring as the silence itself. What had started as a lighthearted race to beat the lunchtime rush now felt like stepping into something far heavier.

The mess hall's usual hum of chatter and clinking trays was nowhere to be found. The long wooden tables remained untouched, the scent of food absent. Only the rhythmic echo of boots on stone as more recruits arrived behind them broke the hush.

Yet the source of the tension was unmistakable.

Arch-Bringer Roland stood at the far end of the hall, his back straight, hands clasped behind him in perfect stillness. His eyes, sharp as cut obsidian, swept over the gathering recruits with an intensity that made even the most confident among them hesitate.

Nysara swallowed hard, her earlier excitement dimming under the weight of his authority.

"Did we…miss lunch?" Alarion whispered, though even his usual sarcasm faltered. "No way, right? Please tell me we didn't miss a meal."

No one answered.

More recruits continued to file in, their chatter joining the growing undercurrent of confusion. Whispers buzzed like static — speculation, nervous questions, and half-formed theories.

Yet Roland remained silent.

The weight of his presence filled the space like a drawn blade — taut, expectant. Not threatening, but charged, as though the room itself was holding its breath.

Liam shifted uncomfortably beside Nysara, his hand brushing the pommel of his sword as if seeking some unspoken reassurance.

Nysara clenched her fists, heart beating faster. This wasn't just some routine assembly.

It felt like a test.

4

The Herald of New Trials

Roland's voice echoed through the silent hall, each word measured, each syllable weighted with authority. "Recruits, today marks a significant step in your journey. In times of peace, it is easy to grow complacent — to mistake quiet for safety. But vigilance is our foundation. Strength comes not just from skill, but from unity and trust in those beside you."

He let the words settle, his eyes sweeping over the gathered recruits with piercing intensity.

"Recently," he continued, speech tightening, "a series of thefts have plagued the guilds. Supplies vital to our operations — components, weapon stock, even Incada Cells — have gone missing. This is not mere carelessness. We suspect organized interference, and it cannot be ignored. Today, you will take part in addressing this threat directly."

A whisper rippled through the crowd, but Roland's gaze silenced it in an instant.

"You have not reached this point in your training as mere students," he pressed, the words deliberate. "You are recruits of Ileydria — envoys of its legacy and defenders of its future. Conduct yourselves as such. Your orders are to investigate the thefts, recover what has been taken, and return with answers. You represent more than just yourselves. Do not forget that."

Nysara shifted, her fingers curling into the fabric of her jacket. The weight of his words pressed heavily on her chest, stirring that familiar knot of anxiety. Liam, standing beside her, caught the movement and leaned closer, his response a quiet reassurance.

"It's all good, Nysara. We've got this."

Roland began calling out names, dividing the recruits into teams, each assigned a different sector of the guild complex. The groups departed in organized pairs and trios, the heavy doors opening and closing with the rhythm of duty.

Finally, Roland's eyes landed on them.

"Liam, Nysara, Alarion, and Celeste," he called, his words carrying above the quiet banter. "Step forward."

The four exchanged glances before approaching, standing at attention as Roland lowered his voice, his stern composure softening — though only slightly.

"Yours will be a particularly delicate assignment," he said, folding his hands behind his back. "Storage Facility Three reported a theft of Incada Cells — an entire batch, unaccounted for. These cells were not secured in combat-grade containers. If handled improperly, even a minor rupture could result in total energy loss — or worse, instability. We cannot afford such a failure, not with the Challenger's Tournament approaching. Supplies are already strained."

His expression narrowed, "Precision and control will be paramount. I expect nothing less. Understood?"

"Yes, Arch-Bringer," they responded in unison, the gravity of the task fully setting in.

As they gathered their things and moved toward a quieter corner of the hall, Liam clapped his hands together in a halfhearted attempt to cut through the tension.

"Well, looks like we're all in this together. Should be fun, right?" His grin didn't quite land the way he'd hoped.

Celeste, arms crossed and already focused, gave him a flat look. "Liam, this is serious. People are stealing Incada Cells — one mistake and we're talking citywide consequences. We don't have time for your usual nonsense."

Liam raised his hands defensively. "Hey, I get it! I'm not making light of it, I'm just saying we work better when we're not all on edge. Tension makes people sloppy."

Nysara nodded, though her arms stayed folded tight against her chest. "He's got a point. If we let this stress us out too much, we're more likely to miss something important."

Celeste exhaled, relenting just a little. "Fine. But let's keep focused. First step, we need information. The guards who were stationed near Storage Facility Three might've seen something."

Alarion, leaning casually against the stone wall, added, "I could check in with some of the locals near the southern perimeter. Rumors travel faster than official reports — someone might've seen something they didn't think to mention to the higher-ups."

Celeste nodded, already falling into her natural role as the team's organizer. "Good. Let's split up, gather what we can, and meet back here in an hour. Stick to the facts. No assumptions."

With that, the group dispersed to their tasks.

Liam made his way toward the storage yard, where two guards leaned lazily against the stone archway, arms folded and clearly unimpressed with their midday shift.

"Hey," Liam started, keeping his tone casual but direct. "I heard you two were on duty when the cells went missing. The Arch-Bringer sent my team to investigate — think you could help us out with some details?"

The guards exchanged a look. One of them, a burly man with a grizzled beard, smirked.

"Oh, the Arch-Bringer sent you, huh? First years, right?"

The second guard, a younger man but no less condescending, chimed in with mock gravitas. "'The Arch-Bringer commands it!' Always the same song with you recruits. Where's the paperwork, kid? Or do you expect us to start spilling classified details just 'cause you asked nicely?"

Liam felt his jaw tighten. He was trying to be professional, but this felt more like hazing than protocol.

Then the older guard's eyes dropped — just for a moment — to the crest stitched into his jacket. The silver-threaded Valoria emblem.

Liam caught it.

His stance shifted, just enough to make the crest more visible.

"Look, I get it," he said, voice lowering as he worked to smooth his tone. "Maybe I came off the wrong way. Truth is, we got this assignment dropped on us fast — no time for formal orders, just straight here from the hall. One Envoy to another, I'm just trying to do my job without anyone getting hurt. If you'd rather wait for orders to land on your desk...I can go back and ask Roland himself."

Silence.

The older guard cleared his throat, glancing toward his companion before nodding.

"Alright, alright. No need to make this difficult. Look, it was late — somewhere around midnight when we noticed a couple of figures moving near the eastern fence line. I couldn't get a clear look before they vanished, but it felt off. No alarms triggered, no sign of forced entry."

Liam nodded, filing the details away. "And you're sure the cells were accounted for before that?"

The younger guard shrugged. "They were. Next shift came on, did their count — crates were missing. No signs of damage, no open locks."

"Appreciate it," Liam replied, feeling the tension in his shoulders finally ease. "That helps more than you know."

Turning back toward the rendezvous point, he couldn't shake the feeling that something was still missing. No forced entry? No damage?

It felt too...clean.

Still, he had information — and that was a start.

"The guards mentioned seeing some suspicious figures around midnight," Liam explained, crossing his arms. "They think there might be a hideout nearby, but nothing confirmed yet."

"I found traces of concentrated Incada leading out toward the city's edge," Nysara added, tucking her scanner back into her satchel. "It's faint, but definitely recent — probably within the last day."

Alarion nodded, arms loosely folded as he leaned against a nearby pillar. "A few locals mentioned seeing shadowy figures near storage facility three too. They figured it was late-night deliveries, but the timing matches what the guards reported."

Celeste, standing slightly apart from the group, let out a slow breath. "That's enough to act on," she said, her expression tightening into focus. "We have a trail.

Let's follow it but stay sharp — if whoever did this took the risk of stealing active Incada Cells, they won't be careless. They know what they're doing."

They moved out from the guild complex together, the towering spires of the capital rising behind them. The streets were alive with the midday bustle — merchants calling out from their stalls, carts rattling over cobbled paths. The scent of spices and fresh bread mingling with the tang of heated Incada from nearby streetlamps. Children darted between stalls, laughter ringing out as they played, oblivious to the tension tightening in Nysara's chest.

The further they traveled from the heart of the city, the sharper the contrast became. The well-maintained stonework shifted, giving way to cracked paving and dimmer lights. Ornate lanterns fueled by carefully regulated Incada faded to flickering, uneven glows.

The pulse of residual Incada energy along the path grew more distinct here. Nysara's scanner beeped softly as she checked it again.

"It's stronger here," she noted, voice hushed as she gestured toward a narrow side street. "Whatever they used...they must've carried more than one cell."

Celeste nodded, eyes narrowing as she led the group forward. "Good. Stay close. No assumptions. We follow the evidence."

The city's noise faded behind them, replaced by the quiet hum of distant machinery and the echo of their footsteps against worn stone.

Liam scanned the narrowing streets with a careful eye, the worn stonework and sagging rooftops pressing in around them. The once-bustling industrial edge of the city had long since been reclaimed by rust and dust. "Feels like we're getting close," he mumbled, his hand brushing the pommel of his sword.

Ahead, the silhouette of an old foundry loomed, its massive gears and chimneys frozen in silent decay. The place felt...hollow. As though the echoes of past work still lingered beneath the quiet.

Nysara slowed, kneeling beside a faint shimmer along the cracked cobblestones. She ran her fingers just above the trace, watching it pulse faintly in the dim light. "The Incada residue is stronger here — more concentrated. They must've come this way recently."

Alarion shifted beside her, his violin case strapped tight across his back. "If they were carrying unshielded cells through here, it makes sense. Residual energy clings to porous stone like this." He gave a wry grin. "Did I mention growing up near an old mill? You pick up things when half your childhood was spent cleaning off grain dust."

Nysara blinked, glancing up with mild surprise. "I thought you were from the countryside — wasn't your family all farmers?"

"Yeah, we were. Mostly wheat and barley," he replied, a note of nostalgia creeping into his delivery. "My parents and sisters still run it. Simple life, but comfortable. My parents always knew I couldn't stay there though. Always something about my music being a 'higher calling.'"

Nysara nodded, brushing her fingertips over the trail again as they continued forward. "I get that. My house wasn't exactly calm though. Both my parents are Originators. I swear, half my childhood was spent in workshops listening to tools clanging or the hum of power coils. It felt like I was breathing metal filings most days."

Celeste, who had been keeping watch at the rear, let a small smile slip. "Honestly? That sounds nicer than my upbringing. My parents were scholars here in the capital. All strategy, structure, and 'legacy-building.' No space for mistakes — just expectation."

Liam cast a glance back at her, his expression softening as he caught the familiar thread beneath her words. "Yeah...I know a bit about that." His voice was quieter now, less playful. "Valoria's have been a part of every guild since the founding. I grew up with people reminding me of that history. It's like...you don't get to figure out who you are. You're already part of the story, and you're supposed to play your part."

The group fell into a thoughtful silence, the only sound their footsteps echoing along the empty street and the distant hum of city life behind them.

Nysara broke it gently, her focus drifting over the neglected edges of the district. "It's strange, isn't it? How different our lives were — farms, libraries, workshops — and somehow, we all ended up here, chasing the same purpose."

Celeste nodded, her usual sharpness softening just slightly. "That's the beauty of the guilds. Different paths. Same destination."

A pulse from Nysara's scanner drew their attention back to the trail. The glow intensified, leading into a narrow alley where the dim energy seemed to hang heavier in the air.

"Trail's fresh," she whispered. "They didn't just pass through here. They stopped."

Liam's hand rested instinctively on his sword hilt. "Then we're closer than we thought. Stay sharp."

The trail led them to the outskirts of the city, where the stonework of the capital gave way to weathered warehouses and forgotten industrial ruins. The structure before them was massive — its windows dark, the heavy iron doors slightly ajar as if beckoning them into its depths. The faint trace of Incada energy remained just outside, barely perceptible now, but unmistakable.

The silence pressed in heavier here, broken only by the distant hum of the city far behind them.

Liam exhaled softly, his hand resting on the hilt of his sword as he eyed the towering structure. "Why is it always an abandoned warehouse? It's like we're living in a storybook. Next thing you know, we'll find a secret tunnel or — "

"Shhh," Nysara hissed, kneeling once more. She ran her fingertips along the edge of a worn stone slab where a faint pulse of blue still glowed beneath the grime. "There's a residual Incada charge here. Weak, but close enough to mean those cells weren't properly shielded. They were definitely here."

Alarion's eyes swept the shadows along the warehouse perimeter, his expression tightening. "If they're still inside, they'll be on edge. If we're not careful, we could walk right into their line of sight."

Celeste nodded, her voice calm but commanding. "Then we keep close. Quiet. We're here to investigate, not get into a fight we can't win."

They moved as one, slipping through the heavy doors and into the cavernous interior.

The air was thick with the scent of rust and stale wood, the kind of cold, dry decay that clung to long-forgotten places. Crates were stacked high along the walls, some half-collapsed, others neatly arranged. Shafts of dim light filtered through the broken upper windows, illuminating the swirling dust in pale ribbons across the floor.

But it wasn't just the silence that put them on edge.

It was the sound beneath it.

Faint. Whispered words. Close.

Liam exchanged a glance with Celeste, his expression hardening. She nodded, gesturing toward a maze of crates along the right wall where the voices seemed strongest. They crept closer, pressing into the shadows as the hushed chatter became clearer.

"...Move faster. We're behind schedule — just load them. We'll be gone before anyone notices."

Nysara peered through a gap between the crates. Figures moved in the dim light — four, maybe five people, clad in dark work clothes, their faces partially obscured. The stolen Incada Cells were unmistakable, their pale blue glow casting eerie reflections against the thieves' anxious faces as they sorted them into reinforced carrying frames.

"We need to be smart," Celeste whispered, her speech barely audible. "We can't confront them head-on. We wait, gather information — "

Clang!

Everyone froze.

The sound of metal striking stone echoed like a thunderclap.

Alarion winced, his foot still half-raised where it had nudged a stray wrench off the edge of the crate platform. The tool bounced once, then twice, finally coming to a dead stop in the center of the floor.

Silence fell — tense, razor-sharp silence.

One of the thieves straightened, hand drifting toward the dagger at his hip as he scanned the shadows.

"Who's there?" one of the thieves barked, voice echoing through the warehouse as he drew a dagger. Another figure, broader and more deliberate, shifted toward the crates of Incada Cells, fingers brushing the edge of one as though preparing to use it.

Liam's grip tightened on his sword. "Now or never," he muttered under his breath.

Without waiting for a signal, he sprang from cover, steel flashing in an intense arc. The first thief barely had time to react before Liam's blade struck, knocking the dagger clean from his grasp with a loud clang. He followed through in the same fluid motion, stepping into the thief's space with a shoulder check that sent him stumbling back.

Two more closed in.

Liam pivoted, catching the first blow on the flat of his blade. Sparks danced along the steel as he countered, twisting his wrist to disarm the nearest attacker with a clean, deliberate motion. The second came low, aiming for his legs, but Liam shifted, letting the strike glance off his armored shin before kicking out, driving his attacker back with a grunt.

To his left, Nysara was already moving. Her fingers slid across the activation switch of a compact device clipped to her belt. A resonant hum filled the air as the device flared to life, casting a soft amber glow across the warehouse. Thin pulses of light rippled outward — highlighting delicate strands of energy crisscrossing the rafters and floor.

"Liam, stop — traps!" she called, delivery-tinged warning.

Liam twisted mid-swing, the blade halted just shy of a glowing beam. His foot hovered an inch from crossing another, close enough for the heat to prickle along his boot.

"Could've mentioned that sooner!" he hissed, rolling back a step as the thief he'd disarmed scrambled away.

"I'm a little busy saving your life here!" Nysara shot back, already reaching for another device. She flung a small, silver orb toward the base of the nearest emitter. It clattered against the stone floor and detonated in a pulse of concentrated light, severing the beam just before it could activate.

But the thieves weren't done yet.

One lunged for the crates where the stolen Incada Cells were stored. Nysara reacted instinctively, snapping her wrist and releasing a second device. The palm-sized disk bounced once, pulsing brightly before releasing a blinding flash. The thief recoiled, clutching his eyes.

Nysara didn't waste the opportunity. She dashed forward, sweeping his legs out from under him with a precise kick. He hit the ground hard, groaning.

From the far side of the room, Alarion's voice rose in an ancient melody. The peculiar song reverberated through the space, threads of energy shimmering into existence around him. Three mirrored versions of himself fanned out, each moving in perfect synchronization as they closed in on a cluster of thieves.

"Which one's real?" one thief growled, swinging wide — only for the blade to pass harmlessly through an illusion.

Another tried to dart around, but Alarion shifted with the rhythm of his song, the real him ducking low beneath the strike. His voice crescendoed, and with a quick downward gesture, the ground beneath them shuddered.

A deep, resonant pulse vibrated the stone, throwing the group off balance.

The nearest thief staggered — and Alarion seized the moment. A flick of his wrist sent a concentrated pulse of energy rippling along the ground, sweeping the attacker's legs from beneath him. As the man toppled, Alarion caught him by the collar and spun, hurling him directly into Liam's waiting path.

Liam didn't hesitate. His sword twisted in a precise disarming arc, knocking the dagger from the man's grip before he planted a boot against the thief's chest, pinning him to the ground.

"Stay down," he warned, speech low.

Behind them, Celeste held her ground, her staff planted firmly as she tracked the entire battlefield. She wasn't just watching — she was commanding.

"Liam, left flank! Nysara, check the crates — Alarion, hold the perimeter! Don't let them regroup!"

A shadow shifted at the edge of her vision.

A thief, unnoticed until now, emerged from behind a stack of barrels, his blade raised. His footsteps were too quiet for most ears — but Celeste sensed him at the last moment.

She didn't even turn.

The faint glow of Incada energy pulsed up her arm, coiling from her grip on the staff like pale-blue threads of silk. In a single fluid motion, she shifted her stance and thrust the staff backward, jabbing the butt into the thief's chest with a sharp crack.

He gasped, stumbling — but Celeste wasn't finished.

In one sweeping motion, she spun to face him, both hands tightening on the staff as she slammed it against the ground. The energy surged. A pulse of radiant blue energy rippled outward, a controlled shock wave that lifted the thief off his feet and sent him sprawling into a pile of shattered crates.

The air seemed to hum with lingering power as the echoes of the blast faded.

Liam, chest rising with constant breaths, pressed his boot lightly against the wrist of the last thief still conscious, ensuring no further resistance.

The warehouse fell silent.

Alarion's illusions faded one by one, the final echoes of his song dissipating into the dim light.

For a moment, none of them spoke, the adrenaline was still fading. Then Liam exhaled heavily, breaking the tension.

"Everyone in one piece?"

Nysara nodded, scanning the scattered crates. "Yeah...but we're not done yet."

Nysara knelt near the crates of stolen goods, brushing dust aside to reveal the faint glow of multiple Incada Cells nestled within the shipment. Yet something else caught her eye — a bundle of papers tucked beneath the cells. She unfolded the top sheet, her brow furrowing.

"Look at this," Nysara said, holding up the paper, the strange symbols and markings catching the dim light. "These symbols...they're not just random marks. They have to mean something."

Celeste took the paper carefully, her brow furrowing as she examined the unfamiliar notations. "It could be coded supply logs. Nothing more. I just reported our location to the Arch-Bringer, the recovery team will be here soon — this is probably just standard procedure."

Liam let out a dramatic sigh of relief, leaning back against a crate. "Thank The Everlight. I thought we were gonna have to haul all this back ourselves after everything." He ran a hand through his hair, still catching his breath.

Minutes passed in quiet as the recovery team arrived, their movements efficient as they secured the stolen Incada Cells and loaded them into reinforced transport containers. The group found seats along the edge of the vehicle as the supplies were hauled back toward the guild complex.

The silence was only interrupted by the rhythmic clatter of the wheels on the road — until Liam, ever unable to stay quiet for long, suddenly sat up straighter, his energy returning in full force.

"Wait, wait, wait — hold on! We have to talk about those moves, Alarion," he said, grinning broadly. "I mean, Nysara and I were out there battling, but you — what was that? You flipped, then there were, like, a bunch of you? And the ground started *shaking*?"

Alarion shrugged, clearly trying to suppress a smile. "Less wild sword swings and more time connecting with The Everlight, and maybe — just *maybe* — I could teach you a few tricks."

Nysara, laughing, cut him off before the banter spiraled further. "Hold on, forget that — did anyone else *see* the look on that thief's face when Celeste spun around on him? I thought he was going to faint."

Celeste raised an eyebrow, lips curling in the slightest smirk. "I wasn't that intimidating...was I?"

The group exchanged glances, holding back while they could — before all four of them burst into laughter.

By the time they rolled through the gates of the guild complex, their spirits were lighter, the weight of the encounter left behind — for now.

The team was escorted directly to Roland's quarters. The Arch-Bringer stood behind a broad stone desk, the recovered supplies already secured nearby. His focus, however, was fixed on the documents they had brought back, the faint glow of Incada lighting the edges of the schematics as he studied them in silence.

The lines of his face grew heavier with each passing moment, his brow furrowing deeper as he traced the strange symbols with a gloved hand. Finally, he exhaled through his nose and straightened, his expression unreadable as he addressed the group.

"Well done," Roland said, though the praise carried the weight of deeper concern. "You've recovered the supplies and avoided harm to yourselves. That is no small accomplishment."

Liam, still catching his breath, grinned and offered a salute. "First of many, sir. Let us know how we can help — "

Alarion, standing just behind him, muttered with a smirk, "Dial it back, Liam. You're laying it on a bit thick."

Roland's stern eyes flicked up from the documents, but the tension in his face eased just slightly.

"You've done well. But there's more to this than a simple theft. I'll need time to review these findings more closely." His voice softened, the authority giving way to something more personal. "For now, get some rest. You've earned it."

The team exchanged quiet glances, the adrenaline of the mission finally ebbing into exhaustion. Without further protest, they nodded in unison and departed the hall, leaving Roland alone with the mysterious documents — and the unspoken weight of what they might mean.

5

Harmony and Discord

Alarion stood by the tall arched window of his quarters, gazing out over the heart of Ileydria as dawn crept across the horizon. The guild complex rose around him; its ancient stone walls bathed in pale hues of morning light. The architecture was a testament to the city's long history — polished marble columns, high vaulted ceilings, and stained glass inlaid with veins of dormant Incada that only pulsed to life during ceremonies. The echoes of tradition remained here, grounding the space in the weight of its legacy.

Beyond the complex, however, the capital stretched like a living tapestry — an endless maze of rising spires and innovation. Incada lanterns still glowed faintly along the winding streets, their crystalline cores pulsing with soft blue light as they dimmed with the rising sun. Farther out, the city's industrial quarter shimmered with modern advancement, where glass-paneled towers hummed with power drawn from carefully stabilized Incada cores. Elevated trams wove between the districts on gleaming rails, their energy lines sparking faintly with each pulse of movement.

Yet, despite the beauty, the noise never stopped. The distant hum of energy conduits. The rhythmic clang of the forges. The constant buzz of life beneath the surface.

It was nothing like home.

He exhaled, his breath fogging the window as he stared past the modern skyline. Four months. Four months since he had left behind the quiet simplicity of his family's farm — the gentle rhythm of sunlit fields and the soft melodies of his father's songs as they tended the crops. The kind of life where days ended with the scent of fresh earth and the comfort of familiar routines.

"Life here is so different," he whispered under his breath, the sound nearly lost in the quiet hum of the waking city. "Everything's...louder. Faster."

The endless drills, the performances, the expectations. The weight of proving himself every single day. Yet, despite it all, the guild had given him something precious — room to create. His music, his craft, felt unshackled here. But there was always that slight discomfort, the fear of his talents being shaped by someone else's hands. Would his music remain his, or be twisted into something he barely recognized?

Still, not all of it was a struggle. Faces surfaced in his mind — people who had made this new life feel less overwhelming.

Ava. The head of the whole guild had taken to working with him directly. Her voice was as captivating as the music she sang, but it was her kindness that had truly struck him. She had never demanded perfection from him, only honesty. He could still hear her whisper before that nerve-wracking recital in the grand hall. "You've got this, Alarion. Just let the music flow through you." He had, and it had been enough.

Then there was Jezreel, head of the Weavers' defensive arts team. Stern, but patient. She had been the one to show him how Incada-infused instruments could create barriers, protective fields woven directly from sound. His first attempt had been clumsy, the shimmering barrier barely large enough to shield a single person — but Jezreel's grin had been genuine as she clapped his shoulder. "You've got a knack for this, kid. Trust yourself more."

And, of course, Evander. The relentless taskmaster of offensive tactics. If Jezreel had taught him to shape his music gently, Evander had shown him how to turn it into a weapon. His harsh, cutting words still echoed in Alarion's mind. "Stop hesitating. Music can be fury too. Use that fire inside you — stop hiding it." Those grueling lessons had left him exhausted, but stronger. Prepared.

Prepared enough for what happened with the thieves, he thought grimly, fingertips brushing the worn wood of the window frame.

His focus moved to the guild courtyard below, where early risers were already moving between the training grounds and the forge halls. So much motion. So much purpose.

His voice was quieter this time, as if speaking aloud would break the fragile calm.

"I'm thankful to be here...even if it wasn't my plan."

A hard knock at his door broke the fragile quiet.

Alarion blinked, pulled from his thoughts as the echoes of the city beyond his window faded. Straightening his jacket, he crossed the room and opened the door. A young courier stood there, his guild-marked satchel slung across his chest, back straight with professional stiffness.

"Summoned to the main guild hall," the courier said briskly, handing over a sealed notice marked with the Weavers' crest.

Alarion's stomach knotted as he accepted it. A formal summons. Not a request.

"Do you know what this is about?" he asked, but the courier merely offered a slight bow before turning on his heel and starting down the corridor.

"Well, if you don't can you please tell Nasara Thandor to get the others and meet me in the commons?" He yelled. The courier simply nodded his head in approval as he rounded the next corner.

Alarion stared at the folded parchment for a beat longer before tucking it into his sleeve and setting off through the guild's stone corridors.

The hallways felt colder than usual — the light from the Incada sconces casting pale reflections across the polished floors, the faint hum of energy underscoring the silence. He could feel the weight of expectation pressing closer with each step, his mind already racing with possibilities. A new assignment? More training? Some correction for how he'd handled the theft investigation?

By the time he reached the grand hall, the tension had settled in his chest like an iron weight.

The chamber was vast, sunlight filtering in through the high, stained-glass windows — each panel depicting scenes from the guild's founding. The images were familiar, yet today, the colors seemed more muted, the stories harder to draw comfort from.

The leadership of the Weavers' Guild sat in a semicircle at the far end of the chamber. Their faces illuminated by both natural light and the faint glow of the Incada-laced designs carved into the marble floor. Ava sat at the center, her presence as composed as ever, her golden cloak draped neatly over her shoulders. To her left, Jezreel stood tall, her arms crossed, an ever-watchful sentinel. And to the right — Evander, his eyes fixed on Alarion the moment he entered, unreadable but intense.

Alarion took a steadying breath and approached, bowing with respectful precision.

"Alarion," Ava began, her voice even but not unkind, the warmth carefully measured. "We have a task for you. One that requires both your skill and leadership."

He nodded, though the unease remained. "Of course. What would you have me do?"

Ava's expression softened. "We want you to compose the opening piece for this year's Challenger's Tournament. Not just compose it — you will also lead the Weaver Orchestra in its performance during the opening ceremony."

The words struck like a hammer blow.

Alarion's pulse quickened. "Compose...and lead?" he echoed, the words twisting in his chest.

"You have shown remarkable growth these past months," Ava continued, her expression encouraging, though her posture remained formal. "We believe you are ready to step forward as an example of what the next generation of Weavers can accomplish. The city deserves to hear your work — your voice."

The knot in his stomach tightened.

"I...I appreciate the trust," Alarion began, choosing his words carefully. "But this is a massive responsibility. Surely, there's someone more experienced, someone with —"

"There is no one more capable," Ava interrupted, though her delivery remained gentle.

But before Alarion could respond, Evander leaned forward in his chair, the scrape of his gauntleted fingers against the marble sharp enough to cut through the air.

"This isn't a request, Alarion," he said. "You've been given every resource, every advantage. It's time to stop second-guessing yourself and meet the expectations placed on you. Stop hesitating. Be a man. Fulfill your duty."

The words struck like a slap.

Alarion's jaw tightened, heat rising unbidden to his face. "I never asked for this," he snapped, the frustration spilling free before he could stop it. "I never wanted to join a guild at all. I didn't come here by choice. My parents —"

The words caught in Alarion's throat, like a chord left unresolved.

The chamber blurred — Ava's calm expression, Evander's unyielding stare — all fading as a memory seized him with relentless clarity.

He was back in the passenger seat of the family vehicle, a simple work truck with three seats. The soft glow of the energy core pulsed steadily beneath the dashboard, but his pulse raced faster, louder. Beyond the reinforced glass, the towers of the guild complex loomed closer, their stone and steel facades catching the pale morning light. The soft hum of elevated trams echoed in the distance, weaving through the heart of the capital like veins carrying life into the city.

His parents sat beside him — his father at the controls, his mother silent in the middle seat. They had spoken in quiet tones earlier, when the journey began. But as the guild gates came into view, silence had taken over.

The spires of the complex stretched skyward — beautiful, imposing. Crystalline conduits pulsed faintly along the outer walls, Incada energy running through them in slow, controlled rhythms. It felt...cold. The air was too still, the city's vibrant hum dimmed here, as if tradition itself muffled everything else.

His mother had finally broken the silence, her voice soft but careful. "This will be good for you, Alarion. Trust us."

But he hadn't trusted them.

The words felt hollow, rehearsed. They spoke of opportunity and growth, yet all he felt was the ache of being cast out from the life he knew. His father's hands stayed steady on the controls, his face unreadable — except for that one tightening at the corner of his mouth, the way his jaw clenched ever so slightly.

They were doing this because they thought they had to. Because they believed it was what was best for him.

But that hadn't made it hurt any less.

The vehicle slowed, coming to rest beneath the grand archway leading into the guild courtyard. Sunlight filtered through the stained glass overhead, catching hints of dormant Incada crystals embedded in the stone.

The door had opened with a hiss.

He'd wanted to run. To beg them to take him back to the farm, where music wasn't an obligation and the world felt...safe. Familiar.

But no such mercy had come.

His father's voice had been quiet. Final.

"This is your path, Alarion. We're giving you a future."

And they had left him there.

The memory wrenched him back to the present like a sudden drop. The grand chamber felt smaller now, suffocating under the weight of expectation pressing down on his chest.

Evander's words cut through it all, like forged steel.

"You can't run from this," he said coldly. "You swore an oath to The Everlight. It's too late to walk away from responsibility now."

The words stung deeper than they should have.

And then Evander was gone, the echo of his footsteps fading as the chamber door closed behind him.

Silence hung heavily in his absence.

Ava remained, watching him with the same calm, joyful look that she always seemed to have. There was no judgment in her expression. No anger.

Jezreel waited too, arms crossed, her face unreadable — but softer than usual, as though giving him space to speak first.

Alarion said nothing.

Because he wasn't sure whether the pressure building in his chest was anger at being forced into this role —

Or shame for simply wanting to go back to his own work.

Alarion left the guild hall with his head down, his steps heavy against the polished stone floor. The echo of Evander's words still rang in his mind, sharp and unrelenting, "You swore an oath. Stop running."

The corridors of the guild felt colder than usual, the elegant arches and crystalline sconces failing to pierce the storm of frustration knotting in his chest. He kept on though; his friends should be waiting for him in the common area by now.

He was so lost in thought that he nearly collided with someone rounding the corner.

"Alarion —"

Nysara staggered back, clutching a carefully balanced cake, its frosting swirled in neat golden patterns. She barely managed to keep it upright, blinking up at him with wide eyes. "Hey! What —" Her focus narrowed. "What just happened in there? We could hear Evander shouting from, like, three rooms away. When I got the word from the courier earlier and told the others, we thought we'd be celebrating some good news."

Alarion forced a smile, but it felt brittle, a mask barely holding together. "It's...complicated. Let's just go meet the others."

She hesitated, concern flickering across her face as she fell into step beside him. The scent of sugar and vanilla from the cake hovered between them, oddly out of place against the tension pressing in on his chest.

Nysara glanced sideways. "Complicated? How? What did they want you to do?"

Alarion exhaled, his hands curling into fists at his sides. "They want me to compose the opening piece for the tournament. And lead the entire Weaver Orchestra for the ceremony."

Her eyes widened. "Wait — seriously? That's incredible! Alarion, that's...a huge honor! Why do you look like someone just told you you're being banished?"

He gave a bitter laugh, shaking his head. "It's not the task. It's Evander. He acted like...like I'm failing just because I hesitated. Told me I needed to 'be a man' and stop running from responsibility." His voice dropped lower, rawer. "I never wanted this. Not like this."

Nysara's expression softened, her grip tightening slightly on the cake box. "Look...Evander's intense. Yeah, his methods are harsh, but he pushes because he believes in people. He's trying to make you stronger, not tear you down."

Alarion shook his head. "Sometimes it feels less like pushing and more like being shoved off a cliff."

Silence hung between them for a beat longer than comfortable.

Then, in classic Nysara fashion, she broke it with a determined, almost too-cheerful tone.

"Well...at least we've got cake."

Alarion blinked — then, despite himself, felt the tension crack just a little. A quiet laugh escaped him as he finally met her gaze.

"Yeah," he muttered, lips curling into a genuine smile. "At least we've got cake."

When they reached the common area, the warm glow of suspended Incada lamps cast soft patterns along the stone walls. Liam and Celeste were already waiting, seated on the low circular benches near the hearth, a few open books and half-finished mugs of tea between them. Liam was the first to look up, his usual grin fading the moment he caught sight of Alarion's expression.

"So…?" Liam leaned forward. "What happened? Good news...right?"

Alarion set his hands on the back of a chair, gripping it just a bit too tightly. His voice felt heavy in his throat. "They want me to compose the opening piece for the tournament. And lead the Weaver Orchestra during the ceremony."

"That's amazing!" Liam's face lit up — until Alarion shook his head, jaw tight.

"Evander didn't see it that way," Alarion muttered, his response sharpening. "He acted like...like I've been running from this. Said I needed to 'step up and be a man.' Like I wasn't already doing my best."

Celeste, who had remained quiet, finally spoke as she crossed the room, her expression calm but thoughtful. "Alarion, you are doing your best. You've worked for this. No matter how Evander speaks, you belong here. We all do."

Liam nodded, resting his elbows on his knees. "Yeah, man. Remember when we first got here? We all had our doubts. You thought the city was too loud, and I was convinced I'd get thrown out in a week —"

Celeste raised a brow. "You almost did get thrown out, if I recall."

"— Details," Liam shot back, waving her off. "Point is, you've come so far since then. We all have."

For a moment, Alarion almost let the words sink in. But the knot in his chest tightened instead. He exhaled slowly, his speech quieter now.

"I need to be honest with you." His grip on the chair loosened, but he didn't meet their eyes. "I didn't want to come here. Not to the capital. Not to the guild. I didn't even bring my instruments when I left home."

Nysara blinked. "Wait...what?"

Alarion's voice wavered, the words coming faster now, as if they'd been bottled too long. "I didn't plan on joining the Weavers. My parents forced me. I've been trying, but this pressure — it's...crushing. I don't want to be the guild's next rising star. I don't want to be a leader. I just...want to create. Without expectations."

Silence settled over the room, broken only by the faint crackle of the hearth.

Finally, Liam spoke, his usual bravado gone. His speech was softer now, genuine. "Look, Alarion...we're not here because of what you can do. We're here because of who you are. You're not alone in this. You're one of us."

Nysara nodded, stepping closer. "You've had our backs since day one. We're not going anywhere. No matter what."

Alarion felt the words — heard them — but the pressure hadn't eased. Not yet. There was too much tangled inside. Too much he hadn't sorted out.

"I...need some time." His manner was quieter, strained as he stood straighter. "I just need to think."

The warmth of their words rested behind him as he turned toward the door, but the weight pressing on his chest hadn't quite lifted yet. Not completely.

The corridors of the guild complex stretched long and empty as dusk settled over Ileydria. Incada lanterns flickered to life along the archways, casting soft blue glows against the stone, but their light felt distant — muted beneath the storm twisting inside Alarion's chest.

His footsteps echoed softly, the rhythmic tap of his boots swallowed by the restless hum in his mind. The words his friends had spoken repeated themselves, clashing against old fears he couldn't quite shake.

They care about you, not just your talents.

But how could he be sure? Wasn't that always how it started? The well-meaning encouragement...until people saw what he could do. Until their admiration soured into expectations, and suddenly he was no longer Alarion, just a performer, a vessel for whatever others wanted from him.

The weight pressed heavier with every step.

It's not the same here. They've stood with you. Haven't they?

The thoughts spiraled, colliding until his chest felt too tight, the ache unbearable. He staggered, leaning against the cold stone wall as his breath hitched. His hands curled into fists at his sides, nails biting into his palms.

"No...No more."

The words barely escaped his lips before his composure shattered.

With a broken cry, Alarion dropped to his knees, clutching his head as frustration and confusion poured out in a raw, unrestrained release. The sound echoed, then faded, swallowed by the stillness of the complex.

Silence.

And then — Drip.

The faint sound, barely louder than a whisper, met his ears.

Drip.

A single droplet of water, hanging from the edge of a leaf just off the pathway, fell — striking the stone below with a delicate, consistent rhythm.

Drip...drip...drip.

His breathing slowed. The ache in his chest didn't vanish, but it dulled, the rhythm anchoring him. Simple. Constant. Honest.

His fingers relaxed as he stared at the leaf, watching the water gather again, trembling at the edge before it fell once more.

There.

The pulse of inspiration ignited, quiet at first but growing stronger. The rhythm. The simplicity. The truth of it.

It wasn't about grandeur or pressure. Music was expression. Music was clarity. And he could hear it now — a melody forming, delicate yet powerful. He had to capture it now.

Tearing himself from the spot, Alarion wiped his damp face, breath ragged as he sprinted for the Weavers Hall. His heart pounded with the echo of that rhythm, each step aligning with the pulse in his mind.

The heavy double doors loomed ahead. He didn't slow.

The doors burst open with a loud clap against the stone as he nearly skidded to a stop, chest heaving. The front desk attendant — an older man with half-moon glasses and a raised brow — blinked in surprise.

"I...need..." Alarion gasped, struggling for breath. "Practice room. Now. Please —"

The attendant studied him for a beat before speaking, clearly unfazed. "We're almost fully booked. The front hall is open, but it's visible from the gallery. If you're planning to, ah...'make a ruckus,' you'll likely have an audience."

Alarion shook his head, the urgency overriding everything else. "Fine. It doesn't matter. I can't lose this idea."

The attendant slid a key across the desk without another word.

Alarion grabbed it, already moving before the man could finish saying, "Good luck."

Liam remained in the common area long after Alarion had left, drumming his fingers idly on the arm of the chair, but his mind wasn't nearly as calm as his posture. Something about the way Alarion had walked out bothered him — an unease Liam couldn't quite shake.

With a sigh, he pushed himself up, adjusting his jacket as he made his way toward the Weaver's Guild Hall.

The towering structure was quieter than usual, most of the day's lessons concluded, leaving the grand stone corridors filled with little more than the distant hum of Incada conduits lining the walls. Yet, as Liam approached the front desk, a curious sound drifted faintly from deeper inside — notes, distant but powerful, resonating in the walls themselves.

The desk attendant looked up, arching a brow as Liam approached.

"Hey," Liam began, voice laced with concern, "I'm looking for my friend — Alarion. Short, black hair carries a violin case. He left the group earlier, and I wanted to check on him. Have you seen him?"

The attendant's expression shifted to something caught between amusement and admiration. "Oh, yeah. Came barreling in about half an hour ago — completely out of breath, ranting about needing a practice space. He's still here."

Relief was short-lived. The attendant's smirk widened as he gestured toward the large glass-walled practice room across the foyer. "You'll have to get through the crowd if you want a better look. He's got half the guild watching him right now."

Liam blinked. "Crowd?"

But as he turned, the reason became painfully clear.

A massive gathering had formed — students, guild members, even a few instructors watching from the grand window of the practice hall, pressing in so close it was nearly impossible to see inside. From his position at the back, all Liam could catch were flashes of pale Incada light and the soft pulse of faint melodies seeping through the thick glass. Every few moments, the crowd would let out soft gasps, the kind reserved for witnessing something truly extraordinary.

Determined, Liam edged his way forward, muttering apologies as he shouldered past the spectators.

When he finally broke through to the front of the glass, his breath caught.

Alarion stood at the center of the practice hall, completely consumed in his work.

The space around him shimmered with threads of light — Incada energy woven so seamlessly into the instruments that they seemed almost alive beneath his touch. Violins suspended mid-air thrummed with soft, beautiful harmonies as his bow brushed their strings. A nearby cello resonated in time, its frame aglow with delicate blue tracing along its edges. Percussion instruments pulsed with steady rhythm, the low thrum of a bass drum vibrating faintly through the floor.

But it wasn't just the music — it was him.

Alarion's entire being seemed to pulse with the energy of creation. His hands flowed from instrument to instrument, weaving sound as though guided by instinct alone. One moment, his fingers danced over the keys of a shimmering piano, then suddenly, he was scribbling furiously in a notebook, his expression shifting from fierce concentration to unrestrained wonder.

Liam had never seen him like this.

Gone was the hesitation, the weight of self-doubt he so often carried. Instead, there was something raw and pure in his focus — a kind of joy, radiant and wild.

And then, just for a moment, Alarion paused.

He closed his eyes, head tilted slightly, as if listening for something just beyond hearing. The entire room seemed to hold its breath. Then his face lit up, breaking into a wide, almost childlike grin as he moved back to the violin, bow raised.

And the music surged to life once more.

Liam couldn't tear his gaze away.

Whatever Alarion was creating — it wasn't just music. It was alive.

Liam slipped into the practice room as quietly as he could, the door clicking shut behind him. The resonance of Alarion's music still hung in the air, like the echo of a heartbeat just fading.

Alarion's bow stilled mid-stroke. He looked up, slightly startled but not displeased, his expression shifting from creative focus to self-consciousness.

The music ceased. The Incada light dimmed. Energy once vibrant seemed to dissolve into the stillness, like mist dispersing at dawn.

"That was… incredible," Liam said, unable to keep the awe from his voice. His arms were folded, but his expression was soft, sincere. "You're incredible."

Alarion immediately shook his head, his demeanor dropping as he set the violin back on its stand. "It's nothing, really," he muttered, the earlier fire now retreating behind familiar walls.

Liam raised an eyebrow, stepping further into the room. "Alarion, stop. It wasn't 'nothing.' That was one of the most amazing things I've ever seen you do."

Before Alarion could protest again, his eyes drifted toward the glass window — and the crowd still gathered outside. More had joined since Liam's arrival, pressed close with wide eyes, murmuring as they watched.

Alarion's face flushed a deep red. With a frantic wave of his hands, he gestured at the spectators to leave, mouthing a silent Go away! before turning his back to them entirely.

Liam fought the urge to laugh but kept his expression calm.

"Look, I get it," Liam said gently, crossing his arms as he leaned against a nearby music stand. "But you can't just brush this off. You have a gift. And it's not just skill, Alarion — it's meant for something greater. Don't run from it."

Alarion hesitated, shoulders tense, but he listened.

Liam's voice softened further. "You know, in my family — the Valorias — we were always taught our gifts aren't ours. They come from The Everlight. It's not about how good we are or how talented we feel. It's about trusting the one who gave those gifts. That's what gives us confidence, not our own strength."

Alarion exhaled, his fingers tightening slightly around the edge of the music stand. "I suppose you're right...I know that, but...it's hard to trust my abilities. I keep wondering if it's enough. If I'm enough."

Liam shook his head, stepping closer. "That's the thing — it's not about you being enough. The Everlight is. Even when we feel unsteady. Even when we mess up. That strength never fades. That's what my family's faith has always been about. Not confidence in ourselves...but confidence in the one who's enduring, unshaken."

Alarion blinked, studying him carefully. "...So, you're telling me all those crazy, reckless moments where you take the lead? That's not just because you believe you can do it? You're not that sure of yourself?"

Liam laughed, loud enough that a few heads turned at the window. "Oh, if you knew how scared I was half the time? You'd lose your mind. I'm always second-guessing myself. But that's the point — I just remind myself to give my all for The Everlight. And trust that where I fall short... He won't."

Alarion's expression softened, the tension in his shoulders finally beginning to ease.

For the first time in a long while, he felt heard.

Liam clapped a hand on Alarion's shoulder, his grin returning with full force. "Alright, now that we've had our heart-to-heart, you did say you'd teach me some of those fancy moves. I'm pretty sure now's a good time for a lesson, don't you think?"

Alarion raised an eyebrow, his arms crossing. "I said I'd teach you what I could. You do realize Envoys aren't exactly known for using Incada in...indirect methods, right?"

Liam smirked. "Come on, that thing you did in the warehouse — the floor bomb pulse or whatever? That seemed pretty direct to me. I bet I could figure it out. It's just like an empowered swing, right? All about impact?"

Alarion blinked, half surprised. "Well...in theory, yes. But the trick isn't just force. You have to release the energy in the air — dissipate it, not drive it straight into the ground, or — "

THUD.

Alarion's head snapped around just in time to see Liam mid-air — knees tucked, arms wide — plummeting toward the floor with all the grace of a boulder.

"LIKE THIS?!" Liam shouted, eyes wide.

"NO! Not here!" Alarion's hands shot up, panic seizing his chest. "This room is full of priceless instruments, Liam!"

With a burst of energy from his hands, Alarion threw a pulse of shimmering air beneath Liam, softening the impact enough for him to hit the ground with a controlled thud instead of a crater.

They both froze.

Several instruments on the nearby racks swayed precariously. A single violin slid an inch before settling.

Silence.

Alarion's pulse pounded in his ears.

Then, slowly, he exhaled.

"Okay. New rule." He extended a hand to help Liam up. "We're practicing outside from now on. Because if Evander catches us wrecking this room, we'll both be cleaning artifact chambers until next winter."

Liam grinned sheepishly. "Yeah...fair point. But admit it — that was almost cool."

"Only if you're measuring coolness by sheer recklessness," Alarion muttered, but a smile tugged at the corner of his mouth despite himself.

The tension between them, so heavy earlier, had dissolved into something warmer. The weight on Alarion's chest felt lighter, the knot in his stomach finally starting to untangle.

As they left the practice hall, their footsteps echoing along the stone corridors, the conversation shifted — jokes, halfhearted challenges, even a debate about whether a pancake was technically a cake.

By the time they reached the mess hall, the golden glow of the lanterns wrapped around them like a welcoming embrace. The scent of baked bread and warm cider remained in the air, a comfort in the quiet after everything the day had held.

Celeste and Nysara waved them over from a corner table, plates half-filled with pastries and late-night rations.

Liam flopped into the chair with exaggerated exhaustion. "You would not believe the workout I just had. Alarion practically threw me across a room with magic. Nearly died. Heroic stuff, really."

Nysara raised an eyebrow. "Heroic or...clumsy?"

Alarion grinned, shaking his head as he sat. "Definitely, clumsy."

The laughter that followed felt real — easing the weight of expectations, of pressure, of everything they had faced that day.

And as Alarion leaned back, the warmth of shared stories and familiar voices surrounding him, he closed his eyes for just a moment.

"Maybe Mom and Dad were right, maybe this is good for me."

6

Shadows of the Bringers

Celeste stood at the threshold of the Bringer Dungeon, the cool draft from the underground passage curling around her ankles like a whispered warning. Dim Incada sconces lined the stone walls, their pale blue glow barely piercing the shadows that pooled deeper within. The scent of ancient stone and faint traces of incense hung in the air — a reminder of the many who had passed through these halls before her.

On either side, Olive the Seer and Counselor Rhane stood in silent contrast. Olive, draped in flowing white robes, seemed ethereal against the gloom, her presence calm but unreadable, while Rhane's broader frame and lined face carried the quiet weight of a guardian long acquainted with this place. Their presence should have been reassuring, yet it only made the air feel heavier. This was more than just another task.

For the past month, Celeste returned here nearly every day. Each visit had been a test of patience — hauling supplies, taking inventory, performing the monotonous duties expected of a Bringer-in-training. It was a cycle of quiet repetition, yet she knew it was designed for something more. This place had a way of revealing truths, breaking down barriers within. And now, standing at the entrance again, her pulse quickened with a tension she couldn't quite explain.

"Are you ready, Celeste?" Olive's voice broke the silence, calm but measured as the soft glow from her staff reflected faintly in her eyes. "This phase of your training is pivotal. It was in these very halls I found my calling as the Seer."

Celeste forced a nod, clenching her fists just enough to keep them still. "I've been here enough times. It's always just...hard work."

Counselor Rhane, his expression unreadable, stepped closer. His hand, firm yet warm, rested on her shoulder. "Don't mistake repetition for insignificance. The work tests more than your strength — it tests your spirit. And when the dark presses close, remember —" His eyes sharpened. "Darkness cannot push back the light."

The words endured, pressing heavier than the shadows around her.

Olive offered a soft smile, her eyes searching Celeste's face as if trying to glimpse something beneath her stoic mask. "The dungeon isn't just a vault. It's a crucible where Bringers confront the limits of their connection to The Everlight. My first time here, I was afraid. But it's where I learned the truth about what I was capable of. You may find more here than you expect."

Celeste drew in a slow breath; the weight of their words settled in her chest. She straightened her posture, squaring her shoulders against gnawing uncertainty.

"I'll do my best," she said softly, though a whisper of doubt stayed at the edges of her mind.

All the while, Celeste's mind kept circling the same thought. This feels pointless.

Day after day, she had returned here with the mentors, repeating the same endless cycle of tasks as if she hadn't already proven herself.

"I've already connected with The Everlight. I can use most of the ancient skills better than half my class. Why am I still being held back?"

She hadn't meant to let the frustration show, but Rhane's quiet chuckle made it clear he had noticed.

"I was the last in my class to have an encounter here," he said, his voice calm but pointed. "It's not about how quickly it happens, Celeste. What matters is that you keep seeking The Everlight. Your connection isn't something to check off a list."

Celeste shifted her weight, her arms crossed tightly. "I'm not just checking boxes. I am seeking. I've been coming here every day for weeks. If nothing's happening, isn't that proof I'm ready to move on?"

Rhane shook his head. "No, it proves you're still holding on to something. The artifacts stored here aren't just relics of the past. They're remnants from the days of the Obsidian Shade — a reminder of what happens when power is misused. That darkness consumed entire guilds once. The Bringers were entrusted not only to guard these objects but to ensure they never twist someone's spirit again.

Understanding why we protect them is just as important as the skills you've developed."

Olive, standing beside him with her hands gently folded, added, "We are asking you to see the dungeon for what it is, Celeste. It's a lesson. A place where The Everlight reveals truths — about us, about what we're ready to face. And what we're still resisting."

Celeste shook her head. "I'm not resisting. I respect the responsibility we have here. But it's been a month. How am I supposed to learn something from just...sorting through old artifacts?"

Olive's lips curled into a faint smile. "I thought the same thing once. The first time I came down here, I thought it was just a storeroom — ancient, yes, but nothing special. I spent days doing mundane tasks, same as you. Then, one afternoon, it shifted. I started hearing things. At first, whispers I couldn't quite place. Later, clearer. I heard my mentors speaking about assignments I hadn't been given yet. I saw friends eating in the mess hall, talking about things that hadn't happened — at least not yet. Two days later, I heard the same conversation word for word."

Celeste blinked, a chill running down her spine. "You...saw the future?"

"Not quite," Olive replied gently. "It wasn't a vision of the future, but rather a deeper awareness. Fragments of what The Everlight had already begun revealing. It was enough for my mentors to realize my gifting as a Seer was awakening."

Celeste's gaze dropped to the stone steps descending into the dark. She swallowed hard, the weight of her mentors' words pressing heavier now. "But I've already felt connected. I know the light is with me. What else am I supposed to prove?"

Rhane's speech softened. "It's not about proving yourself. The Everlight isn't something you master. It reveals the truth. Including truths, we might not want to see yet."

The words cut deeper than Celeste expected.

She had spent so long focusing on control, on mastering every skill and discipline the guild had taught her. But the way Rhane said it — truths we might not want to see — felt far too personal.

Her grip on her staff tightened. "I'm ready," she said firmly, even as her heart pounded harder in her chest.

With a final nod from her mentors, Celeste took her first step down, the shadows stretching long beneath her as she descended into the Dungeon alone.

The entrance yawned wide before Celeste, the ancient stone archway carved with intricate depictions of Ileydria's most harrowing days. The rise and fall of the Obsidian Shade unfolded in jagged relief — scenes of battle etched into the walls, warriors clashing with figures cloaked in darkness, their faces twisted in agony and triumph alike.

As she stepped deeper, the air cooled, the warmth of the upper halls fading behind her. A pale-yellow luminescence shimmered faintly along the edges of the corridor. Incadise.

The deeper she moved, the stronger the oppressive energy felt, clinging to the edges of her senses. The dungeon was vast; a labyrinth of tunnels and vaults lined with containment fields — each holding relics touched by corruption.

Her footsteps echoed softly as she passed the artifacts sealed behind shimmering barriers of pale light. A cuirass of midnight-black steel caught her eye, its surface so dark it seemed to devour the ambient glow around it. Inlaid along the chest plate, faint yellow stones pulsed with rhythmic light — Incadise, the corrupted twin to the pure energy they had been trained to wield.

Celeste paused, tracing the strange way shadows shifted around it. The stones didn't radiate power like Incada. They seemed to pull, drawing light inward, casting distorted silhouettes that felt too fluid, too unnatural.

Another step. Another containment bay.

Weapons twisted by that same corruption lay before her — swords with blades that rippled as if alive, shields emitting a murky haze, gauntlets etched with markings that pulsed to the rhythm of some unseen force.

The artifacts whispered a quiet malevolence, as if the dungeon itself was holding its breath.

She adjusted her grip on her staff, exhaling slowly. It's just another task. Do the work. Stay focused.

Her first assignment was inventory. Simple, repetitive. Methodical.

Moving from bay to bay, she checked the list engraved on the small crystalline tablet at her side. Verify the containment field. Confirm the item. Log the integrity. One by one, she worked through the chambers.

Cool metal. Polished stone. The quiet hum of protective wards.

Each item accounted for. Each barrier is intact.

Yet the silence pressed heavier with every hour that passed.

"Another day spent, another day wasted," she muttered, finishing the last vault in her section. The work was necessary, but it felt so...empty.

She had expected more.

With the final check complete, she stowed the tablet back at her belt and brushed her hands together. Just a few more menial tasks — sweeping the lower corridors, shifting a few crates of documents — and she could call it a day.

Celeste glanced back toward the main corridor, her mind already repeating the directions on instinct.

"Second left. Second right. First right. Third left. Stairs. Second left. Second right. First right. Third left. Stairs."

She whispered the path under her breath, counting each turn. The dungeon wasn't dangerous, not really. The leaders could track her location at any time. But getting lost? That was a mistake recruits never live down.

And with her family's legacy...that wasn't a joke she was willing to be the subject of.

Not today.

Celeste worked in silence, the regular rhythm of the broom sweeping across the stone floor echoing faintly through the dim corridor. The scent of dust clung to the cool air, mingling with the constant, gentle hum of the Incada containment fields lining the walls.

She moved methodically, pushing the debris into neat piles, her focus narrowed on the simple, repetitive motions.

And yet...

Something was different.

The blue glow of the containment fields seemed just slightly dimmer. Or perhaps the shadows around them felt heavier, stretching a bit further beyond their usual boundaries.

"No. You're imagining things."

Grabbing the next crate of documents, Celeste adjusted her grip and hauled it toward the designated storage alcove. The papers shifted within, the edges rustling with a soft, familiar whisper. The sound was ordinary. Comforting, even.

But as she passed one of the older bays, a strange weight pressed against her chest. The artifacts stored within — tarnished armor, shattered blades, a staff glowing with Incadise corruption — pulsed faintly behind the shimmering barriers. Pale-yellow threads of Incadise energy coiled and flickered, contained but never quite still.

A whisper brushed the edge of her hearing.

"Celeste."

She froze, the crate growing heavier in her hands.

The corridor remained quiet. The Incada fields held, fixed and firm. Nothing stirred behind the barriers.

She forced herself to keep walking, setting the crate gently on the stone shelf. The tension in her shoulders remained as she returned to her sweeping, the sound of the bristles scraping across stone louder than before.

"It's just your mind playing tricks," she muttered under her breath. "Focus."

The broom moved in rhythmic strokes. Dust stirred. Light flickered.

The containment fields dimmed — just slightly.

"Celeste."

The voice was closer.

The broom clattered from her hand as she spun, heart hammering.

Nothing.

The corridor was empty. The artifacts remained silent behind their barriers, the blue Incada glow constant and unbroken.

She exhaled shakily, pressing her hand to her chest as she bent to retrieve the broom.

"Come on. If I didn't know better, I'd think Liam was behind this. The guy practically lives to get a rise out of me."

The thought was almost enough to break the tension. Almost.

But then the voice came again.

"Careless."

It wasn't a whisper this time. It felt colder.

"You'll never be enough."

The containment fields shuddered. Only for a moment — barely more than a flicker — but the blue light wavered.

And behind the barriers, the corrupted Incadise flared in response.

Celeste flinched back, her pulse racing.

"Who's there?!"

Silence answered.

And yet the shadows shifted, curling along the edges of the halls as though reaching for the cracks in the light.

Her breath caught.

"It's all…in my head."

But the voice persisted.

"Why did you even try? You're alone, Celeste. Always alone."

The words dug deep.

Her mind flashed back to the quiet moments alone in the training halls. The way she was stuck in the Dungeon while her peers had moved forward.

The ache of waiting.

The quiet shame of being left behind.

"No," she whispered, voice shaking. "I'm not alone. I am enough. I serve The Everlight."

"Do you? You're just another recruit. Forgotten. Left behind."

"Stop it!" Her words echoed, raw and trembling, but the darkness only seemed to press closer.

"You can't silence me, Celeste."

The broom slipped from her hands.

She ran.

Her boots pounded the stone as she fled, the corridor shrinking tighter around her, casting twisted shadows that seemed to reach for her.

Second left. Second right. First right. Third left. Stairs.

The directions hammered in her mind, but the halls felt wrong — narrower. Longer.

The voice was louder now.

"You will fail. You always do."

"It's not real. It can't be real. Keep moving. Find the stairs."

The whispers didn't fade.

They followed her. Closer. Louder.

"You'll never escape. You're weak. Unworthy."

"STOP IT!" Celeste's scream echoed through the stone corridors, but the voices only grew stronger, relentless as they closed in from every direction.

She ran harder, heart hammering, her boots slamming against the uneven stone. The dim blue glow of the Incada containment fields blurred past her. She'd lost count of the turns — had she passed the second right already? Or was it the first?

Her own thoughts were being drowned out.

"Now you're lost… They're going to have to come find you. How embarrassing. What will Daddy have to say? What a failure."

Each word felt heavier, pressing into her chest like weights she couldn't shake.

Then it happened — her toe caught the edge of a loose stone.

She stumbled —

— and the ground vanished beneath her.

The impact knocked the breath from her lungs, the stone floor cold and unforgiving beneath her palms. But the pain was...distant. Distant because when she blinked, the dungeon was gone.

The oppressive containment fields, the whispering shadows — all of it melted away.

Celeste sat up, blinking against the sudden warm light filtering through soft curtains.

No.

This wasn't real.

But it felt real.

She pushed herself to her feet, heart pounding harder now for a different reason.

The pale lavender canopy bed, its sheer curtains drawn back just slightly. The mahogany vanity, its surface cluttered with worn books, a half-empty inkwell, and a silver comb. The massive banner of the Bringers' crest, proudly hung on the far wall, its golden embroidery stitched in flawless precision.

Her childhood bedroom.

Exactly as it had been.

"Wait...no. This can't be real." She whispered aloud, yet everything around her seemed so tangible. The soft fabric beneath her fingertips. The scent of the parchment stacked on her old writing desk. Even the faint breeze stirring the curtains — so gentle, so normal.

"Get down here right now, young lady!"

The words struck like a bolt of lightning through her chest.

Her father's voice.

Celeste spun toward the door, the booming echo still reverberating through the walls.

No. This wasn't real.

But her body moved anyway. As if bound by muscle memory, she rushed out of the room, down the sweeping staircase — just as she had on that day so long ago.

And there he stood.

Her father. Tall, stern, the same sharp lines of his face etched with disappointment. His dark green cloak, embroidered with the family crest, made him look larger, more imposing than she remembered.

She knew where this was. When this was.

It had been the afternoon she returned home from school, stomach twisted with dread, knowing her teacher had already called ahead.

Knowing exactly what awaited her.

Celeste had been playing outside with a group of classmates — nothing reckless, just a simple game. A rare moment of laughter in an otherwise rigid schedule.

But that didn't matter.

Her father had made sure the instructors knew she wasn't to waste time with "distractions."

"We don't waste time, Celeste!"

The memory unfolded with cruel clarity.

"How dare you," his voice thundered, pointing toward the family crest hung above the mantle. "Do you see that? We don't play. We don't mess around. We take our calling seriously."

She remembered how small she felt. How the words had pierced deeper than they should have.

"I'm sorry, Dad," she had whispered then, speech trembling. "I'll do better. I just thought —"

"That's the problem." His manner became colder, quieter. The words hurt worse that way. "You think too much, Celeste. Until you get rid of this childish thinking you shouldn't think for yourself. Just listen to instruction and we will teach you what to think."

The weight of it crushed her all over again.

Her hands shook at her sides.

Her younger self had bowed her head that day. She had swallowed the words. She had let them bury themselves deep where they remained — unchallenged.

But this wasn't then.

This wasn't real.

She wasn't that child anymore.

"I was just a kid," she whispered, voice breaking.

The world around her began to waver. The golden light dimmed. The walls of her home dissolved into shifting shadows.

And then, like a candle snuffed out —

She was back in the dungeon.

The icy stone beneath her knees. The pale Incada light from the containment fields pulsing steadily once more.

Yet the whispers lingered.

"You'll never be enough."

Tears streamed down Celeste's face as she slumped against the cold stone wall, her chest heaving with ragged breaths. The icy dampness pressed against her back, but it was nothing compared to the crushing weight pressing inside her chest. Fear. Exhaustion.

"I can't do this," she whispered, speech barely more than a breath. "I'm not strong enough."

The darkness pressed closer.

It wasn't just the dim corridors now — the shadows themselves seemed to creep from the cracks in the stone, shifting and pulsing just beyond the containment fields. The pale blue Incada glow holding back the corrupt artifacts had dimmed to the faintest pulse. Almost like they, too, were struggling under the same weight she felt inside.

"You're failing."

"You always were."

"You'll never be more than a disappointment."

The voices were louder now, circling her like vultures.

And yet —

A different voice echoed faintly, piercing the storm.

"Darkness cannot push back light."

Rhane's words.

The memory hit like a spark in the void.

Celeste forced her trembling hand to her staff, its carved surface warm beneath her fingertips. A reminder.

She gritted her teeth, summoning what little strength she had left. The darkness fed on fear — she could feel it, pressing closer with every whispered lie. But fear wasn't the only thing she carried.

She raised her staff and drove its base hard against the stone.

A brilliant flare of blue Incada light surged outward, rippling along the cracks in the walls and forcing the shadows to retreat.

The voices hissed — pained, distorted — but they didn't vanish entirely.

Celeste's breath slowed, but she didn't let go of the staff. The light pulsed steadily, illuminating the corridor in a way that felt...warmer. Familiar.

"I am a Bringer," she whispered, the words firmer now. "And I will overcome."

The voices began to fade, but something else stirred — filling the silence.

A presence.

Not a voice of condemnation, but one that felt ancient, sure. Like the warmth of a flame in winter.

The Everlight.

The glow around her intensified, though this time it didn't blind. It clarified.

And suddenly, she wasn't in the dungeon at all.

The darkness fell away, replaced by the gentle warmth of sunlight reflecting on water. She stood on the edge of a vast, endless lake, its surface rippling softly as though stirred by a breeze she could not feel. The reflection of herself stared back — yet it was not the cold, calculating version she'd crafted to protect herself.

This Celeste had softer eyes. Unburdened.

Whole.

"You are more than your past," came a voice — steady, resonant, yet impossibly gentle. It filled the air, not from the lake, but through it, like the words were woven into the fabric of the moment itself.

Celeste's pulse slowed as the presence pressed further into her mind.

"Embrace who you are. Not who others say you are — but who I say you are."

She felt her knees weaken, the weight of unworthiness rising like a tide. "Who am I to be worthy of this? I've doubted. I've failed."

The voice did not scold.

"Strength is not found in being flawless. It is found in understanding. Did you think I never delight? That I do not know joy? You are mistaken."

The image in the water rippled — and in its place, flashes of her friends filled the reflection.

Liam's reckless grin, teasing and lighthearted even in the midst of battle. Nysara's quiet humor, the way she diffused tension. Alarion's calm, unwavering presence.

"Joy is not a weakness, Celeste. It binds. It strengthens. The laughter you share with them — the moments of vulnerability — this is not a distraction from your calling. It is your strength."

The words struck deeper than any condemnation.

She had been so focused on control. On perfection. As if shutting out the lighter parts of herself would make her more worthy.

It was a lie.

The rippling water stilled. The vision faded —

And she was back.

The dungeon. The containment fields glowing steadily once more. The shadows no longer pressing in.

Her staff was still glowing, the light was steadier than before. Stronger.

Celeste took a calming breath, standing taller as the knot in her chest loosened.

She could feel it now — the connection to The Everlight wasn't just power. It was trust. It was truth.

Celeste followed a figure of light through the dim corridors, its presence both brilliant and gentle, illuminating the path ahead with steady pulses of pale blue. Though the rational part of her mind whispered questions, "Was this truly The Everlight? Could it be?" The truth settled deeper than logic.

She knew.

The presence was unmistakable.

And yet, she told herself no one would ever hear of this. No one would believe it — visions and voices were things whispered about in ancient texts, not spoken openly. Besides, how could she begin to explain what had just happened? How could she describe the way the shadows had seemed alive, pressing in with words that felt designed to break her?

She wouldn't try.

As the final stair came into view, the figure of light faded, its warmth lingering just long enough for her to find her footing.

The heavy wooden doors at the top of the dungeon loomed larger than they ever had before. And yet, Celeste didn't hesitate. She climbed the last step and pushed them open.

The cool evening air rushed against her face.

She had made it.

Olive and Counselor Rhane were waiting at the entrance, the sunlight catching on the deep purple accents of their Bringer robes. The tension in Olive's face eased the moment she saw Celeste — though her eyes narrowed as she took in her appearance.

Celeste's robes were torn; dirt smudged across the fabric. Stray strands of hair clung to her damp face, and her breathing was uneven. She leaned heavily on her staff, every step careful, controlled — but her grip didn't waver.

Rhane was the first to step forward, concern flashing beneath his usual calm. "This...doesn't look like someone who had a normal day in the dungeon." His manner was light, but there was gravity behind it, his eyes scanning for injury.

Celeste let out a breath, standing as straight as her exhausted body would allow.

"I had my encounter," she said quietly, but the words carried a new weight. A steadiness.

Olive's face softened, her hands pressing together just below her chin. "You're sure?"

Celeste met her eyes without hesitation. "I'm sure. I'm ready for whatever comes next."

The two leaders exchanged a brief glance — one of knowing. Relief.

"Well, thank The Everlight," Rhane said, stepping beside her to offer his arm for support. "Because we were only a few minutes away from coming after you. Honestly, I was already preparing my lecture about wandering off just to keep us on edge."

Celeste shook her head with a tired smile. "I didn't wander. I just...needed to find my way."

Olive moved closer, her expression gentler now. "No one can question what you are anymore, Celeste. You are a Bringer. I hope you understand that now."

There was something different in the way Olive said it — not as praise, but as recognition. As if she'd seen it the moment Celeste emerged.

Celeste felt it too.

The weight of uncertainty had lifted.

"Thank you," she said softly, her speech thick with emotion. "For believing in me...even when I wasn't sure I could believe in myself."

Rhane chuckled, his tone breaking the moment's intensity. "Alright, alright — so am I going to have to carry you back to your quarters, or do you think you can make it under your own power?"

Celeste shook her head, a faint laugh escaping her lips despite the ache in her muscles. "I think I've got it. Barely."

Olive stepped back, gesturing toward the guild hall with a wide, encouraging smile. "Then go. Get some rest. You've earned it. Besides —"

Her smile sharpened slightly.

"We've only got a few weeks until the tournament. I expect you to be at the top of your game."

Celeste nodded, the exhaustion was still heavy, but a quiet strength had taken root alongside it.

On her way back to her quarters, Celeste spotted her friends waiting just outside the entrance of the Bringer Guild Hall. Liam, Nysara, and Alarion sat near the stone steps, the soft blue lanterns casting long shadows across their faces as the evening settled in. Their conversation quieted the moment they noticed her; concern etched clearly in their expressions.

"Celeste!" Liam called, pushing himself up first and striding toward her. "You look like you went twelve rounds with a bear. Everything okay?"

She let out a breathless laugh, the ache in her muscles momentarily forgotten. "You could say that. I... had my encounter."

That was enough to make Nysara's eyes widen as she stood, her earlier sleepiness evaporating. "In the dungeon? Seriously? That place is terrifying. What happened?"

Celeste hesitated, gripping her staff tighter as she took a moment to choose her words. They weren't Bringers. They wouldn't fully understand the purpose of the dungeon — or the weight of what she'd just faced. But they were her friends. They deserved the truth, or at least as much as she could share.

"It was...intense," she admitted. "I heard voices. I felt like something was trying to get inside my head, pushing all my worst fears in front of me. But then —" She paused, manner softening. "The Everlight was there. He helped me find my strength when I didn't think I had any left."

Alarion's brow furrowed, his curiosity evident. "Wait — you saw The Everlight? As in, a vision? What...what did he say?"

Celeste swallowed. Part of her still felt that protective instinct, the same one that told her no one would believe this. But they were looking at her differently now — not as if she were frail, but with awe. Respect.

She recounted as much as she dared — the weight of the shadows, the voice echoing her fears, and how The Everlight's words had cut through the darkness like a flame. When she finished, her friends were silent for a moment, absorbing it all.

"That's incredible," Nysara said softly. "You faced that...and came out stronger. That's what being a Bringer is all about, isn't it?"

Celeste nodded, then lowered her response. "Please don't tell anyone else, okay? You're probably the only people who would even believe me. I —" She exhaled, shaking her head. "I don't want people thinking I've lost it."

Liam grinned, crossing his arms. "Celeste, you're probably the toughest person we know. Seriously. We're lucky you're on our side."

Celeste felt warmth rise in her chest, the knot of isolation that had weighed on her for so long finally easing.

"Thanks, guys," she whispered. "I mean it. I don't think I could've gotten through this without you."

Suddenly, a soft snore broke the moment.

Everyone turned toward Nysara, who had somehow drifted off standing up, her head tilted slightly to the side.

"Are you serious?!" Liam barked, nudging her shoulder.

Nysara jerked awake with a dramatic blink. "Huh — wha —? Oh, sorry! I was...resting my eyes. Totally paying attention."

Alarion snorted. "How do you even do that? You fell asleep standing up."

Nysara smirked sleepily. "It's a gift, really."

Liam rolled his eyes but softened. "Well, come on, sleeping beauty. Let's make sure Celeste makes it back to her quarters in one piece."

The walk was quiet but comfortable, the tension of the day finally beginning to ease as the guild hall's lanterns cast their soft blue glow across the stone pathways.

When they arrived at her door, Nysara was the first to step forward, wrapping Celeste in a tight hug. "We're always here for you, okay? No matter what."

Celeste smiled, feeling something settle within her at last.

"Thanks, all of you. Really."

As the door clicked shut behind her and the quiet of her quarters wrapped around her, Celeste finally let herself exhale fully. The ache in her body was still there, but beneath it was something stronger — something steady.

She lay back on her bed, staring at the faint patterns of light dancing across the ceiling from the window's glow.

"Maybe there's more to this than strategy," she thought, closing her eyes. "Maybe...there's more to me than that too."

7

The Dawn of Challengers

The sun crested over the capital of Ileydria, painting the towers and spires in hues of gold and amber. The light caught on the polished stonework of the guild complex, its towering marble arches and crystalline inlays gleaming as the city stirred awake. At the heart of it all, the Duriel Arena stood in quiet majesty — its high walls and intricate carvings a living testament to the kingdom's strength, history, and unity.

From its highest tiers, the banners of the four great guilds rippled proudly in the morning breeze. The golden crest of the Envoys, bold and unyielding like the warriors it represented. The slate blue cogwheel of the Originators, symbolizing invention and progress. The crimson insignia of the Weavers, elegant and sharp as the melodies they commanded. And the radiant violet sigil of the Bringers, glowing bright with the authority of those entrusted to guard The Everlight's truth.

Within the arena, the air buzzed with anticipation. Thousands of spectators filled the stands, their voices blending into a rising tide of excitement. Towering screens, powered by the refined hum of Incada energy, illuminated the faces of this year's challengers alongside highlights from past tournaments. A celebration of legacy — and a challenge to the next generation.

At the center of the arena floor, Alarion stood poised before the Weaver Orchestra, his hands trembling as they gripped the baton. From the corner of his eye, the vastness of the crowd loomed, pressing in — more people than he had ever performed for in his life.

Okay...okay, you can do this, he told himself, drawing a short breath. It's no different than rehearsal. Except...the entire kingdom is watching. No pressure.

The weight of it pressed heavily on his chest. Then, he thought of Ava's words — gentle and even. "Just start playing. The music will carry you from there."

With a breath, Alarion raised the baton — and the first note bloomed.

The grand ballad he had composed unfurled in a rising cascade of sound, a powerful blend of triumph and reverence. Strings, brass, and percussion melded as one, the music carrying through the arena with shimmering trails of Incada light that drifted above the performers, weaving patterns of energy that pulsed with each note.

Then, the procession began.

The Envoys entered first, their golden armor catching the morning light as they marched in perfect formation, each step a declaration of discipline. Next came the Originators, draped in slate blue, their complex devices gleaming with faint Incada pulses at their belts — living testaments to ingenuity. The Weavers followed in flowing crimson robes, carrying banners embroidered with swirling patterns of energy, some plucking gentle notes from lyres to compliment the grand orchestra as they walked. Finally, the Bringers stepped forth, their staves raised high, their presence calm yet commanding, a reflection of their sacred charge.

The crowd's applause swelled as the final guild crossed the threshold, voices rising in celebration for the protectors of Ileydria's way of life.

From a broadcast booth high above the arena, two commentators presided over the unfolding spectacle.

"The annual Challengers of the Realm Tournament — what a sight!" came the words of Garrick, smooth and confident as it echoed across the venue's crystalline speakers. "I'm Garrick, your host for today, bringing you coverage of this extraordinary tradition. And joining me, as always, is my co-host, Lyra!"

Lyra's response rang out with infectious enthusiasm. "That's right, Garrick! You can feel the energy in the air! Challengers of the Realm isn't just about competition — it's about unity. These guilds define our way of life, and the tournament events will test both individual skill and teamwork. Stay tuned, everyone. This year's lineup? Absolutely unforgettable."

The crystal screens shifted, displaying sweeping aerial views of the three primary arenas designed for the tournament's trials. Each was crafted to test different aspects of a challenger's skillset, emphasizing both individual excellence and teamwork.

"The Combat Arena," Garrick's voice echoed above the crowd, "a massive open battleground marked by a central square, will push our competitors' fighting abilities to the limit. Expect to see the most intense one-on-one duels unfold here."

The image shifted to the very arena they stood in — the Duriel Arena — its grand architecture a reflection of Ileydria's rebirth. Towering columns and gilded carvings told the story of King Duriel, the ruler who had restored the kingdom after the fall of the Obsidian Shade.

"And here in the Duriel Arena, where the opening ceremonies are underway, strategy and teamwork will be put to the test. Only those who can truly work as one will rise to victory in these cooperative trials," Lyra added.

The screen shifted once more, revealing a vast, ever-changing space. Forested glades blended into frozen tundras, jagged cliffs bordering rivers of lava — a landscape in constant motion.

"And finally," Garrick continued, "The Grand Arena, a dynamic, multi-environment space built to simulate the complexity of large-scale warfare scenarios. Only the most adaptable will endure its challenges. And remember — "

Lyra jumped back in, finishing the thought. "Points are awarded based on performance in each phase. The top three participants from the solo rounds will earn points for their guilds, while cooperative events hold higher stakes, rewarding coordination. But the grand finale? Guild Wars, the ultimate test — victory there grants the most significant point reward of all!"

Down in the preparation chambers beneath the arena, Nysara adjusted the straps of her combat gear, the worn leather familiar against her skin. Her pulse fluttered with anticipation — and just a touch of nerves.

She wasn't about to let that show, though. Not today.

The sound of distant cheers echoed from above as she caught sight of her friends near the entrance. Liam, Alarion, and Celeste stood together, already lost in conversation.

Nysara grinned and jogged over, her expression lighting up as she reached them. "Alarion, that was incredible!" she exclaimed, pulling him into a quick hug. "Seriously, you crushed it out there!"

Alarion blushed slightly, rubbing the back of his neck. "Thanks...I was terrified. Thought my hands were going to stop working halfway through the first stanza."

"Well, they didn't," Liam chimed in with a teasing grin. "Now let's see if you can keep that momentum when you're not holding a baton."

Alarion shot him a playful glare. "Oh, I'm more than ready. I came here to win, thank you very much."

Liam crossed his arms, the cocky grin never fading. "Yeah? We'll see about that. Because if it's a straight fight, I'm taking the gold, no question."

Celeste, standing quietly until now, finally spoke up — her tone dry but tinged with amusement. "Well, provided my plan goes the way I've calculated, the only thing you three will be 'winning' is a trip to the infirmary."

Liam snorted. "Pffft — look at you, Celeste. Trying so hard not to crack a smile. If you keep that up, people might actually think you're soft."

"Or," Nysara interjected, smirking, "maybe someone other than you finally has the winning plan this time."

Celeste raised her cloak, covering her mouth, but the faintest shake of her shoulders gave her away. Then, muffled through the fabric, she muttered, "At least I'm guaranteed to be awake for the entire tournament...unlike some people."

That was it.

The tension broke as Celeste finally burst into laughter, the sound echoing through the ready chamber. Nysara doubled over, barely containing her own amusement, while Liam dramatically clutched his chest, pretending to be wounded.

The stress of the day seemed to melt, replaced — at least for a moment — by the shared warmth of friendship.

And as the laughter faded, the four of them exchanged quiet looks, the unspoken promise clear between them: They would each give this their all.

The tournament bracket illuminated the towering screens above the Combat Arena, each competitor's name slotting into place with a soft pulse of Incada light. Sixteen names, sixteen contenders for the first-year individual competition.

Celeste Osman's name appeared alongside her first opponent: Orin Veyne of the Originators Guild.

The Combat Arena stretched out before her — a massive stone platform with clearly marked Incada boundary lines, glowing softly under the mid-morning sun. The space was designed for precision duels, every inch crafted for clarity and fairness in combat.

From her place in the entrance tunnel, Celeste could hear the crowd's growing anticipation. Thousands of voices blending into a dull roar above as the final moments before the match ticked away.

She adjusted her grip on her staff, steadying her breath.

This was it.

The massive screens shifted again as the commentators' words filled the arena.

"Welcome back, Ileydria! I'm Garrick, and we're just moments away from the opening match of this year's first-year solo tournament! Facing off in our first bout, we have Celeste Osman of the Bringers Guild and Orin Veyne from the Originators! Remember, victory comes by either forcing your opponent out of the ring or rendering them unable to continue — non-lethal engagements only!"

Lyra's voice followed, brimming with excitement. "And what a match-up to kick things off, Garrick! Celeste represents the Bringers, master strategists and visionaries who excel at controlling the flow of battle with precision tactics and mystical insight. On the other side, we've got Orin from the Originators — known for pushing the boundaries of innovation and crafting some of the most unpredictable battle tech we've seen. This clash of careful strategy versus raw technological power should be incredible!"

Celeste stepped into the arena, her boots echoing against the stone as the crowd's roar swelled.

Across from her, Orin entered with a confident stride, the deep slate-blue accents of his Originators uniform glinting under the sunlight. On his left arm, a gauntlet of polished steel and crystalline channels pulsed with faint energy — a custom piece of tech designed for ranged combat.

The commentary buzzed above them.

Lyra whispered, "Look at that gauntlet, Garrick! Classic Originators work. Channeling pure Incada energy directly through a modular crystal array. If Celeste lets him control the tempo, this could get dangerous fast."

Garrick replied, "No doubt — but don't count out the Bringers' discipline. Celeste's known for her calculated defenses and her ability to turn an opponent's momentum against them. If anyone can keep their cool under pressure, it's her."

The match was seconds from beginning.

Celeste's focus narrowed. She could already see Orin adjusting his gauntlet, the crystals shifting slightly as he ran a quick calibration.

"He's gauging power levels. Fine-tuning before the first strike. Watch the patterns. Stay calm."

The announcer's voice cut through the air.

"Fighters — take your positions!"

Orin raised his gauntlet. Celeste shifted her stance; staff angled just slightly across her body.

"Three… two… one… FIGHT!"

Orin moved first.

A blast of energy erupted from his gauntlet, a focused bolt of white-hot Incada streaking across the arena.

Celeste reacted on instinct — her staff swept outward, and a shimmering barrier expanded from its tip. The blast struck, scattering harmlessly across the curved shield in a burst of sparks.

Orin's gauntlet whined again. He was already recalibrating, the crystals shifting in subtle pulses of light.

Another blast.

Celeste angled her barrier, deflecting it once more, but her focus stayed keen on him — not the blasts.

He was looking down at the gauntlet every time he recharged.

"He's checking the settings after every shot. That delay...it's exploitable."

She shifted, holding her ground, pretending to stay fully defensive. Let him think she was playing cautiously.

From the stands, Liam nudged Nysara with a grin. "You see that? She's baiting him."

"Yeah," Nysara replied, leaning closer, eyes narrowing. "She's not even trying to counter yet."

Below, Celeste watched Orin prepare his next attack, the gauntlet pulsing brighter as he dialed up the energy output.

There it was again — his eyes flicked down to check the charge.

"Now."

Celeste surged forward.

The head of her staff slammed into the stone with a resonant force. A pulse of energy rippled outward, flooding the ring with brilliant light.

Orin flinched, blinded by the flash. His shot went wide, fizzling out against the arena barrier.

By the time his vision cleared, Celeste was already there.

Her staff swept low, striking his legs and knocking him off balance. Orin hit the ground hard, his gauntlet sputtering as the crystals lost charge.

Before he could react, Celeste planted the tip of her staff lightly against his chest.

The boundary wards flared.

Match Over.

The arena erupted with cheers.

Lyra's voice rang out.

"Celeste Osman takes the win! An absolutely flawless victory! Did you see that, Garrick? The patience, the control — she let Orin reveal his pattern and shut him down completely!"

Garrick added, "That was Bringer strategy at its finest. Calculated. Defensive, then explosive. Orin put up a great fight, but Celeste's read was just too sharp today."

Celeste exhaled, the tension melting from her shoulders. The crowd's noise faded to a distant hum as she extended her hand toward Orin.

He blinked, still catching his breath, but accepted the offer.

"Good match," he muttered, managing a faint smile. "Guess I'll have to rethink my gauntlet design."

"You fought well," Celeste replied. "And I'm sure your next design will be even better."

As she turned toward the stands, her eyes caught on Liam, Alarion, and Nysara — cheering loud enough to be heard over half the crowd.

Celeste felt the edges of a smile break through her usually calm demeanor.

As the match concluded, Nysara jumped up from her seat, her excitement barely contained. "Guess I'm up next! Wish me luck, Liam."

Liam raised a brow, leaning back with a smirk. "Hold on, aren't you and Alarion matched up? You sure you'll be able to take him down, or am I gonna have to make it to the finals just to deal with him myself?"

Nysara grinned, adjusting the straps on her gear. "You know I'm giving it my best — regardless of the outcome."

Without another word, she headed for the preparation area, leaving Liam shaking his head with a chuckle.

In the arena, Lyra's words rang out, amplified across the stadium. "Alright, Ileydria, you're in for a treat! This next match features someone you've already seen in action today. Give it up for Alarion of the Weavers — composer of that breathtaking opening performance earlier! And now, let's see if his skill with music matches his skill in the ring!"

Garrick added with a laugh, "And trust me, folks, every Weaver has a few tricks up their sleeves. Don't let the music fool you!"

The cheers echoed as Alarion and Nysara stepped into the Combat Arena, meeting each other in the center with a shared nod of respect. The sunlight caught the crimson trim of Alarion's Weaver cloak as he adjusted it. Nysara, clad in slate-blue Originator armor lined with faint energy conduits, rolled her shoulders, already in motion as she mentally reviewed her strategies.

"Fighters ready?" Lyra's speech echoed. "Three...two...one...FIGHT!"

Alarion moved first, the bow sliding across his violin in a long, sustained note. A shimmering illusion of himself split into three copies, each shifting unpredictably as they circled Nysara.

But she was ready for this.

"Not this time, Alarion." Nysara's hand shot to her belt, and a trio of small, metallic devices clattered to the floor. They spun up with a soft hum, each one surrounded by a faint blue glow as Incada energy coursed through them.

The spinning tops whirled faster, rising into the air as she flicked her wrist. They hovered around her like a protective barrier, crackling with kinetic potential.

"You're not dealing with a common street thief," she taunted. "You're gonna need more than parlor tricks today!"

The hovering devices began launching pulses of energy outward, striking the illusions one by one. Each false image dissolved with a burst of light until only Alarion remained, already retreating to the edge of the ring.

His fingers danced across the strings, the melody shifting. A translucent barrier of Incada energy rippled into place before him — soft blue, shimmering like waves on water.

"That should hold for a bit," Alarion thought, steadying his breath as the barrier solidified. "But she's planning something better to make her come to me."

Nysara tilted her head, eyes narrowing as she watched the glowing shield pulse in rhythm with his music. Without hesitation, she raised her hands, recalling the spinning tops. They returned to her grip and with a twist, she realigned their configuration into a larger device, the three pieces interlocking into a triangular formation.

"Alright, Alarion. Let's test how strong that barrier really is."

The modified device spun faster, releasing a focused pulse of Incada energy as it shot forward, colliding with the shield. The impact sent ripples across the surface, but it held. For now.

"You can't hide behind that forever," she called, advancing step by step as the device continued hammering against the barrier.

Alarion's eyes narrowed, fingers slowing ever so slightly on the strings.

"She's overconfident. That's it...just a little closer."

The barrier flickered.

Nysara grinned. "Gotcha."

She lunged, sending the battering ram straight for the weak point in the shield.

But Alarion had been waiting.

With a subtle shift in his bowing, the barrier shattered — not from strain, but by his design. The moment it collapsed, he sidestepped the incoming blow and, with a burst of speed, planted his hand into Nysara's side. The strike sent her stumbling backward, feet just crossing the boundary line as she fought to regain balance.

Realization hit too late.

Her boots scraped the ground just beyond the edge of the ring.

The crowd fell silent.

Then Lyra's voice exploded over the speakers. "Victory to Alarion!"

The arena roared with applause as the containment fields pulsed brighter in response to the excitement.

Nysara, still catching her breath, stared at the ground in disbelief. Then, with a shake of her head, she laughed.

"You tricked me," she admitted, smiling despite herself.

Alarion smiled in response, "Had to. You were incredible. If I hadn't — well, I'd be the one on the ground right now."

"Next time," Nysara said with a playful grin. "Next time, you're the one going out of bounds."

Alarion offered his hand to Nysara, helping her up from where she sat just outside the combat ring. She dusted herself off with a playful groan, shaking her head as they exited the arena together.

"I can't believe I fell for that," she muttered, though her grin betrayed the sting of her loss.

Alarion chuckled softly. "Hey, it was close. I had to pull out every trick I had — next time, I might not be so lucky."

They parted ways to clean up after the match. The preparation chambers were quieter now, the echoes of the previous fight replaced with the constant hum of Incada lighting along the walls. Alarion had just finished changing when Liam strolled into the room, stretching his arms overhead with a satisfied sigh.

Alarion blinked. "Wait. Wasn't your match right after mine and Nysara's? Shouldn't you be out there?"

Liam flashed a grin. "Already done."

Alarion stared, incredulous. "What? How?"

Liam shrugged, leaning back against the wall with an exaggerated yawn. "They matched me against a Weaver."

Alarion narrowed his eyes. "Come on, man. Seriously. What happened?"

Liam snorted. "I'm serious! Listen, I'm not saying he wasn't talented — he had solid form. But solo combat? Not his thing. His defensive patterns were slow, and by the time he tried to set up some musical countermoves, I already had my blade at his chest."

Alarion sighed, rubbing his temples. "Let me guess...Cedric?"

Liam nodded. "Yeah, I think so. Why?"

Alarion shook his head. "I've been on him for weeks about focusing more on solo defense. His skill set is built for team coordination. They should've never put him in the singles bracket."

Liam clapped him on the shoulder with a smirk. "Not your problem today. But hey, speaking of next matches...you seen the bracket yet?"

Alarion raised a brow. "Not really. Why?"

Liam's grin widened. "Because my next match is against Celeste. So, you know, guess she's the next one to lose." He gave an exaggerated thumbs-up.

Alarion laughed under his breath, shaking his head. "You do realize she's been training like crazy for this, right? You might be in for a rough time."

Liam just shrugged. "Please. I've got this. And besides, we've got some time to relax before then."

The two of them returned to the stands, where Nysara was slouched so deeply in her seat it looked like she might slide right out of it. Celeste sat a row ahead, arms crossed, clearly focused on the current match while the crowd roared in excitement.

"So, Celeste," Alarion said with a teasing lilt as they settled in, "Liam seems pretty convinced you're going down next round."

Celeste turned, arching a brow at Liam. "Oh, does he?"

Liam folded his arms, feigning nonchalance. "Yeah, well… you know, I don't plan on losing anytime soon, so I guess that makes you next."

Celeste smirked, leaning closer. "You sure about that, Liam? Because I've been watching your fights. I think I've got you figured out."

Alarion exchanged a glance with Nysara, who snorted. The tension between Liam and Celeste was so thick it might as well have been part of the match itself.

"Okay, you two," Alarion cut in, waving a hand. "Save it for the ring. Some of us are trying to enjoy the rest of the tournament without your pre-fight commentary."

As their playful bickering continued, Alarion let his attention drift back to the arena. The next match was fierce, but he was more interested in the bracket projections. If Celeste and Liam were matched up next, then his potential finals fight would be determined by whoever won between them.

Suddenly, he noticed Nysara had gone completely quiet.

Glancing over, he found her slouched further down, arms folded, eyes closed.

"Nysara!" he yelled, nudging her shoulder.

She jolted upright with a dramatic gasp. "What — did I miss it? Who won?"

Alarion smirked. "Nothing yet. They both just headed down to prepare for their match. Celeste insisted we let you sleep. She said — and I quote — 'If she naps through my whole fight, I'll never let her live it down. It'll be sooo funny.' So, naturally, I'm waking you now to spare us both from that endless teasing."

Nysara groaned, rubbing her eyes. "I swear, if I hear her tell that story for the next six months..."

Alarion grinned. "You will. Definitely. But hey, at least you'll be awake to watch Liam get knocked flat next round."

"Ha! I wouldn't miss it," she replied, still shaking off the nap. "Let's see if Mr. Overconfident actually holds up under pressure."

Lyra's words filled the arena, clear and energetic as the crowd's cheers began to settle. "And we're back for round two, Garrick! I hope you're all ready — because if the first round was impressive, things are only going to heat up from here!"

"Oh, absolutely, Lyra," Garrick chimed in with his usual enthusiasm. "Next up, we've got a matchup guaranteed to turn some heads. Liam of the Envoys versus Celeste Osman, representing the Bringers Guild! But — wait a second...Lyra, am I seeing this right?"

Liam had just emerged from the far side of the Combat Arena. Gone was his typical polished armor, replaced by a simple dark training uniform. No reinforced chest plate, no shoulder guards, just the basic sparring gear worn for drills. Across from him, Celeste approached with her Bringer staff in hand, her expression shifting from focus to bewilderment as she took in his appearance.

Lyra sounded equally confused. "Well, Garrick, that's...unexpected. An Envoy stepping into the ring without his armor? Maybe he's trying to throw her off mentally — though I have to admit, it seems like a risky move against someone as calculated as Celeste. From what we've learned, these two worked together on a guild investigation earlier this year. Could Liam be counting on familiarity to his advantage?"

Celeste's voice cut through the arena as she cupped her hands around her mouth. "Are you trying to lose, Liam? At least *pretend* to take this seriously!"

Liam only offered a grin, resting both hands on the hilt of his sword, the tip of the blade pressed lightly against the stone floor. "Maybe I am. Or maybe I'm just making it fair," he called back, his manner teasing but controlled.

In truth, his mind was anything but relaxed.

"Stay calm. Stick to the plan. She knows how I fight — if she's on her game, I probably can't beat her straight up. I need her frustrated. Unbalanced."

Celeste narrowed her eyes, shifting her stance. The familiar blue light of Incada energy flared to life along the edge of her staff as she swept her cloak forward, summoning a shimmering shield of light in front of her. Her signature defense — stable, precise, and nearly impossible to break head-on.

Liam had been expecting it.

He didn't move.

From the stands, Nysara shifted forward in her seat, brow furrowed. "What's he doing?" she whispered. "Liam never just...stands there."

Alarion sat beside her, arms crossed, watching closely. "He's baiting her. Look how he's holding his sword — tip down, completely passive. He's waiting for her to make the first move."

"But why? She's too smart to fall for that," Nysara replied, though her delivery was uncertain.

Alarion shook his head. "Celeste relies on calculated defense. She waits for mistakes and punishes them. Liam knows that. So, he's forcing a different kind of mistake. If he can frustrate her, drain her stamina, she'll break her own rhythm. And when she does..."

"It'll be over," Nysara finished, her response quieter now, her eyes fixed on the arena floor.

The crowd noise faded to a hush as the tension in the arena coiled tighter.

"Alright, alright," Garrick's voice echoed over the speakers. "No more stalling. Let's get this match underway! Lyra, you ready to call it?"

"Ready as ever," she replied. "Fighters, prepare yourselves! On my count — three...two...one...FIGHT!"

Neither moved.

Celeste's shield held firm, the blue energy casting rippling patterns on the stone beneath her. Liam hadn't so much as shifted his stance. The only motion was the subtle rise and fall of his breathing.

"Why isn't he attacking? He always starts aggressively. Is this some kind of bluff?"

The shield wavered slightly as her focus shifted. She could feel the constant drain it caused — the energy wasn't limitless. *He's trying to wear me down.*

Liam's words cut through the quiet. "Come on, Celeste. You know how this ends if you wait me out. Drop the shield. Take your shot. Or..." He tilted his head, smirking. "...are you scared?"

Celeste's grip on her staff tightened.

"He's trying to make me act first. But if I hold the shield too long, I'll burn out. If I drop it, he'll rush me."

Her pulse quickened, the frustration bubbling beneath her calm exterior. Liam's stance hadn't shifted an inch. Sword still grounded. Just *watching* her.

She took a half step forward, shield pulsing brighter. Testing him.

No reaction.

The crowd stilled, the tension thick enough to hold them silent.

Liam's fingers flexed slightly around the hilt of his sword.

"That's it...just hold the line...one more second..."

Celeste's mind raced. *If I wait, I lose. If I attack recklessly, I lose. So —*

She took a slow breath.

"Then I won't play your game, Liam. I'll make you move."

The shield dropped. The energy dissolved in a crackling pulse, her staff shifting into a two-handed guard as she braced for his charge.

Liam finally moved — but not forward. He stepped *back*.

Celeste blinked. *What?*

And then his sword was already in motion. A sweeping arc, low and controlled, the tip carving through the air — sending a sudden, precise gust of energy slicing toward her ankles.

Celeste vaulted back, barely clearing the strike as the energy crackled against the stone where she'd stood.

"He's still holding back! He's trying to keep me reacting."

Her eyes narrowed. "Fine," she muttered under her breath.

And she struck.

Her staff spun in a blur as she lunged, the tip crackling with a surge of Incada energy, aiming for his exposed side. But Liam was already moving, pivoting just enough for her strike to graze his sleeve, the fabric singed but not connecting fully.

He met her gaze. Smirked.

And whispered, "Gotcha."

In a blur, Liam reversed his stance — pressing forward this time. His sword swung high, not aiming to hit but forcing her to block. Celeste's staff came up, the impact ringing out like a bell. But the force sent her sliding back a step.

Then another.

She gritted her teeth. *He's faster without the armor. He's pushing me back —*

Liam adjusted his grip, pressing the offensive now. "Not bad," he taunted, "but you're off balance, Celeste. I can see it."

Celeste's jaw clenched as she adjusted her footing. *No more holding back.*

The duel had only just begun.

Celeste made the next move, lunging forward with her staff raised high, the crystalline tip shimmering as it caught the sunlight. She aimed for a sweeping strike, hoping to break Liam's balance and force an opening.

Liam reacted in a split second, his blade snapping upward to meet hers with a resonant *clang*. The impact echoed through the Combat Arena, drawing a quick breath from the crowd. For a short time, they were locked together, strength against strength — until Liam shifted his footing, twisting sharply. His sword slid along the length of her staff, leveraging her momentum just enough to send the weapon spinning from her hands.

The staff clattered across the stone floor, the sound cutting through the roar of the audience.

Celeste's eyes widened — but only for a moment.

Without hesitation, she dropped low, rolling with the momentum of his disarm. Dust kicked up as she twisted back to her feet, her hand snapping out toward the fallen weapon.

It jerked sharply, as though answering her will — ripping free from the stone and flying back into her outstretched grip.

Liam's sword was already in motion.

A powerful overhead strike came crashing down toward her, but Celeste met it just in time, her staff raised horizontally to catch the blow. Sparks of blue Incada energy flared between the weapons as the impact echoed once more, the force trembling down her arms. She gritted her teeth, bracing hard against his strength.

The crowd surged with excitement.

For a breath, they both held their ground. Then, as if silently agreeing to reset, the fighters stepped back, each catching their breath.

Celeste's shoulders rose and fell as she reset her stance, her grip sure but her breathing heavier now. Across from her, Liam shifted, lowering his blade slightly as he adjusted his footing. His eyes narrowed — not with frustration, but calculation.

"She's keeping up better than I expected. But now it's time to change the rhythm."

The moment stretched. Liam's pulse slowed, his mind quickening as he exhaled, steadying his focus.

No more testing.

Now, he would press the advantage.

Without warning, he exploded forward.

Celeste barely had time to react before he was on her, his sword a blur of silver arcs. The sudden burst of speed was jarring — faster, more aggressive than before. She parried, barely deflecting the first strike, then the second, but each one came faster than the last.

The sound of clashing steel echoed like a drumbeat.

Liam's strikes came relentlessly — fluid, unpredictable, forcing her back step by step.

"This isn't like him," Celeste thought, struggling to keep pace. *"He's holding nothing back now — no hesitation. No armor slowing him down."*

She adjusted her stance, planting her feet more firmly, trying to reclaim control — but Liam pressed harder. His sword sang as it sliced through the air, a precise rhythm designed to overwhelm, to leave her reacting instead of thinking.

The edge of the combat ring loomed closer behind her.

"Come on, Celeste, keep up!" Liam called, his grin sharp but focused as he pressed his advantage.

The crowd's energy surged with every strike, but Celeste barely heard it over the ringing steel. Her muscles burned, her staff trembling slightly in her grip as she deflected another powerful swing.

From the stands, Alarion leaned forward, his eyes narrowed as he studied the match. "Liam's not fighting like himself," he whispered, voice low enough only for Nysara to hear. His arms were crossed; his usual calm tinged with concern. "He's sacrificing power for speed — pushing her pace, trying to keep her on the defensive."

Nysara nodded, her eyes locked on the duel below. "He's trying to wear her down. If Celeste doesn't shift her approach soon, he's going to box her in completely."

In the arena, the pressure was mounting.

Liam's relentless strikes came faster, tighter — each blow calculated, keeping Celeste pinned near the edge of the ring. Her arms burned from deflecting the rapid succession of attacks. She tried to backpedal, to create space and reset her footing, but the uneven stone of the arena floor betrayed her.

Her boot was caught.

She stumbled.

Liam saw the opening.

With a fierce step forward, he swung in a wide arc — not for a direct hit, but for pure disruption.

Celeste raised her staff just in time, the impact rattling her entire frame. The force was overwhelming. She felt the strength leave her stance as she was thrown backward, her staff wrenched from her hands. It clattered across the stone, sliding just out of reach.

The arena seemed to slow.

Celeste hit the ground hard, the breath forced from her lungs as she lay sprawled on the cold stone. Her vision swam, heart pounding louder than the muffled cheers echoing from the stands.

No. Not like this.

She pushed up, struggling to rise, but before she could fully regain her footing —

Thud.

Liam's boot pressed gently but firmly against her shoulder, halting her movement. His sword, lowered but strong, hovered just above her chest.

"Not this time, Celeste," he said, his voice controlled but softer than expected.

Celeste clenched her jaw; frustration flared beneath the sting of defeat. She had been outpaced, outmaneuvered — but the fight wasn't without meaning. She could feel it.

The arena was silent, the tension hanging thick in the air. Then —

Lyra's words cut through the quiet.

"Liam Valoria wins! What an incredible display! Celeste gave it her all, but in the end, Liam's speed and strategy proved unstoppable!"

The crowd erupted, cheers rolling over the arena like thunder.

Garrick's voice echoed through the arena as the crowd's cheers continued to swell. "What a masterful display of skill! Celeste Osman's resilience was incredible, but

Liam Valoria's decision to ditch his armor completely changed the dynamic. His speed was simply unmatched!"

The applause rolled over them in waves as Liam extended a hand toward Celeste. She hesitated before clasping it, his grip steady as he helped her back to her feet.

Celeste's chest still heaved from exertion, but a small smile broke through her exhaustion. "You really got me there, Liam." She dusted off her cloak, shaking her head. "But I'll get you next time. Count on it."

Liam grinned, brushing his hair back from his damp forehead. "I'm holding you to that, but seriously — that roll when your staff went flying? I thought you were done right there." He gave her a playful pat on the shoulder. "You fought like a champion, Cel. Respect."

As they crossed the boundary line, the cheers finally beginning to settle, Nysara and Alarion were already waiting at the arena's edge.

"Nice fight," Nysara said, leaning closer to Celeste with a teasing smirk. "If he hadn't pulled every trick he had, you would've had him easy."

Celeste's smile widened as she shot Liam a mock glare. "Turns out Liam's *full* of surprises, huh? But don't think for a second this is over."

Alarion chuckled, arms crossed as he exchanged a glance with Liam. "Well, I guess I'm next. Don't get too comfortable, Valoria."

Liam's grin turned. "Oh, I'm plenty comfortable. Question is — are you ready to lose?"

"Ha. We'll see." Alarion's reply was calm, confident. "But don't expect it to be easy."

"Easy?" Liam shrugged. "I never expect easy. I just make it *look* that way."

Celeste rolled her shoulders, wincing slightly from the fresh soreness in her muscles. "Alright, I'll give you this, Liam. That whole no-armor thing? Completely threw me off. For a second, I thought you'd lost your mind."

Liam winked. "Nah. Just had to get in your head somehow. Looks like it worked."

Celeste narrowed her eyes, smirking. "You're lucky you had a trick up your sleeve. Next time? I'm flattening you."

Nysara snorted, rolling her eyes. "Sure, Celeste. Keep telling yourself that. Now let's focus on the real event — *tomorrow*." She turned toward Alarion, her grin shifting. "Think you can take him after all that? Liam's on a roll."

Celeste raised a brow, eyes narrowing playfully. "Deflecting already, huh, Nysara? You're really gonna side with him?"

Nysara's face flushed slightly, but she held her ground. "Oh, come on! I'm just saying the finals are going to be *epic*. Besides, I'm curious — Alarion? You feel ready for this showdown?"

Alarion shrugged, his calm confidence settled back into place as he gave Liam a measured look. "I've watched you fight enough to know your strengths — and your weaknesses. I'll manage."

Liam folded his arms, a playful grin widening across his face. "Oh, *you think so*, huh? Just remember, Alarion — this isn't the orchestra. At some point, you'll have to do more than put on a show."

Without missing a beat, Alarion tapped his violin case, the polished wood catching the arena's fading lights. "You should know by now, Liam — this old thing does more than just play a tune." His smirk was subtle but unwavering. "My solo act? A bit different from the ensemble performance."

The tension between them was thick, but not hostile. Friendly, competitive — like a game neither was willing to lose.

Nysara, unable to resist, leaned in with a teasing grin. "I don't know, Alarion. Liam *did* just pull a few surprises on Celeste. Maybe he's more unpredictable than you're giving him credit for?"

Alarion's focus didn't waver. "Trust me. I'll be ready."

Celeste, smiling now, clapped Alarion on the shoulder. "You'd *better* be. I'm rooting for you. We can't let Liam walk around thinking he's as good as everyone else *thinks* he is."

Liam gasped in mock offense, hand on his chest. "Hey! Aren't you supposed to be on my side? If I'm the Champion, that means you only lost to the best!"

Celeste raised a brow, smirking. "You *might* be right...but honestly, I'd rather see you knocked down a few times."

The tension broke with laughter and the four friends left the arena together, their footsteps echoing softly against the stone as the city's lights bathed the courtyard in a soft, golden glow.

"Get some rest, you two," Nysara said as they reached the edge of the guild hall. "Tomorrow's going to be...interesting."

Liam and Alarion exchanged one final glance, the rivalry returning but softened by mutual respect.

"See you in the finals, Alarion," Liam called over his shoulder, voice light but charged with confidence.

Alarion nodded, the corner of his mouth twitching into a small smile. "You too, Liam."

Hunter Fowler

8

Together We Are Stronger

The morning sun cast a golden glow across the Combat Arena, its pale stone polished to perfection after the intensity of the previous day's matches. Banners of the four guilds rippled gently above the stands

The air felt charged, anticipation crackling as thousands of spectators filled the towering stands. The murmurs of the crowd blended into a low hum, waiting for the final round of the first-year solo tournament to begin.

At the center of the arena, Liam and Alarion faced each other beneath the midmorning sun. The stone beneath their feet still bore faint scuffs from earlier battles, but all other details faded into the background.

To Liam, nothing existed beyond the figure standing across from him.

Alarion stood tall, his crimson-trimmed Weaver cloak shifting slightly in the breeze, violin resting in his steady hands. His expression was calm, unreadable — focused.

Liam exhaled slowly, rolling his shoulders to shake off the tension coiling in his chest. This wasn't just any match. This was Alarion. His best friend. Someone who had seen him at his best and worst. Someone who knew every flaw he tried to hide.

"I've got to be at my best," Liam told himself, tightening his grip on his sword. "He won't give me an inch. If I lose focus for even a millisecond — it's over."

The crowd's hum swelled as a voice boomed from the crystal amplifiers above.

"Welcome back, Ileydria!" Garrick's words echoed across the arena, rich and confident. "It all comes down to this — the final round of the first-year solo tournament! Facing off today: Liam Valoria of the Envoys, known for his relentless strength, and Alarion of the Weavers, a master of creative combat. This promises to be a match you won't forget!"

The cheers surged, a thunderous wave of sound as Garrick's voice built to the countdown.

"Three...two...one...FIGHT!"

Liam exploded into motion, his sword slicing through the air in a powerful opening strike. He aimed straight for Alarion's center, hoping to end this quickly.

But Alarion was ready.

The bow of his violin danced across the strings in a singular, resonant note. A shimmer of Incada energy rippled outward — and in the next breath, Alarion's figure fractured into a haze of light. A perfect illusion remained where he had stood, while the real Alarion blurred out of sight, reappearing several paces away with a soft pulse of energy.

Liam's blade cut through empty air.

His pulse hammered in his ears as he twisted to face the new form.

"Okay...that's new."

The illusion wavered for a beat — then multiplied.

Three, then four, then six identical copies of Alarion spun around Liam in a tightening circle. Their movements were fluid, synchronized, and eerily silent. The reflections shifted in and out of phase, shimmering in the sunlight like heat mirages.

Liam tightened his grip on his sword. His heart pounded, but he forced himself to stay calm.

"Focus. One of them must be real. Wait for the tell...look for the mistake."

But there was no mistake. No sign.

Every time he lunged, his blade met nothing but fading light. Every strike was just barely too late.

"He's not even giving me a chance to fight back," Liam thought, frustration coiling tight in his chest. "How can I win if I can't land a single hit?"

Above, in the stands, Nysara leaned forward, eyes darting between the flickering forms. "He's completely overwhelming him with those illusions," she muttered. "If Liam can't figure this out, it's over before it even begins."

Celeste, watching just as intently, folded her arms. "Liam's resourceful. He'll find a way. But Alarion isn't holding back this time."

Nysara tilted her head, watching the patterns shift again. "Have you ever seen him use this many projections before?"

Celeste shook her head slowly, her brow furrowed. "Not like this. It's almost like...echoes of where he's been. He's been saving this technique for today."

Liam forced a breath through clenched teeth, trying to calm the pounding in his chest. He couldn't let the illusions break his focus. If he lost control, Alarion would dismantle him piece by piece.

But how could he fight back when he couldn't even see the real threat?

Suddenly, one of the illusions shifted — too fast to track. It lunged from the right, blade shimmering with the same pale blue light as Alarion's real weapon. Instinct kicked in. Liam's sword snapped up, deflecting the strike with a metallic clang.

But the illusion dissolved on impact, vanishing in a swirl of mist.

Before Liam could recover, another flickered forward from the left. This one came even faster. Liam barely twisted in time, his blade catching the phantom's slash — but there was no weight behind the blow. Nothing real.

He staggered a step back, heart racing.

"I'm barely keeping up. Every time I block, there's another. It's like fighting a shadow — there's no rhythm. No pattern."

The illusions circled tighter.

Alarion's chatter echoed from all around him, calm and measured, layered beneath the hum of the violin's melody. "Losing your focus, Liam? Strength won't help you here. You can't just swing your way out of this one."

Liam growled, the taunt sparking heat behind his eyes.

"Fine. If you want brute strength — "

With a defiant shout, he swung his blade in a wide arc, a sweeping strike aimed at carving through the entire circle of mirages.

But they shifted effortlessly, bending with the motion. The illusions slipped just out of range, untouched, as if the arena itself was working against him.

Liam's breathing hitched, frustration mounting.

"He's right. I'm swinging at nothing. This isn't working. I —"

The thought caught, ice creeping into his chest.

"I'm going to lose."

The crowd's roar blurred into a dull hum, drowned beneath the growing weight pressing against his shoulders. The expectations. The pressure. The fact that it wasn't just any opponent — this was Alarion.

And for the first time all tournament — Liam felt outmatched.

But he couldn't stop now.

"No. I've come too far to break here."

He forced the doubt back, gripping his sword tighter.

"I just need...a way through. An opening. There has to be something I'm missing."

As if sensing his hesitation, the illusions moved again.

Closer.

Sharper.

Blades of pale light lashed out in perfect unison. Liam blocked high. Parried low. But the attacks kept coming — faster, more relentlessly — forcing him back step by step.

Then, a voice behind him.

Too close.

"You're running out of time, Liam," Alarion's words echoed softly, still calm, still in control. "You've always been the stronger fighter — but strength doesn't matter here. Focus. Control. Without those, you've already lost."

Liam's jaw tightened, his pulse thundering in his ears.

"He's right. But I can't — "

He shook the thought away.

"Think, Liam. Find the real one. Break the pattern. You can do this."

A memory ignited — clear and vivid, cutting through the chaos.

A training session. Months ago.

Alarion standing beside him, violin in hand. The echo of his words resurfaced in Liam's mind: "Control the space. If your opponent controls the rhythm, disrupt it. Clear the board."

The technique.

A shock wave.

Liam had practiced it — once. A way to unleash a burst of Incada energy so forceful it would fracture illusions, disrupting the entire field. But it was unpredictable, draining.

And he hadn't even considered using it here.

Until now.

"A shock wave," he realized, heart pounding harder. "That's my shot. My only shot."

Liam shifted his stance, tightening his grip on the hilt of his sword. Incada energy surged along the blade's edge, the pale blue glow intensifying.

"Focus. Channel it — just like Alarion showed you."

With a powerful burst of motion, Liam leapt into the air.

For an instant, the arena seemed to hold its breath.

Then he brought his sword crashing down.

The blade struck the stone floor with a deafening crack, a pulse of brilliant blue energy detonating from the point of impact. The ground quaked. Cracks spiderwebbed outward as the wave expanded in a perfect circle, rippling across the entire arena.

Illusions shattered like fragile glass.

One by one, they fractured — shimmering figures splintering apart, dissolving into nothingness beneath the force of the pulse.

And when the dust settled —

There he was.

The real Alarion.

Standing alone at the heart of the battlefield, his bow hand still raised, his calm mask slipping just slightly — eyes wide, lips parted in disbelief.

The crowd gasped as one, the sound echoing in the sudden quiet.

Alarion's mind raced. "He used it. The shock wave. I taught him that technique...and he just outplayed me with it."

Across the arena, Liam staggered slightly, chest heaving, the surge of energy clearly draining him. But even through the exhaustion, his expression was fierce. Steady.

The fight wasn't over.

And Liam wasn't giving him the chance to reset.

Liam didn't hesitate.

The moment the last illusion shattered, he charged.

Alarion, still recovering from the shock wave, staggered slightly as Liam closed the distance. His bow scraped across the strings, summoning a faint shimmer of Incada energy — too faint. Too slow.

Liam's blade swung in a precise arc.

Clang!

The flat of his sword struck the violin cleanly, knocking it from Alarion's hands. The instrument clattered to the stone, its strings reverberating with a hollow, dissonant note.

Before Alarion could fully recover, the blade's edge hovered just above his chest, glowing softly with pale Incada light.

A hush fell over the Combat Arena.

The crowd, the cheers, the world — faded into quiet.

Liam, breath ragged, stood over his friend, the sword shaky in his grip. Victory was his.

But he didn't lower the blade further.

Instead, his expression softened. He drew back and extended his free hand.

An offering.

Alarion blinked up at him, chest heaving, the disbelief still evident in his wide eyes. But there was something else beneath it now — admiration.

He remained still for a brief moment. Then, with a quiet exhale, he grasped Liam's hand.

Liam pulled him upright with a firm tug.

"You really are full of surprises," Alarion said, manner softer than before, but the slightest smile tugged at the corner of his lips. "Using my move against me? I didn't see that coming."

Liam grinned, the weight of the match still pressing on his shoulders but easing. "Had to keep you guessing, right?"

The silence broke.

The arena erupted.

The crowd's roar surged like a tidal wave, voices blending into a thunderous ovation as banners unfurled and the massive crystal screens flashed Liam's name above the arena floor.

Liam and Alarion stood together, both breathless, both grinning despite the ache in their limbs. They had given everything.

As the cheers rang on, Garrick's voice echoed once more across the arena.

"And there you have it, Ileydria! The final standings for the first-year solo tournament: Liam Valoria of the Envoys claims first place, followed closely by Alarion Cyrus of the Weavers in second, and Celeste Osman of the Bringers securing third! What an incredible showing from our young challengers!"

Lyra chimed in. "But let's not forget the veteran bracket results as well! The Originators took first in a stunning upset, with the Bringers claiming second and the Envoys in third!"

The crystal screens shifted, displaying the updated guild rankings. The golden crest of the Envoys, the blue slate of the Originators, the crimson Weavers, and the violet Bringers all gleamed above the crowd, their current scores beside them.

The applause swelled again as the competitors began to exit the arena floor.

The next morning, the city was quieter, but the energy from the tournament was still present.

At their usual corner table in the guild hall café, Liam, Alarion, Celeste, and Nysara sat with trays of breakfast spread between them — plates piled with toast, eggs, and fruits from the outer provinces.

Nysara was mid-bite when she finally spoke, shaking her head with a smirk. "That final move, Liam. I can't believe you pulled that off. Using Alarion's own technique against him? Absolutely wild."

Liam shrugged, chewing on a slice of toast, clearly enjoying the praise. "Hey, had to do something unexpected. Alarion knows all my standard moves — I figured it was time to give him a taste of his own medicine."

Alarion let out a soft chuckle, swirling his tea. "I'll admit, you got me. But don't get too comfortable, Liam. Next time, I'll be ready for whatever tricks you've got up your sleeve."

Celeste, leaning back in her chair, smirked over her cup. "At least I didn't get completely outclassed. Third place isn't so bad. Someone had to make sure you both didn't get too full of yourselves."

Nysara snorted, propping her feet on the bench beside her. "You all did great, but it's a new day. We've got the cooperative events ahead — and I'm so ready to show everyone what we can do."

Liam nodded, his expression more serious. "Yeah. Two from each guild, paired up. This isn't just about individual skill anymore. It's about trust — and knowing how to work as a team."

The group fell quiet for a moment, the weight of the challenge ahead settling in.

The stands of Duriel Arena buzzed with anticipation, the crowd's energy building as the rescue event prepared to begin. The arena had been transformed overnight into a massive maze — towering walls of stone interlaced with shimmering force fields and patches of simulated urban terrain. Illusory rooftops, narrow alleyways, and shifting barriers created a constantly changing battlefield designed to test more than just combat ability. Teamwork, strategy, and adaptability would be the true deciding factors here.

Liam and Nysara sat side by side in the stands, trays of half-eaten food forgotten as they leaned forward, studying the complex layout below. From their elevated vantage point, they could see the maze slowly rearranging itself — the force fields rippling and shifting position like pieces of a living puzzle. At the very center, hidden beyond layers of barriers, was the objective: a glowing figure wrapped in golden light, the "hostage" that each team had an attempt at "defending" and "rescuing."

"Look at the way the maze keeps shifting," Nysara muttered, shielding her eyes from the glare of the midmorning sun. "That's going to be a nightmare to navigate. Alarion and Celeste are going to have to think fast if they want to hold the lead."

Liam nodded, his arms crossed but his focus sharp. "They'll manage. They've got the right balance — Alarion's illusions can keep the other team chasing shadows, and Celeste…" He allowed a small grin. "Well, you know she's the best tactician out here."

Down on the arena floor, Alarion adjusted the strap of his violin, his eyes sweeping the constantly shifting maze with quiet calculation. At his side, Celeste rolled her shoulders, her Bringer staff resting easily in her grip. The violet trim of her cloak rippled as she moved, the gleam of Incada energy dancing faintly along the patterns etched into the staff's length.

They weren't alone. Two additional recruits — Leila from the Weavers and Cron from the Bringers — stood with them. While both were skilled, there was a noticeable tension in their stances, the kind of nervous energy that revealed they weren't yet as comfortable in the arena spotlight.

Leila, a tall, wiry girl with a sketchbook tucked under her belt, gave Alarion a hesitant smile. "You're going to use the illusions, right? Keep them guessing?"

Alarion met her eyes with a calm nod, offering the same quiet reassurance he'd given before every performance. "I've got it covered. Just stick to your role and stay sharp. Remember, we're working Celeste's plan."

Cron, broader in the shoulders and carrying himself with the weight of quiet confidence, gave a knowing grin. "The defense is ours to lose. A Bringer and Weaver combo? We can stop wars together — let alone a simple match." He glanced toward Celeste, the faintest challenge in his tone. "So... you do have a plan for the rescue too, right?"

Celeste's smirk was immediate, her eyes narrowing with playful confidence. "Who do you think I am, Cron?"

The sound of the announcers returning to their commentary echoed across the arena, drawing the final moments of preparation to a close.

Across the arena floor, the opposing team — composed of Envoys and Originators — stood in a tight formation, heads bent together in hushed conversation. Four figures, clad in the bold hues of their guilds, prepared for the challenge ahead.

At the front stood Kellen, a towering Envoy with his arms crossed over his chest, wearing his guild's gold-trimmed combat gear with a confident smirk. His reputation for brashness wasn't undeserved. Beside him, Ylana, a Shield Guardian and defensive specialist, adjusted the straps of her reinforced gauntlets, her expression stoic as she scanned the maze.

The remaining pair, Roen and Raya, Originator twins in slate-blue tunics, fiddled with a set of small crystal-etched devices hanging from their belts. The soft hum of Incada energy pulsed faintly from the gadgets as they exchanged quiet, rapid whispers, clearly making last-minute adjustments to their tech.

Kellen cracked his knuckles, speech low but carrying authority. "Listen up. We're taking the fight to them. Roen, Raya, be ready to shut down any traps or barriers they throw up. Ylana — keep me covered. We're going straight for the center, fast and direct."

Roen exchanged a look with his sister before nodding. "No problem. We've got a few tricks for their force fields." Raya's grin mirrored his.

High above, Garrick's voice boomed across the arena as the crystal screens flared back to life.

"Ladies and gentlemen, welcome to the first cooperative event of the day — the rescue challenge! Today, our two teams will be put to the ultimate test of strategy and coordination. One side will defend the simulated hostage, while the other attempts a daring rescue before time runs out!"

Lyra added with a burst of excitement, "That's right, Garrick! On one side, we have the Weavers and Bringers — masters of illusion and battlefield control. On the other, the powerhouse combo of the Envoys and Originators, bringing sheer force and technological precision. Let's see who can outsmart who!"

The crowd erupted as the massive crystalline horn sounded, echoing like a bell across the arena.

At once, the maze shifted — the glowing force fields rippling as barriers rearranged themselves, warping the battlefield into a fresh pattern of corridors and cover.

The match had begun.

Celeste took command the moment the horn echoed through the arena; her words calm but pointed. "Alarion, create projections of the dummy — make them unpredictable. Leila, you and I will keep shifting the force fields. Cron, track their movements and keep feeding us intel. Our goal is confusion. Keep them chasing shadows. Stick to your positions and don't let them close in."

Alarion nodded, his bow gliding across the violin strings. Faint trails of Incada energy followed each note, and in an instant, shimmering copies of the glowing hostage appeared throughout the maze. Each duplicate pulsed faintly, moving independently as they flickered between the maze's twisting barriers. It was impossible to tell which was real — by design.

On the opposite end of the maze, Kellen's eyes lit up as one of the glowing figures came into view. "There!" he barked, charging forward with his sword drawn. Roen and Raya followed close behind, their gadgets primed, the faint hum of Incada energy rising as they synchronized their devices.

But just as Kellen's hand reached out, the figure rippled and burst into mist.

He blinked, his hand swiping through empty air. "What the —?" He spun around, face twisting into a scowl. "It's a fake!"

Hidden behind the maze's barriers, Alarion's fingers continued to dance along the strings, his expression calm but focused. A hint of a smile tugged at the corner of his lips. "Good luck finding the real one, Kellen."

Raya adjusted her wrist-mounted disruptor, the crystalline device glowing brighter as it pulsed in rhythm with the shifting walls. "These barriers keep moving too fast. I can't get a proper lock — every time I recalibrate, they reset."

Roen muttered, adjusting his own device. "We need to get closer. If we can pulse directly into the barrier's core frequency, it should disrupt the entire layer."

High in the stands, Nysara grinned, leaning forward as the opposing team stumbled through yet another dead end. "They're completely lost. Alarion's got them chasing ghosts."

Liam gave her a sideways glance, raising her eyebrow. "You do remember who you're cheering against, right? Those are your Originators getting wrecked down there."

Nysara blinked, hesitating as her grin faded into a thoughtful expression. "...Oh. Yeah. Right." She shifted awkwardly, then shook her head. "I mean, technically... but I can't help it. They're my friends. I want them to win too."

Liam blinked, taken aback by the softness in her voice. Nysara, always so fiercely loyal to her guild, was rarely this conflicted. He offered a small, genuine smile. "I get it. I like that about you, you know. You care."

Nysara gave a bashful laugh, nudging his arm playfully. "Well, don't tell the guild council. I'm pretty sure they'd disown me."

Liam chuckled. "Here's hoping we can keep cheering for each other — win or lose."

"Look at that!" Nysara pointed, leaning over the railing as the shimmering maze shifted again. "Kellen's changing tactics."

Down in the arena, Kellen's scowl was sharp as he gestured his team into a tight huddle. "Forget the hostage. We're wasting time playing their game. We need to flush them out."

Roen nodded, already reaching into his belt pouch and producing a compact, sphere-shaped gadget etched with glowing runes. "I've got just the thing. A resonance disruptor — this pulse should destabilize both the force fields and Alarion's illusions. But we need to get close enough."

The twins moved in sync, Roen and Raya weaving through the maze's shifting corridors. Their movements were precise, calculating — each step closing the distance toward the center where the real dummy was hidden behind layers of defenses.

Raya knelt, pressing the disruptor against the nearest shimmering wall. "Activating it now — stand back."

A burst of energy pulsed outward in waves, distorting the surrounding force fields. The maze shimmered violently, flickering like a glitching projection. For a few seconds, the illusions faltered — faint outlines peeling away — and there, among the fading copies, the real glowing hostage stood clearly visible.

"There!" Kellen's eyes lit up, and he surged forward, sword drawn.

But Celeste had been waiting.

Her staff spun in a fluid arc, energy rippling outward as the barriers shifted yet again, seamlessly rearranging to seal off the path Kellen had just cleared. At the same instant, Alarion's bow slid across the strings, and a new cluster of shimmering figures burst into life, surrounding the exposed hostage.

Kellen's charge met an abrupt stop. His sword struck a solid reinforced barrier materializing just as he lunged. The impact sent him sprawling back with a grunt.

From her position deeper in the maze, Celeste lowered her staff, lips pressing into a confident smirk. "Not so fast."

Up in the stands, Liam shot to his feet, eyes wide. "They almost had it! That pulse was a perfect setup — but Celeste...she's already two steps ahead."

Nysara nodded, arms crossed but smiling. "She's got them boxed in. If they keep reacting instead of adapting, they'll run out of time."

Kellen, still on the ground, slammed a fist into the arena floor. "Again! Disrupt it again!"

But Roen shook his head, his disruptor now flickering weakly. "It's shorted out! I told you; we only had one shot!"

The remaining seconds ticked down, each passing moment solidifying Celeste's defensive web further. Alarion's illusions danced between barriers while the shifting walls forced the opposing team in circles.

The horn blared.

"Time's up!" Lyra's voice echoed, triumphant over the crystal speakers. "The Weavers and Bringers have successfully defended the hostage!"

The crowd erupted into cheers as the arena walls shimmered, resetting for the next phase.

"Nice work, everyone." Celeste wiped sweat from her brow, her breath controlled despite the exertion. "Now it's our turn to go on the offensive."

The teams switched sides, the shimmering walls of the maze resetting around them. Celeste and Alarion regrouped at the starting position while the opposing team adjusted their defensive stance near the hostage's position.

Alarion drew in a large breath, fingers flexing as he raised his violin. The strings shimmered with pale blue Incada energy as he spoke. "Let's keep the pressure on. Same strategy — illusions to spread them thin." His bow touched the strings, energy rippling outward.

Celeste's eyes narrowed as she scanned the maze. "Not quite the same. Last round, we let them adjust. This time? No breathing room. We end this quickly."

The horn sounded, launching the second round.

The Weavers and Bringers wasted no time. Alarion's illusions burst to life — this time far more complex. Echoes of himself, Celeste, Leila, and Cron fanned out across the maze, flickering between barriers with uncanny fluidity. Each figure shifted in perfect synchronization, blurring the lines between reality and trickery.

On the defensive side, Kellen's grip tightened around his sword, frustration already evident. "Not this time!" he barked, rushing toward the nearest Alarion projection. His blade slashed clean through the figure, which dissolved into harmless mist.

"Again, with the illusions!" he spat, whirling around.

Meanwhile, Celeste and the real Leila had broken off from the main group, using the cover of the false images to move deeper into the maze. The glowing blue figure of the hostage was lightly guarded — Ylana and the twins holding their positions but clearly struggling to track the shifting threats.

"Form up on the hostage!" Ylana yelled. "Defensive circle!"

Roen glanced between the approaching illusions, his brow furrowing. "Which ones do we defend against? There's too many!"

Kellen's jaw clenched, his tone turning defiant. "Forget it! I'm swinging at everything — just keep them back!"

Celeste's lips curled into a knowing smirk as she heard the outburst echo through the maze. "That's exactly what I needed."

Kellen lunged toward another false figure, his sword carving wide arcs through the air — reckless, powerful, and wildly inefficient.

"Now."

Celeste surged forward. Blue Incada light flared along the length of her staff as she swept it low. The crystalline tip struck the ground, sending out a pulse of blinding light that erupted across the maze. The force sent Kellen stumbling, his vision overwhelmed in a burst of pale blue.

In the same breath, Leila dashed through the opening. She darted past the disoriented defenders; her smaller frame barely noticed amid the chaos. With a fluid motion, she seized the glowing hostage and thrust it high above her head.

"It's over!" she called out, her words echoing through the arena.

The horn blared, confirming her words.

Garrick's voice rang out, booming over the thunderous roar of the crowd. "And that's it! A decisive victory! The Weavers and Bringers take the win with a masterful display of strategy and precision! What an incredible finish!"

The crowd's cheers echoed through the arena as Alarion and Celeste returned to the preparation area with their teammates, still riding the high of their victory. Celeste exchanged a brief smile with Alarion, their teamwork having paid off in full.

As the energy in the stadium began to settle, a familiar figure approached. Olive the Seer, her violet-trimmed cloak flowing with each step, caught Celeste's attention with a proud smile.

"That was brilliant, Celeste," Olive said, her speech calm but warm. "You've come so far since your first days training in the dungeon."

Celeste exhaled, the compliment cutting through her adrenaline. "Thank you...really. That means a lot coming from you."

Olive nodded. "You're leading well. Keep it up. The Bringers and Weavers are tied for first — 100 points each. The Envoys and Originators are holding at 75, but the day's far from over. There's still time for them to catch up."

The arena was already transforming for the next event. As the crowd resonated with renewed excitement, massive sections of the arena floor shifted, revealing an expansive body of water stretching across the center. A shimmering lake, broken up by floating platforms and twisting currents, dominated the space. On the far end, towering wooden structures formed a massive obstacle course of climbing walls, balance beams, and rope bridges.

To make matters more complicated, bursts of blue Incada energy rippled across certain parts of the course — defensive wards designed to hinder progress. And as if the challenges themselves weren't enough, stationed along key checkpoints were guild veterans, ready to act as active "obstacles" for any team unlucky enough to cross their path.

This was the Obstacle Race, a test of both physical and strategic mastery. Speed, strength, coordination, and clever thinking would all be essential to claim victory.

Nysara and Liam took their places at the starting line, each leading their respective squads.

Nysara, representing the Originators and Bringers, stood flanked by a sharp-eyed team of the two guilds already tinkering with various propulsion gadgets strapped to their belts.

Liam, leading the Weavers and Envoys, stretched his arms, his confident grin set as he exchanged glances with a squad evenly split between the constant strength of Envoy warriors and the agile precision of the Weavers.

Liam's response carried easily across the short distance between them. "Guess we're not rooting for each other this time, huh?"

Nysara chuckled, shaking her head as she adjusted the straps on her gauntlet. "Don't think so, Valoria. I'm giving this everything I've got...hope you're ready for that."

From the stands, Celeste and Alarion watched the exchange with keen interest.

Alarion, still feeling the thrill of their earlier victory, leaned forward in his seat. "This could be close. Liam's team has speed and experience on land, but...well, you know Nysara. She always has some crazy backup plan."

Celeste nodded, her eyes sweeping the shimmering lake below. "And with those gadgets? She'll dominate the water phase. Liam better gain ground fast once they hit the obstacle section, or they won't catch up."

As the teams completed their final preparations, Garrick's voice echoed through the arena.

"Welcome back, everyone! It's time for the second cooperative event of the day — the Obstacle Race! Teams will need to work together to overcome a series of challenges, including a lake crossing, navigating shifting barriers, outsmarting guild leaders acting as obstacles, and a final sprint to the finish. First team across the line claims victory!"

Lyra chimed in, energetic as ever. "That's right, Garrick! But speed alone won't win this. Strategy, teamwork, and creative problem-solving will be the key to victory. Let's see which guilds can rise to the challenge!"

The starting horn blared.

The first phase began: the lake crossing. Each team had been provided with a sleek longboat, but the methods of propulsion would make all the difference.

Nysara wasted no time. "Roen, propulsion systems — now!" she called.

Roen nodded, his hands already working the controls on his wristband. From beneath the boat a soft hum began to build, and with a surge of blue Incada energy, twin jets of water burst from the back, propelling their vessel forward at remarkable speed. The boat skimmed the water's surface, practically gliding as the crowd gasped in awe.

On the other side of the lake, Liam's team had no such advantage. Without Originator tech, they were forced to rely on pure physical effort. Liam stood at the front, calling out, "Steady rhythm — together! Don't fall behind!"

The oars dipped in unison, blades slicing cleanly into the water. Despite his leadership, the difference was obvious.

"Liam, they're pulling too far ahead!" shouted Darian, one of the Weavers, his breath ragged as he kept pace with the others.

Liam's jaw tightened, his arms burning with effort. "Let them go! We hold here — our time comes on land!"

As the teams neared the halfway point of the lake, the first set of floating obstacles came into play. Massive, brightly colored buoys drifted in unpredictable patterns, creating a tangled maze across the water's surface.

Nysara's team, still riding the surge of speed from their propulsion system, was forced to ease back. The rapid bursts of energy made precise navigation difficult.

"Throttle down, Roen!" Nysara called, leaning forward as she steered with tight, deliberate motions. "Keep control — don't let the momentum get ahead of us!"

Roen nodded, adjusting the propulsion controls. The jets sputtered slightly as their forward momentum slowed, the boat weaving carefully between the obstacles.

"This is getting tricky," Roen muttered under his breath, eyes scanning the moving barriers. "One bad turn, and we'll be off course."

Meanwhile, Liam's team, though rowing manually, was closing the gap. Without the added challenge of propulsion adjustments, they cut a clean, measured path through the maze. Their rhythm was nearly perfect, Liam's calls keeping the strokes in sync.

"They're gaining on us!" Roen hissed, casting a quick glance over his shoulder to see Liam's boat narrowing the distance, now halfway across the obstacle zone.

Nysara's grip on the tiller tightened. "Hold steady. We've still got the lead — just keep it clean!"

By the time both teams reached the far shore, Nysara's team still held a lead, but the gap had shrunk significantly. As her group leapt from their boat, the pulse of urgency in Liam's eyes made it clear — he wasn't done yet.

The second leg of the race began — the land obstacle course. Towering wooden structures loomed ahead, crisscrossed with ropes, ladders, and narrow ledges forming a tangled maze of physical challenges. Blocking the way at the first major checkpoint were two guild leaders: Hadassah of the Originators and Roland of the Bringers, both renowned not just for their skill but their tactical mastery.

"These two aren't playing around," Liam muttered, eyes narrowing as the pair of veteran competitors took position at the first barrier.

Hadassah's grin was sharp as the teams approached. "You want through?" Her voice carried easily over the crowd's hum. "Then prove you're ready. Think you've got what it takes?"

Nysara's team reached the checkpoint first. Without hesitating, she barked commands. "Roen, take the high path. The rest of you, go low and keep moving. I'll draw their focus."

Roland stepped forward, his staff glowing with its pale blue aura as he twirled it into a defensive stance.

Nysara activated her bounce boots, the modified gear hissing softly as they powered up. With a burst of energy, she vaulted onto a narrow ledge above Roland's position, aiming to get the height advantage.

But Roland was ready. His staff pulsed, sending a controlled wave of Incada energy rippling through the ledge. The stone trembled beneath her feet, forcing her to wobble dangerously.

"Good idea, but I've seen that trick before," Roland called, smirking.

Gritting her teeth, Nysara recovered, pivoting midair as she landed in a crouch. She quickly signaled Roen, who was already scaling a rope ladder nearby. "Roen, I need a distraction!"

Roen nodded, flipping a dial on his wrist gadget. A pulse of distortion energy rippled toward Roland, not enough to harm but causing his vision to blur for a moment.

It was all Nysara needed. She launched from her crouch, flipping off the ledge and landing behind Roland before he could fully recover. Sprinting forward, she cleared the checkpoint and raced toward the next section of the course.

Meanwhile, Liam's team had reached Hadassah, who planted herself firmly in the lower path, arms crossed and unshaken.

"You're not just powering through me," she challenged, the faint blue shimmer of defensive wards pulsing around her gauntlets. "I hope you've got more than brute force this time, Valoria."

Liam offered a confident grin but kept his grip on his sword relaxed. "Oh, I do."

Instead of charging headlong, he raised two fingers and signaled his teammates. Without a word, they spread out, moving along both sides of the barrier.

"What's he doing?" Celeste muttered from the stands, eyes narrowing as she watched Liam hold his ground, sword lowered, feet planted.

Alarion leaned forward, studying his posture. "He's baiting her. Liam never just freezes like that. He's forcing Hadassah to split her focus."

Down in the arena, Hadassah shifted her weight, eyes flicking between the spread-out members of Liam's team. The subtle tension in her stance betrayed her growing uncertainty.

Liam remained perfectly still, his sword resting lightly at his side, eyes locked onto Hadassah's.

"Well?" she called, raising a brow. "Lost your nerve, Valoria?"

Liam's smirk was razor-sharp. "Not quite."

In a heartbeat, the trap was sprung.

Two Weavers on his team moved first, conjuring a veil of shimmering Incada energy that momentarily obscured the field. The light danced like heatwaves, distorting the space between Hadassah and the rest of the course.

Before she could react, the remaining Envoys surged forward, darting around the barrier with practiced agility. Liam followed close behind, vaulting past the stunned guild leader as her line of sight restabilized.

Hadassah's eyes narrowed, realizing the deception too late. "Crafty," she muttered under her breath, pivoting to give chase, but Liam's team was already halfway to the next challenge.

Liam allowed himself a grin, the rush of adrenaline mixing with satisfaction. "That's how you get creative," he whispered, pressing on.

Ahead, Nysara's team had just cleared the last major obstacle, reaching the final stretch — a grueling uphill sprint toward the finish line. The terrain was unforgiving, scattered with loose stones and uneven inclines designed to test stamina more than speed.

But Liam wasn't done.

Planting his foot harder with each stride, he surged forward, his powerful steps eating up the ground beneath him. The gap between them began to close, and within moments, he was right beside Nysara, matching her pace stride for stride.

She glanced at him, eyes narrowing as she saw the determined grin spreading across his face.

"You're not getting past me that easily, Valoria!" she shot back, pushing herself harder as her boots kicked up dust behind her.

The crowd's energy surged, the tension in the air thick as the two racers fought for every inch.

As the finish line drew closer, Liam couldn't resist. He shot a sideways grin at Nysara, throwing a glance over his shoulder at the trailing competitors.

"Better luck next time, Nysara!" he called, the words bursting out with the confidence of a sure win.

But Nysara wasn't done either.

With a sly grin, she reached into her belt and triggered a small device. The same propulsion system she had used on the boat, now repurposed for a folding cart she'd quietly been carrying in her pack. The crowd collectively gasped as the mechanism ignited with a burst of blue energy, sending Nysara rocketing forward in a blur of speed.

Liam's jaw dropped. "What the — ?!"

The finish line rushed toward her as Liam's steps faltered. In seconds, Nysara skidded across, arms raised in triumph as the final crystal marker flared bright.

The arena exploded with cheers.

Garrick's voice boomed overhead. "Bringers and Originators take the win! What a spectacular finish! Nysara just left Liam in the dust with some classic Originator ingenuity!"

Liam stumbled to a stop, panting as he watched her celebrate. His face twisted in disbelief, then shifted to reluctant amusement. "You gotta be kidding me," he muttered, running a hand through his hair.

From the stands, Alarion practically doubled over with laughter. Celeste grinned, leaning over the railing to call out, "Liam! You might want to save the victory speech until after you cross next time!"

Nysara, still catching her breath but clearly pleased, walked back toward Liam and clapped him on the shoulder. "Well, at least now I can go back to rooting for you again."

Liam huffed but couldn't help cracking a grin. "Alright, alright. You got me. That was...impressive."

Later that evening the four friends lounged together in the guild hall, the soft glow of Incada lanterns casting a warm light over the room. Laughter echoed between them as they replayed the day's highlights.

"You should've seen your face, Liam," Nysara teased from her spot on the couch, smirking. "You really thought you had it wrapped up."

Liam groaned, sinking deeper into his chair with his hands over his face. "Don't remind me."

Celeste nudged him playfully. "Maybe next time, don't start the victory speech before you've actually, you know...won?"

Liam groaned louder.

Alarion leaned back with a knowing grin. "You do realize, Nysara's the only one of us who's actually beaten you in the tournament now, right?"

Liam's head shot up, eyes narrowing. "Hey, hold on —"

Alarion raised a hand, continuing smugly. "And since I beat Nysara earlier...well, that technically puts me in the lead."

Liam sat up straight. "First of all —"

Nysara waved him off with a laugh. "It's a joke, Liam. Relax."

As Liam made his way back to his quarters, the distant echoes of laughter gave way to a quieter tension. Passing by one of the arena's crystal displays, he caught the current point standings.

275 – Originators

200 – Bringers

200 – Weavers

75 – Envoys

Liam exhaled slowly, the weight of the numbers pressing heavily on his chest.

"We're falling behind," he thought, his jaw tightening. "If the Envoys don't start turning this around, we won't just lose — we'll be out of the running entirely."

Clenching his fists, Liam turned toward his quarters, resolve settling in his chest like stone.

Tomorrow would be different.

It had to be.

9

What Lies Beneath

The Guild Leadership convened in the dimly lit chamber at the heart of the guild complex. It was a circular space with walls carved from smooth stone, adorned with intricate mosaics depicting the formation of Ileydria and the guilds' shared victories. At the center stood a raised platform bearing the crest of Ileydria, its polished metal catching the faint blue glow of Incada sconces lining the walls.

Alexander leaned forward, his tone even but commanding. "The first years have shown promise, no question there. But let's not kid ourselves — promise doesn't mean readiness. They've got miles to go before they can hold their own outside these walls."

"Come on, Alex," Cobus grinned. "You saw Nysara in that race. That propulsion trick? Genius. She had that win dialed in."

Sunniva raised an eyebrow, her arms crossed as she leaned on the table. "Genius? Maybe. But she's too reliant on her gadgets. What happens when something fails? Out there, you can't just slap a patch on a broken device and hope for the best. She needs to learn to adapt without all the bells and whistles."

Cobus chuckled, his grin widening. "And here I thought adaptability was part of the job, Sunniva. She adapted just fine by using her tools to win. Or are we pretending you don't lean on your shields and armor out there?"

Sunniva smirked, tilting her head. "The difference is, my shields are an extension of me, I'm never without them."

Bella cleared her throat, when she spoke it cut through the banter with measured calm. "She handled herself under pressure, and that's worth something. But Sunniva's not wrong — growth means learning to stand on your own. The race was clever. Now it's up to us to make sure her ingenuity has depth."

Roland nodded, his response low and measured. "Each of you has a point. Nysara has strengths, but those strengths will only carry her so far if she doesn't shore up the rest. That's our task: not to celebrate her successes alone, but to guide her through her weaknesses."

"Speaking of successes," Jezreel cut in, her excitement barely contained, "did anyone else catch Alarion and Liam's duel? That was artistry, plain and simple. Alarion's illusions were flawless — he had Liam on the back foot almost the entire time."

"Had him," Evander interjected, his tone clipped. "Until Liam turned it around. Let's not gloss over the fact that Alarion lost. Fancy tricks only get you so far when you're up against raw determination."

Jezreel narrowed her eyes, leaning toward Evander with a knowing smirk. "Determination? Or brute stubbornness? Liam's strength is impressive, sure, but Alarion was steps ahead in skill. If he'd adjusted his approach a moment sooner, Liam wouldn't have had a chance to counter."

"Stubbornness is a strength," Evander shot back, his tone cutting. "It's what keeps you in the fight when everything's stacked against you. Alarion may have finesse, but finesse doesn't mean much if you can't finish the job. Liam did."

Elise chimed in, her delivery smooth and deliberate. "You're both right in your own way. Alarion pushed Liam to his limits with strategy, and Liam proved he could adapt under pressure. That's the balance we aim for. Both of them grew from that match — and both are stronger for it."

Jezreel nodded reluctantly. "Fine. I'll give you that. They're both shaping up to be real contenders."

"Liam's got fight in him," Rhane said, a wide grin on his face. "Kid's scrappy. I like that. Makes him a perfect fit for leadership, don't you think, Roland?"

Roland allowed himself a small smile, but his eyes were distant. "He does have the spirit for it. But no matter who we are talking about, what matters is how they handle the challenges ahead. None of this is static. Growth is continuous — and the lessons only get harder from here."

The table fell quiet for a moment before Roland leaned forward, his tone shifting. "Speaking of challenges, has anyone else been thinking about the thefts?

The shift in tone was immediate.

Elise straightened, her poised expression unflinching. "More missing inventory?"

Bella nodded, folding her hands atop the table. "Three crates this time. Equipment from the restricted armory. But this isn't just about stolen gear anymore. We found residue. Not Incada — Incadise."

A ripple of tension spread through the room.

Jezreel's brows furrowed. "You're certain?"

Bella's voice was grim. "I tested the residue myself. It's unmistakable. Crude, but *there*."

Evander's expression darkened. "Impossible. The process was eradicated a millennium ago. No one *alive* should even *know* how to create Incadise, much less refine it."

Alexander folded his arms. "And yet, it was there."

Sunniva's jaw tightened. "If someone's trying to replicate *that,* they're playing with fire they don't understand. The Shade fell because of what Incadise did to their minds. There's no power worth that cost."

Roland's words were calm but heavy. "The Shade didn't fall because they lacked power. They fell because the *power consumed them.*"

Elise's focus turned toward the mosaics on the wall; she fixated on the fragmented image of a black banner with a jagged golden sigil. "Power corrupts, but Incadise twists. The histories make that clear. It was never just a weapon — it was a *distortion* of strength, designed to break its wielder even as it magnified them."

Sunniva's fists were clenched. "Then we need to stop this. Immediately."

Elise's voice remained level, but there was a point beneath it. "We still don't know *who* is behind this. Or if they even understand what they're tampering with. The thefts could be experimental. Careless."

Bella shook her head. "Careless doesn't explain the symbols carved into those crates. They're not random — they're *Shadian derivatives*. Someone isn't just tampering with dangerous material. They're *studying* it."

Cobus sat forward, the levity in his manner gone. "Then we've got a bigger problem. If they've figured out how to make Incadise, it's not about power — it's about *control*. That's why the Shade used it. Not just for war, but to dominate their own minds. Until it broke them."

Evander's reply was low, his fingers tapping the hilt of his dagger. "Then we end this before it starts."

Alexander shook his head. "We can't risk rash action without clarity. We need solid proof. And we need to ensure we're not chasing shadows."

Silence lingered.

It was Roland who finally broke the silence. "I agree with Alexander. The threat is real, but so is our duty to these recruits. The Grand Tournament is already in motion. If we shift focus now — if we pull resources for an investigation mid-event — we risk compromising both the safety *and* the purpose of this competition."

Bella exhaled, though her expression remained tense. "So, what, then? We wait? Pretend this isn't happening?"

Alexander's voice remained firm. "No. We monitor. Quietly. The stolen supplies are a concern, but there's no evidence of *active* use — only residue. This is not a crisis, yet. The tournament remains our priority. It's too critical for morale. For unity. And for the lessons these recruits *need* to face."

Elise nodded, though reluctantly. "Agreed. The tournament tests not just skill but leadership. If we compromise it, we risk sending the message that fear dictates our choices."

Jezreel exhaled, clearly frustrated but holding her tongue.

Roland's response softened slightly, though the weight of it remained. "Once the tournament concludes, we can divert full resources to uncovering the truth. For now, Guild Wars is a proving ground we cannot afford to disrupt. We owe it to the next generation — to show them strength without panic."

Cobus gave a reluctant nod. "Then we better get over there, this year is like no other… There's a whole mountain inside the arena this year, forests, rivers, we've yet to do something on this scale. Let's go walk the battlefield."

"That's a good point," Alexander said, standing. "We should head to the arena now. There's still plenty to finalize. I've been meaning to discuss some plans for Guild Wars with all of you before the event."

Hadassah smirked. "What's this, Alex? Planning your comeback after the Envoys fell to last place?"

Alexander's expression didn't waver. "Winning matters, Hadassah. But strengthening our recruits matters more. That's what King Ryune's directive has always been: Better individually. Better together. Stronger Ileydria."

Roland rose, "Then let's make it so. Not by controlling the outcomes, but by creating opportunities for growth. That's what they're here for."

They filed out of the chamber, their conversations shifting to the specifics of the upcoming event. Roland paused for a moment, his eyes on the shadows flickering along the walls. "And yet," he thought, "growth may not be enough to prepare them for what's coming."

The guild leaders stepped into the Grand Arena, its vast, circular expanse slowly transforming as the final adjustments were made for the battle royale. Roland, trailing slightly behind the group, took in the scope of the arena, the hum of the massive mechanisms echoing faintly beneath his boots.

At the heart of the arena, colossal mechanical platforms shifted with measured precision. Sections of terrain — lush forest thickets, jagged rocky outcrops, and shimmering desert sands — were being lowered and raised into place, controlled by a lattice of gears, pulleys, and hydraulic lifts hidden within the arena's perimeter. Each biome module was carefully arranged, clicking into position as the familiar glow of Incada along the arena's outer walls pulsed in synchronization with the shifting ground.

It was a feat of engineering. The biomes themselves sat atop reinforced platforms designed for rapid reconfiguration, ensuring maximum flexibility while the solid stone foundation beneath remained untouched. Roland knew that while the surface of the battlefield could be changed in a day, the true bedrock of the arena never shifted.

High above, crystalline projectors embedded along the arena's vaulted ceiling adjusted the light, simulating shifting weather patterns — flickers of rainclouds forming over the mountain, while a blazing midday sun baked the sands. The effect was immersive, designed to disorient and challenge the recruits with dynamic environmental hazards.

Roland's eyes focused on a mountainous formation being drawn into place, the rock face bristling with narrow ledges and concealed alcoves perfect for ambush tactics. It was a carefully curated challenge, meant to teach both positioning and strategic retreat.

"This arena is as much a test of resourcefulness as it is of skill," he thought.

This arena, for all its elegance, was controlled. Curated. Within its shifting walls, risk could be measured, influence carefully calibrated. But the thefts, the residue — *that* was no calculated danger. It was a threat born from desperation. Or ambition. He could feel it pressing at the edges of his thoughts as the stone groaned, adjusting once more to reveal a new zone — jagged icy outcroppings, frost clinging to the arena walls.

Elise gestured toward the shifting ice. "The transitions are seamless today. Better than the last trial run."

Now standing at the edge of the arena, his gaze sweeping the space one last time before the weight of something out of place caught his attention.

To his side was a hallway that led around the perimeter of the arena. Behind a partially drawn curtain, half-obscured by the shifting light, sat several wooden crates. Plain. Unmarked — except for the symbols etched into their sides.

A chill traced down his spine.

The markings were the same.

Roland's chest tightened.

"Not here."

"Excuse me for a moment," Roland said, his voice calm. The others barely registered his departure as he moved toward the crates.

The crates were unremarkable in design — wooden, reinforced with metal, the kind used to transport supplies. But the symbols etched into their sides caught the light oddly, as if they resisted it. Roland crouched, pried one open, and peered inside.

Empty glass jugs lay nestled within, their interiors coated with faint, sickly yellow residue. Roland touched one cautiously. It was warm, and the faint glow made his heart sink.

"Incadise," he muttered. "Why here?"

Roland moved silently down the hallway, his hand gripping his staff as he processed what he had just seen. "Abandoning The Everlight," he muttered under his breath. "After everything we've been through, after all we've rebuilt, what kind of person would make that choice?"

He shook his head, his brow furrowing as he considered the question. "Power, probably," he continued, his voice edged with frustration. "It's always power, isn't it? They think they're in control, think they're clever enough to wield something as dangerous as Incadise without losing themselves. How many times have we heard this story?"

His boots tapped softly on the stone floor as he walked, the quiet rhythm grounding him. "Maybe it's not just power," he mused. "Maybe it's fear. Fear of being powerless, fear of failing or worse, fear of being ordinary." He frowned, his mind turning over the possibilities. "But fear is no excuse. The Everlight is there for everyone. It's not just a source of power — it's a guide. A strength that doesn't ask for more than you can give. How could anyone turn their back on that?"

The hallway narrowed slightly, the walls seeming to press closer as the light from the sconces dimmed. Roland glanced at the flickering glow of Incada crystals embedded in the walls, their soft blue light casting gentle shadows. His grip tightened on his staff. "If it's power they want, they should remember what it cost the Obsidian Shade," he said, his tone sharpening. "Entire cities lost, people enslaved, lives shattered. How could anyone look at that history and think, 'Yes, let's do that again'?"

He paused, staring ahead into the dim corridor. "No," he thought, shaking his head. "It's not just history. It's ignorance. Complacency. A kingdom that has known peace for too long, people forgetting the lessons of the past." His words dropped to a whisper, almost as if he were confessing to the hallway itself. "And maybe we're to blame for that. Maybe we've done too good a job of keeping the dark days out of sight."

As he continued walking, his thoughts grew darker. "And what if it's not just a few people?" he asked himself, his tone laden with worry. "What if this isn't isolated? What if these symbols, these thefts, are the start of something bigger? A rot spreading through the kingdom, right under our noses?" He shook his head again, trying to push the thought away. "No. Focus, Roland. Find the truth first. Then worry about the rest."

He was so lost in his musings that the flicker of light ahead almost went unnoticed. Roland stopped abruptly, narrowing his eyes. A torch? In these halls? He stepped closer to the wall, pressing himself into the shadows as he watched the light bob in the distance. It moved steadily, held by someone walking with purpose. His pulse quickened.

"A torch," he whispered. "Not Incada. Why?" His eyes tracked the light carefully. Roland began to move; his steps deliberate and quiet. "Alright," he whispered to himself. "Stay sharp. They don't know you're here. Whoever they are, they have a destination in mind. You just have to follow."

The torchbearer moved ahead, their steps echoing faintly in the empty corridor. Roland kept his distance; his eyes locked on the light as he followed. "You're no professional," he muttered, noticing the slight unevenness in the person's stride. "Careful, but hesitant. Not used to sneaking around, are you? So, what are you doing here?"

The figure paused at an intersection, and Roland stopped instantly, holding his breath. He watched as the torch shifted slightly, its light casting fleeting shadows on the walls. The figure seemed to listen for something, their head tilting slightly, before turning left and continuing down the hallway. Roland let out a slow exhale, then followed.

"Where are you going?" he wondered aloud, his voice barely audible. "And what are you looking for?" The hallway grew darker as they moved further from the arena entrance. The warm glow of the torch was the only light ahead, and Roland kept his eyes fixed on it, his mind racing.

"If this is connected to the thefts, they're not going to lead me to nothing," he reasoned quietly. "There's something down here. Something they don't want found." He paused, glancing over his shoulder as a thought struck him. "Or someone."

His grip tightened on his staff, his knuckles whitening. "If it's a trap, fine. Let them try. But if they think they're getting away with this..." He let the thought hang in the air, unfinished.

The figure turned a corner, and Roland crept closer. His thoughts churned as he moved, each step drawing him deeper into the mystery. "Who are you working for? How many of you are there? And how much damage have you already done?" The questions burned in his mind, but one stood out above the rest, its weight pressing heavily on his chest.

"How much more will you do before we stop you?"

The torchlight led him to a storage room. Roland pushed the door open cautiously, his staff raised. He stepped cautiously into the storage room, his eyes darting to every corner, expecting to find the torchbearer he had been following. The room was dimly lit, filled with the faint scent of mildew and dust. Shelves lined the walls, holding long-abandoned crates and tools, some rusted beyond recognition. But the room was empty.

He frowned, his grip tightening on his staff as he scanned the area. "Empty?" he muttered to himself. "That doesn't make sense. I saw the torchlight. I followed it here." He turned slowly, his eyes sweeping the room again. "No exits other than the way I came in. No sign of anyone hiding...so, where did they go?"

Roland's brow furrowed as he took another step inside, his boots scuffing softly against the stone floor. He moved to the center of the room, his shoulders tense, and let out a slow breath. "This has to be more than just a dead end," he muttered. "I didn't just imagine that light. It was here."

His gaze shifted to his staff, its smooth surface faintly catching the light. He adjusted his grip, his jaw tightening as his mind worked through the possibilities. "Alright, Roland," he said quietly, his tone clipped with determination. "Time to get some answers."

He planted his feet firmly, drawing his staff up with a fluid motion. Concentration etched deep lines into his face as he spun the staff in a precise, controlled arc. The motion was elegant, practiced — a weapon master's grace tempered by years of discipline. With a decisive move, he brought the base of the staff down against the floor with a resounding crack.

From the point of impact, a pulse of blue energy erupted, spreading out in a wave. The energy rolled across the floor like ripples on a still pond, its soft light illuminating every crevice. The wave climbed the walls, spilling over shelves and crates, reaching into corners, and finally curling across the ceiling like a dome of light. For a brief moment, the entire room glowed in a vibrant, almost otherworldly hue, as if the very air had been imbued with life.

Roland's eyes followed the wave, his mind alert and focused. As the glow blanketed the room, it began to reveal subtle movements. A faint shimmer outlined where air currents flowed, tracing invisible pathways. Around the edges of the doorway, near vents, and even in the cracks between the stones, the energy clung like frost before fading away.

But one point on the wall caught his attention. It was faint, almost imperceptible — a slight disturbance where no vent or doorway should have been. The glow remained there, stubborn and distinct. Roland tilted his head, his focus narrowing as he stepped closer.

"Interesting," he muttered, running a hand along the wall. It felt smooth, unremarkable to the touch, but the energy had marked it. "A hidden door, maybe? Clever. But not clever enough."

He placed the base of his staff against the wall, his eyes narrowing in focus. "Let's see what you're hiding," he said, though he held no malice — only determination. With a deep breath, he steadied himself, closing his eyes for a moment. The staff pulsed faintly, its blue light intensifying as it connected with the wall.

The stone didn't crumble or crack. Instead, it seemed to dissolve into fine dust, falling away in a gentle cascade to reveal a dark tunnel beyond. Roland stepped back, his breath steady as he surveyed the opening. The air that flowed from the tunnel was cool, carrying a faint metallic tang that set his nerves on edge.

He stared into the darkness, his thoughts racing. "This changes things," he muttered, gripping his staff tightly. "If this tunnel leads somewhere significant, it's a direct link to whoever's behind all this."

For a moment, he considered turning back. "The others should know about this," he reasoned aloud. "They'd want to see it for themselves, and if there's danger..." He let the thought hang, his brow furrowing.

But then his eyes flicked to the dust at his feet, the faint yellow residue on the crates still fresh in his memory. "If I leave now, whoever built these tunnels might figure out we've found them. We lose the element of surprise, and they cover their tracks. No, that's too big a risk."

He squared his shoulders, his expression hardening. "I'll go," he decided firmly. "Just a quick look. Map the area, figure out what I can, and then I'll tell the others." He adjusted his grip on his staff, the familiar weight grounding him. "Besides," he added quietly, a hint of wry humor in his tone, "what's the point of being the Arch-Bringer if I can't handle a little danger?"

His mind raced as he walked.

"These tunnels...they're too deliberate. Too well-hidden. Whoever built this wanted to stay unnoticed."

The air grew cooler as Roland descended deeper into the tunnels, the heavy dampness clinging to his robes. His staff cast a dim, steady light that flickered against the jagged walls, the shadows shifting as he moved. Each step was deliberate, the faint echo of his boots carrying just far enough to remind him how far below the surface he must be. The oppressive quiet wasn't comforting — it was weighted, like the tunnels themselves held their breath.

"These tunnels weren't dug by amateurs," Roland pondered to himself, his tone thoughtful but edged with suspicion. His voice sounded small, swallowed up by the darkness. "Too clean. Too deliberate. Whoever built these had resources — and a plan."

He held out his hand, and with a flicker of concentration, an Incada stone flared to life, floating a few paces ahead. Its pale blue glow illuminated the way like a sentinel, casting just enough light to reveal the uneven floor and damp walls. A few drops of water fell from the ceiling in sporadic plinks, the sound distant and hollow.

Roland stopped, his fingers brushing against the wall. The surface was cold and rough, but something about the texture felt wrong. His hand found grooves carved into the stone — lines that were too even to be natural. He ran his fingers along the marks, his brow furrowing.

"Symbols again," he muttered, his breath visible in the chilly air. He glanced back down the tunnel, his thoughts circling. "The crates above had them. Now here, carved into stone? Why go through this much trouble? What are you hiding?"

He straightened, the faint blue light from the Incada stone glinting off his staff. The metallic tang in the air grew stronger — a subtle but unmistakable acrid scent that prickled the back of his throat. He let out a slow breath, his eyes narrowing.

"Incadise," he whispered. The word hung heavily in the silence. "It's faint, but it's here. Enough to disrupt the untrained. Could this entire place be steeped in it? How far does this go?"

Roland pressed on, his movements cautious. His thoughts grew louder in the stillness, each step dragging him deeper into his own mind.

"You'd think we'd learned," he said quietly, shaking his head. "After the Obsidian Shade, after everything we lost, who would choose this path again? Who looks at The Everlight and says, 'No, I'll take the darkness'? Is it desperation? Ambition?" His jaw tightened. "How many people would it take to build something like this? And how many more believe in it?"

The tunnel narrowed, forcing him to stoop slightly. He moved forward, his focus sharpened, when a faint sound broke through the silence. He froze. A shuffle. Soft but distinct. His eyes snapped to the faint glow ahead — the flicker of torchlight casting long shadows on the walls.

Roland extinguished the light of his staff, plunging the space into near-total darkness. He crept forward, his hand brushing the wall for guidance, the faint torchlight his only guide. The figure ahead moved steadily, their steps deliberate but light. Whoever they were, they knew these tunnels well.

"Not a worker," Roland mused under his breath. "No hesitation. No second-guessing. You've been here before." His fingers tightened around the staff as he continued, keeping his distance. "But where are you going?"

The figure turned a corner, the torchlight disappearing from view. Roland quickened his pace, his boots soundless on the damp stone. When he reached the corner and looked around, the torchbearer was gone. The tunnel ahead was empty, the oppressive silence settling back over him.

Roland's brow furrowed. "Gone," he muttered, scanning the space. "Too quick. Either you know these tunnels better than I thought...or you saw me."

He pressed on, his steps more cautious than before. The acrid scent of Incadise grew stronger with each turn, mingling with the earthy smell of wet stone. His Incada stone flickered faintly, the disruption subtle but unmistakable. Roland's jaw clenched as the memories of his studies flooded back.

"Just like the texts," he thought. "Tunnels laced with Incadise. Disrupt the senses. Disable abilities. Classic Shade tactics. But why here?"

Roland slowed his steps, his breath controlled but his pulse quickened. He let the weight of the quiet settle over him as he stopped taking stock. His hands pressed together, his eyes closing for a moment of concentration. Slowly, he pulled his hands apart, the familiar blue glow of Incada energy expanding outward in a wave. It formed a faintly shimmering map of the tunnels he had explored, the glowing lines carving out the labyrinth he had been navigating.

The layout wasn't random.

His brow furrowed as the holographic map hung in the air. The twists and turns, the dead ends and strategic placements — it all clicked into place. He traced a path with his eyes, noting chokepoints and hidden junctions.

"This isn't just for smuggling," he whispered, "It's a staging ground. Ambush tactics. Just like the Obsidian Shade."

The realization sent a chill through him. His mind raced back to the old tomes he'd poured over as a young Bringer recruit. Accounts of how the Shade manipulated terrain, using hidden routes to outflank and overwhelm their enemies. This layout was too similar to be a coincidence.

The soft glow of the map began to fade, and Roland pressed his hands together, letting it dissipate. He adjusted his grip on his staff. Every instinct told him to turn back, to gather the other guild leaders and confront this together.

"But if I leave now," he said under his breath, "they'll scatter. Whoever built this has been careful — more careful than we realized. They'll know we're onto them, and they'll disappear into the shadows again."

He tightened his grip on the staff. "No. The element of surprise is worth the risk."

As if to mock his resolve, the floating Incada stone ahead flickered and dropped to the ground with a hollow clink. Its light extinguished instantly, leaving only the faintest glow of his staff to push back the encroaching darkness.

The acrid scent that had been growing stronger was no longer subtle. It hung thick in the air now, suffocating, oppressive. His Incada abilities were faltering, the interference unmistakable.

A flicker of yellow light ahead snapped him out of his thoughts. The torchlight again, faint but distinct, beckoned him forward. Roland rose, his steps cautious but deliberate. He kept to the shadows, letting the dim torchlight guide him.

"Whoever you are, you're not slipping away this time."

The tunnel twisted sharply to the left, the flickering torchlight growing brighter as he approached. His boots moved silently over the damp stone as he rounded the corner and stopped short.

A makeshift wooden door stood before him, its edges uneven and hastily nailed together. Faint yellow light seeped through the gaps, casting long shadows on the floor. The acrid tang of Incadise was almost overwhelming now, clinging to the back of his throat.

Roland stared at the door, his mind racing. His grip on his staff tightened, and he adjusted his stance, bracing himself for whatever lay beyond. Slowly, he reached out and pushed the door open, its hinges groaning softly in protest.

The sight inside took his breath away.

The room was vast and dimly lit by the sickly yellow glow of Incadise lanterns embedded in the walls. Rows of silhouettes filled the space, moving with precision. Figures clad in dark; armor embedded with cells full of incadise made to look like gems, sorted through crates, and practiced formations. Their movements were efficient and deliberate.

"It's a small army," Roland thought, his heart pounding.

The yellow glow cast their shadows long and distorted, sending a chill down his spine. His fingers itched to raise his staff, to call forth The Everlight and cleanse this place — but before he could act, a hand clamped over his mouth.

His eyes widened as he felt himself yanked backward. The door slammed shut in front of him, the sound reverberating down the tunnel. The sickly glow of Incadise vanished, replaced by total darkness.

Roland struggled, his mind raced, every muscle tensed for action, but the grip on him was ironclad. His captor's breath was hot against his ear, a low voice whispering a single, chilling phrase:

"You've seen enough."

10

A Clash of Guilds

The crowd in The Grand Arena was electric, their cheers echoing like thunder as the anticipation built to a crescendo. High above the battleground, Garrick and Lyra sat in their commentary booth, their faces illuminated by the soft glow of Incada-powered monitors. Behind them, massive screens displayed sweeping views of the Grand Arena, its sprawling terrain rendered in intricate detail by the aerial drones that circled overhead.

The Grand Arena was a marvel of design — a vast expanse that seemed to stretch on forever, divided into distinct zones. Thick wooded areas offered natural cover, while rocky outcroppings provided vantage points for those seeking high ground. The open plains and their rolling hills seemed deceptively serene, but their wide spaces offered little protection from enemy eyes. And there, towering at the far edge, stood the mountain — a jagged sentinel cloaked in mist, its peak shimmering faintly with the energy of embedded Incada crystals.

Surrounding the entire arena floor, a network of protective barriers hummed, translucent walls of blue light ready to rise nearly twenty feet over the stands. These barriers, designed to protect spectators from stray projectiles or energy discharges during intense competitions, were controlled by a central system accessible only from the broadcast booth. Once the event begins the barriers would rise and cut the battlegrounds off from the rest of the kingdom. This ensured that no matter how fierce the battles became, the audience remained completely separated from the action below and the competitors separated from the broadcaster's play-by-play. The system had been refined over decades of tournaments, becoming so reliable that spectators never gave a second thought to the shimmering walls that stood between them and the competitors.

Garrick's voice boomed across the arena,

"Ladies and gentlemen, welcome to the pinnacle of this year's tournament — the Battle Royale in the Grand Arena, or as we like to call it… Guild Wars!"

The crowd erupted, waving flags bearing their favorite guilds' colors. The banners of the Envoys, Originators, Weavers, and Bringers flapped in the wind, their vibrant hues a testament to the loyalty of their supporters.

"This is the event we've all been waiting for," Lyra chimed in, her tone carrying its usual mix of enthusiasm and charm. "Today, our recruits will be tested like never before. Strategy, teamwork, and grit — everything they've learned so far will be put to the ultimate test."

The camera panned across the terrain, zooming in on the central battlefield — a fortified area with a raised platform glowing faintly with Incada energy.

"Here's how it works," Garrick explained, leaning forward. "Teams have two primary objectives. First, control the key position in the center of the arena. Holding it will steadily accumulate points for your guild. Second, eliminations. Every time a recruit is knocked out of the competition, their guild earns elimination points. Simple enough, right?"

Lyra chuckled. "Simple? Sure. But here's the wrinkle, folks! Every year, Guild Wars comes with a surprise twist — an unexpected objective that can turn the tide of battle. So, keep your ears open for the announcement!"

The screens lit up with highlights from the tournament so far. Clips of Nysara's brilliant propulsion device from the obstacle race, Celeste's calculated strikes in the solo matches, Alarion's mesmerizing illusions, and Liam's raw power and determination filled the displays.

"And let's not forget," Garrick interjected, his grin audible in his tone, "this event could very well decide the tournament's standings. The Envoys are trailing, but with the right tactics, they could climb back into contention. The Originators, Bringers, and Weavers are neck-and-neck. It's anyone's game!"

As the cameras panned back to the arena, the participants could be seen in their starting zones, their teams huddled together for last-minute discussions.

Liam finished addressing his squad, his words carrying conviction that steadied the nerves of his teammates. Their collective resolve mirrored his own as they prepared to secure and hold the central position. As the group began final preparations, Alexander approached from the edge of the starting area, his imposing figure commanding immediate attention.

"Liam," Alexander called, gesturing for him to step aside.

Liam approached, his expression sharpening. "What's up?"

Alexander crossed his arms, leaning slightly to speak in a low, deliberate tone. "This match is going to test you in ways you're not expecting. Holding a position like this? It's about more than just brute force. You'll need to trust your squad, delegate, and be ready to adapt."

"I trust them," Liam replied earnestly. "They're solid. We've trained for this."

"Trust isn't just about assuming they'll do their jobs," Alexander countered. "It's about empowering them to make decisions when things go sideways. When the heat's on and you're focused on the bigger picture, you need to know they can handle the details."

Liam hesitated, absorbing the words. "So, ... I can't just do everything myself."

"Exactly," Alexander said, his tone softening. "You're strong, Liam, but don't let that strength make you blind to the power of teamwork. They follow you because they believe in you. Make sure you give them a reason to keep believing."

Liam nodded, his jaw tightening with determination. "Understood. I won't let you — or them — down."

Alexander clapped a hand on Liam's shoulder. "Good. Now go show them why you're their leader."

Nysara stood in the center of the Originator team, her combat gear gleaming with faint traces of Incada energy. Bella hovered nearby, her arms crossed as she observed the group. Nysara held up a cylindrical device, its surface etched with intricate grooves that shimmered faintly in the light.

"Alright, listen up," Nysara said, her voice brimming with confidence. "These are Rotating Incada Cells. They're the game-changer." She held the device higher, her grin widening. "Most people think gadgets like ours are limited by their power reserves, but not today. These cells rotate between multiple charged cores, so when one's tapped out, another takes its place. Essentially, we've got more juice than anyone out there expects."

The team hummed with approval, a few Originators leaning in for a closer look.

Bella cleared her throat, her expression remaining stern. "It's a brilliant piece of tech, Nysara. But don't let that brilliance blind you. If you lean too heavily on these cells and something goes wrong, you'll find yourself with a dead gadget and no backup plan."

Nysara's grin faltered slightly, but she nodded. "I hear you, Bella. Trust me, I've thought it through. We're not going to blow all our resources at once — we'll use them wisely."

Bella's expression softened, and she placed a hand on Nysara's shoulder. "Good. You've got talent, Nysara. Don't let overconfidence trip you up. This arena is going to throw curveballs. Be ready for them."

Nysara straightened, her determination rekindled. "Ready and waiting."

Alarion leaned against a tree at the edge of the Weaver starting area, his violin resting against his leg. Ava and Jezreel stood nearby, poring over a small map of the Grand Arena.

"So, here's the plan," Jezreel began, tapping the map with a gloved finger. "We're not going for the key position immediately. We spread out, lay traps, and thin out their numbers before we even think about direct engagement."

Ava nodded, her eyes flicking to Alarion. "Your illusions will be crucial for this. The more we can confuse and delay the other guilds, the more time we have to set up our traps."

"Understood," Alarion said, his manner calm but resolute. "I've been working on a new variation of my projections. They'll be less obvious but more disorienting. If anyone wanders into our zones, they'll wish they hadn't."

Jezreel grinned. "Perfect. And if we do this right, we won't just slow them down — we'll control the battlefield."

Ava crossed her arms, her tone taking a serious edge. "Just remember, we're playing the long game. No flashy moves until it's absolutely necessary. Patience will win this for us."

"Patience," Alarion echoed, his fingers brushing the strings of his violin. "Got it."

The Bringer starting area was a flurry of controlled preparation. Celeste stood in the center, her staff glowing faintly as she spoke with Olive, who had been named acting leader in Roland's absence.

"High ground," Olive said, her voice even and authoritative. "It's our greatest advantage. From up there, we'll see everything — every movement, every tactic. That's how we'll win this."

Celeste nodded, her expression serious. "And when the time comes to engage?"

"Only when we're sure of the outcome," Olive replied. "The other guilds will burn through their resources trying to outmaneuver each other. Let them. We'll strike when they're at their weakest."

A recruit nearby shifted uneasily. "And what about Roland?"

Olive's look hardened for a moment, then softened. "Roland entrusted me with this for a reason. We'll carry out our mission, and we'll do it well. He'd expect nothing less."

Celeste placed a hand on Olive's shoulder. "We're ready. Let's make him proud."

Olive gave a faint smile. "We will. Now, let's move out."

"This is it," Lyra said, her words tinged with excitement. "The Grand Arena is set, the recruits are ready, and the stakes couldn't be higher. Who will rise to the top? Who will fall short? And what surprises lie in store? Buckle up, folks — it's time to find out!"

The crowd hushed in anticipation as the guild leaders made their way from their respective starting zones, converging for a ceremonial gathering.

Alexander of the Envoys was the first to arrive, his commanding presence undeniable. He moved with measured authority, his focused eyes scanning the vast terrain as if already calculating its every tactical advantage. Bella of the Originators followed, her posture relaxed but her eyes keen as she took in the scene. Ava of the Weavers approached next, her sharp features illuminated by the Incada light, her expression calm but focused. Finally, Olive stepped forward, representing the Bringers in Roland's absence. She carried herself with quiet determination, her head held high despite the weight of her temporary role.

As the four leaders met at the platform, there was no need for words at first. Their presence alone spoke volumes — a moment of unity before the chaos.

Bella broke the silence, her tone light but tinged with an edge of curiosity. "Quite the arena this year. A lot of opportunities...if you know how to look for them."

"Opportunities for the clever, pitfalls for the reckless," Alexander replied evenly. His focus shifted momentarily to Olive, who stood silently, her expression unreadable.

Ava smirked, folding her arms. "Or traps for the overly confident. That mountain's going to make for some interesting plays."

Olive's eyes flicked to the towering peak in the distance. When she spoke, her voice was calm and measured. "Only if you waste time rushing for it without understanding what it costs. Control of the battlefield starts with observation."

Bella raised an eyebrow, her lips curving into a faint smile. "Well said, Olive. I take it the Bringers aren't planning to make the first move?"

"Not unless it's the right move," Olive countered smoothly.

Alexander's gaze lingered on her for a moment before shifting to the mountain. "Cautious. Not a bad strategy. But in a match like this, hesitation can cost you everything."

The tension between them was subtle but undeniable. Though their words were measured, their intense glances hinted at deeper layers — a prearranged plan shared in secret meetings, and the knowledge that this event would test more than just their recruits.

Ava tilted her head, her eyes studying Olive. "You're carrying Roland's mantle well, but I can't help noticing he's...missing. Is everything alright with the Bringers?"

Olive's focus didn't waver. "Honestly no one really knows where he could be, we haven't heard from him since he went off on his own while we were inspecting the arena. However, The Bringers are ready."

Bella's expression softened slightly, though her reply remained practical. "It's unlike him to miss something this important. I hope whatever's keeping him away isn't serious."

Alexander folded his arms, his tone neutral but edged with curiosity. "It's not like Roland to be absent without reason. But I suppose there's no time to dwell on it now."

"Indeed," Olive said firmly. "We have a match to focus on."

High above, Garrick and Lyra watched the leaders' exchange from their booth, their commentary adding to the charged atmosphere.

"Well, there you have it," Garrick said, leaning closer to his mic. "The guild leaders have gathered, and it seems we're starting this event with a bit of intrigue. Roland's absence isn't just surprising — it's unprecedented. What do you think, Lyra?"

Lyra tapped her chin, her expression thoughtful. "It's definitely unusual. Roland's been a fixture of this tournament for years. But Olive's stepping up in a big way. She's poised, confident, and clearly ready to lead."

"True," Garrick replied, nodding. "Still, it makes you wonder — what could be more important than this?"

The camera panned back to the leaders, who exchanged final nods before stepping down from the platform.

Lyra's voice carried a note of intrigue. "Whatever the reason, one thing's for sure: Olive has her work cut out for her. But if anyone can rally the Bringers, it's her. Now, let's see what the leaders' strategies bring to the battlefield."

Garrick's grin returned. "And with that, the stage is officially set. The leaders are ready, the recruits are ready, and we're seconds away from pure chaos. Buckle up, folks — it's time to see who rises to the top!"

The final countdown began, a massive display ticking down from ten. The arena grew quiet for the first time that day, every eye locked on the screens.

"And there it is!" Garrick roared as the final number faded. "The Guild Wars starts… now!"

The arena exploded with sound, the crowd roaring in unison as the recruits surged forward into the chaos of the Grand Arena.

The horn blared, signaling the start of the event. The arena came alive as the recruits surged from their starting positions, each guild executing its carefully planned strategy. The massive Incada screens overhead displayed split views of the Grand Arena, capturing every movement as the recruits fanned out across the terrain.

Liam led the charge toward the central platform, his squad moving in perfect unison. The Envoy recruits carried large shields emblazoned with their guild's crest, their disciplined formation creating a near-impenetrable phalanx as they marched into the battlefield's heart.

"Keep your eyes up," Liam commanded, his manner steady despite the adrenaline coursing through him. "Once we take the position, lock it down. No one gets through us."

The squad reached the platform with precision, moving into pre-practiced positions. Shield Guardians formed a tight circle around the glowing key point, their shields interlocking to create a barrier. Behind them, Envoy recruits armed with bows and spears stood ready, scanning the horizon for threats.

Up in the commentary booth, Garrick's voice rang out. "And there it is, folks — the Envoys have wasted no time in securing the key position! Look at that formation. That's textbook teamwork right there."

Lyra leaned toward her microphone, her tone brimming with admiration. "It's what the Envoys do best, Garrick. They're like a well-oiled machine. If anyone wants that key point, they'll have to fight for it."

Far from the central platform, Nysara and her team sprinted toward the supply caches scattered across the arena. The Originators moved quickly but methodically, their eyes scanning the terrain for potential threats.

"This one's clear," Roen called out, flipping open a supply crate. Inside were spare Incada cells, mechanical components, and a few tools for constructing field gadgets.

"Good," Nysara said, already assembling a small device with practiced ease. "We need to stock up fast. The longer we wait, the harder it'll be to counter the others."

Bella joined her, holding a hand to her ear as a communicator buzzed faintly. "We've got reports of the Weavers moving into the woods. Keep an eye out for traps."

"Let them set their little tricks," Nysara said with a grin, slotting one of her Rotating Incada cells into place. The device hummed to life, glowing faintly. "We're ready for them."

Bella raised an eyebrow, nodding toward the cylindrical device. "Just remember what I said — don't burn through those cells too quickly. They're a massive advantage, but they won't save you if you rely on them too much."

"Trust me, Bella," Nysara replied, giving the device a final twist. "We've got this."

In the dense wooded area, the Weavers moved like ghosts. Alarion's illusions flickered among the trees, creating phantom recruits that darted between the shadows. Jezreel crouched low, setting a tripwire laced with Incada energy that would stun anyone who triggered it. Ava stood nearby, her eyes scanning for potential intruders.

"Remember," Ava said, "we're not here to fight directly. We slow them down, divide their forces, and make them question every step."

Alarion nodded, the faint glow of his violin reflecting in his eyes. "Illusions are in place. Anyone who wanders in here won't know what's real until it's too late."

"Good," Jezreel said, brushing dirt off her gloves as she finished setting another trap. "Let them think they've got the upper hand. When they least expect it, we'll turn this place into a nightmare."

High above the battlefield, Celeste and the Bringers reached a rocky outcrop overlooking the central arena. The elevated vantage point gave them a clear view of the Envoys' formation and the surrounding terrain.

"Olive, look at that," Celeste said, pointing toward the platform. "The Envoys are locked down tight. No one's touching that position without a serious fight."

"Exactly as expected," Olive replied. "Let them sit there and rack up points. They'll burn themselves out holding it while the rest of us conserve our strength."

"And when we do engage?" a younger recruit asked, his voice tinged with uncertainty.

"We strike fast and hard," Olive said, turning to address the group. "But not until we're sure the time is right. For now, we watch. Study their movements. Let the others make the first mistake."

Celeste nodded, gripping her staff tightly. "Understood. We'll wait."

The screen above the arena lit up with the current point totals. The Envoys were already pulling ahead, their disciplined control of the central platform steadily accumulating points.

"Look at that climb!" Lyra exclaimed. "The Envoys are taking firm control of this battle."

Garrick chuckled. "But holding the position this early comes with risks, Lyra. They've painted a big target on their backs. Let's see how long they can hold out."

As the Originators moved to challenge the Envoys, they found themselves drawn into the wooded area. The dense forest was eerily quiet, the stillness broken only by the occasional rustle of leaves.

"Stay sharp," Bella warned, her voice low. "This is Weaver territory. They'll be waiting for us."

She was right. The first trap was triggered by an unsuspecting Originator recruit, who let out a yelp as Incada energy surged through his legs, temporarily immobilizing him. A moment later, one of Alarion's illusions appeared, drawing two more Originators into another trap — a carefully hidden net that snapped them off their feet.

"They're everywhere!" Roen shouted, swinging a device wildly to scan for hidden traps.

"Calm down," Nysara said, pulling out an Incada cell. "We can turn this around."

She slid the cell into a larger gadget strapped to her wrist. The device emitted a low hum, and a few moments later, a massive pulse of energy radiated outward. The glow was blinding, sending ripples of light through the forest.

Tripwires snapped. Illusions flickered and vanished. Jezreel and Ava, hidden behind a tree, exchanged stunned glances as their carefully laid traps were exposed.

"What was that?" Ava hissed.

Jezreel's expression darkened. "Wait… Nysara must have finished those rotating cells she was developing. They've brought more power than we thought."

The Originators pressed their advantage, moving swiftly through the now-cleared woods. Several Weavers retreated, their numbers thinned.

Up in the booth, Garrick's words echoed. "And there's the Originators showing off their tech! That energy pulse just turned the tables on the Weavers. What a play!"

Lyra added, her tone impressed. "But was it too soon? That's a lot of power to burn this early in the match. Let's see how they capitalize on it."

The crowd roared as the Bringers began their descent from the high ground. Celeste led her squad with calculated purpose; Olive's orders echoing in her mind. "Strike fast and hard, but only when the time is right." Now was that time.

Garrick's voice rose in excitement. "And here come the Bringers, folks! They've been watching and waiting, but it looks like they're ready to enter the fray."

"They've chosen their moment perfectly," Lyra added. "The Envoys are holding fast, but can they defend against a two-front attack?"

Celeste scanned the battlefield, her keen eyes locking on the Envoys' entrenched position. The Originators were beginning their charge after their skirmish with the Weavers, and their presence near the central platform created an opportunity.

"Focus fire on the Envoys," Celeste commanded, her tone quick and confident. "Their formation is strong, but if we disrupt their front line, they'll fold."

Her team fanned out, using cover and the terrain to flank the Envoys' position. As they drew closer, the disciplined wall of shields and spears loomed larger, a fortress of cohesion and teamwork.

"Ready the shock volleys," Celeste ordered. Recruits carrying staffs imbued with Incada energy nodded, their weapons sparking to life.

Liam spotted the Bringers' approach and let out a frustrated sigh. "Bringers on the left flank!" he shouted. "Hold positions! Shields up!"

The Envoy recruits shifted slightly, their phalanx formation adjusting to face the new threat while maintaining coverage against the Originators.

"Stay tight!" Liam barked, stepping to the front line. His sword glowed faintly with Incada energy as he prepared to intercept the incoming attack.

The first wave of Bringer recruits struck hard, their shock volleys crashing against the Envoy shields in a dazzling display of light. The crowd gasped as the Envoys absorbed the impact, their formation holding firm.

Garrick's voice boomed over the noise. "And there it is! The Envoys showing off their legendary discipline. That phalanx isn't going anywhere!"

In the chaos, two figures broke through the fray, and what was once a stalwart phalanx became a wild skirmish. Nysara and Celeste advanced toward Liam, their weapons at the ready.

Liam squared his shoulders, his grip tightening on his sword. "Alright," he muttered to himself. "Let's see what you've got."

Nysara struck first, her dual batons humming with energy as she darted forward. Liam parried her blows with quick, precise movements, his sword flashing in the light.

"Still as predictable as ever," Nysara taunted, her grin widening as she twisted away from his counterstrike.

"And you're still overconfident," Liam shot back, using his momentum to force her back a step.

Before he could press his advantage, Celeste entered the fray, her staff sweeping in with a powerful arc. Liam ducked, the staff narrowly missing his head, and rolled to the side to avoid her follow-up strike.

"You're outnumbered, Liam," Celeste said, her tone measured but firm. "You don't have to prove anything here."

"Prove something?" Liam said, his breathing level despite the strain. "I'm not proving anything. I'm holding the line."

He spun his sword in a defensive arc, keeping both opponents at bay. Nysara moved in again, her strikes a blur, but Liam anticipated her pattern and blocked each attack. Celeste capitalized on the distraction, forcing him to split his attention, but Liam's focus didn't waver.

The duel intensified, each blow sending sparks of Incada energy flying. Liam's movements were more fluid, more strategic than they had been in previous matches. He wasn't just fighting — he was adapting.

"Impressive," Celeste admitted, her expression serious. "But let's see how long you can keep this up."

A loud whistle cut through the air, drawing everyone's attention. Elise charged in, leading a small group of Envoy recruits. "Reinforcements are here!" she called out.

Liam grinned despite himself. "About time."

Elise and her squad moved into position, their shields interlocking seamlessly with the existing formation. Together, the Envoys reestablished their phalanx, their disciplined ranks pushing Nysara and Celeste back.

"Phalanx formation!" Elise commanded, her words ringing out over the battlefield. "Hold the line!"

The Envoy recruits moved as one, their shields forming an impenetrable wall. Liam stepped back into formation, his breathing heavy but his resolve unshaken.

"Nice timing," he said to Elise.

"Couldn't let you have all the fun," she replied with a smirk.

As the battle raged on, Celeste and Olive regrouped with their remaining recruits, assessing the situation from a safe distance.

"The Envoys are too entrenched," Olive said, her manner laced with frustration. "We're not going to break that formation without wasting more resources than it's worth."

Celeste nodded, her mind already calculating their next move. "Then we shift focus. Eliminations will give us more points than trying to take the platform outright."

She turned to her squad, her tone decisive. "Target the Originators. They're still vulnerable from their fight with the Weavers. Move quickly and take out as many as you can."

The Bringers descended on the scattered Originators like a storm, their coordinated strikes taking out several recruits in rapid succession.

Up in the booth, Lyra leaned forward, her eyes wide with excitement. "And there it is! The Bringers are shifting gears, focusing on eliminations rather than the central position. It's a bold move — and it's paying off!"

Garrick laughed. "Classic Bringer tactics, Lyra. They're not just fighters — they're hunters. Celeste is showing some serious leadership out there."

The screen displayed a flurry of action as Bringer ambushed the engaged Originators, their precision and timing leaving little room for counterattacks.

"They're making a statement," Lyra said, her reply tinged with admiration. "Don't underestimate the Bringers."

The chaos of the battlefield seemed distant within the calm, sterile walls of the infirmary. The room buzzed softly with the hum of healing devices, their faint blue light casting gentle glows over the rows of cots. Injured participants lay or sat, some wincing as their wounds were treated, while others stared numbly at the ceiling, recovering from the adrenaline crash.

A nurse moved from patient to patient with practiced efficiency, her hands glowing faintly with Incada energy as she stabilized the eliminated participants.

A young recruit sitting on the edge of a cot watched her work with wide eyes. His arm bore the faint trace of an Incada burn, a mark from a stun weapon. "Does it always hurt that much?" he asked, flexing his fingers gingerly.

The nurse smiled, her tone calm but instructive. "The Incada ensures that no permanent harm is done, but the pain is real. It's how the tournament stays authentic — teaches you what real combat feels like without risking serious injury."

The recruit nodded, though he still looked dubious. "But how does it work? I mean, if it hurts that bad, how do you make sure it's not lethal?"

The nurse straightened, holding up a small dagger-like weapon. Its blade shimmered faintly with Incada energy. "It's all about the energy calibration," she explained. "The impact registers in your nervous system, mimicking the sensation of pain. But it doesn't pierce the skin or damage tissue."

The recruit tilted his head, curiosity flickering in his expression. "Could you...show me?"

A ripple of chuckles spread through the other recruits nearby. "Careful what you ask for, kid," one of them muttered, grinning.

The nurse raised an eyebrow, a hint of amusement playing on her lips. "Are you sure? It's not exactly pleasant."

He nodded, though his confidence faltered slightly. "Yeah. I need to understand it."

"Alright then." She stepped closer, holding the dagger aloft. "Hold still."

With a flick of her wrist, she jabbed the blade into his side — not hard, but enough to send a pulse of Incada energy through him.

The recruit's eyes widened as he let out a yelp, clutching his ribs and doubling over. "Ow! That feels like...like I just got punched by a battering ram!" He patted the area frantically, searching for blood or a wound. "But there's nothing there?"

The nurse extended her glowing hands toward him. As she moved her hands over the spot, his expression shifted from pain to surprise.

"Whoa," he gasped as the sensation disappeared. "It's...gone?"

"Gone," the nurse confirmed, stepping back. "See? Pain teaches, but it doesn't have to scar. Now, remember that feeling — and don't get hit next time."

The recruits laughed, the tension in the room easing slightly as the young recruit slumped back onto his cot, shaking his head with a rueful grin.

The battlefield was quiet in the wooded section where the Weavers, Bringers, and Originators converged. The air was thick with tension, the faint crackle of Incada energy hanging in the atmosphere from earlier skirmishes.

Ava of the Weavers stood with her arms crossed, her eyes flicking between Celeste and Bella. Jezreel hovered nearby, her posture wary but ready for anything. Nysara stood close to Bella, while Olive observed silently from the shadows.

"This isn't sustainable," Ava said, breaking the silence. Her words carried an element of frustration. "The Envoys are too dug in. If we keep fighting them separately, we'll burn through everything we have before they so much as flinch."

"She's right," Bella admitted, her tone measured. "We've tested their defenses, and they're airtight. If we want to take the position, we need to work together."

"Agreed," Celeste said, stepping forward. "But this alliance is temporary. Once the Envoys are out, it's every guild for themselves."

"Obviously," Ava replied, her smirk faint but sharp. "No one's here to lose the event."

Jezreel tilted her head. "So, what's the plan?"

Bella gestured toward the platform visible through the trees. The faint glow of the Envoys' phalanx was unmistakable. "We hit them hard-and-fast. Divide their focus. The Weavers will disrupt their formation with illusions and traps. The Originators will strike with our tech to neutralize their defenses, and the Bringers will bring the firepower to finish the job."

"And when the Envoys are gone?" Olive asked, her reply steady but probing.

Bella's gaze met hers evenly. "We'll settle it like fighters. Each guild chooses a champion. They fight, and the winner claims the key position uncontested for the next hour."

The group exchanged glances, weighing the proposal. Finally, Ava nodded. "Fair enough."

Celeste stepped forward, extending her hand toward Bella. "Let's do this."

Bella clasped it briefly, "Don't hold back."

"Oh, I won't," Celeste replied with a faint smile.

As the group dispersed to prepare, Garrick's voice filled the arena once more. "What's this? It looks like the other guilds are regrouping — and judging by their movements, something big is brewing."

Lyra leaned forward, her eyes sparkling with anticipation. "Could we be seeing an alliance, Garrick? If so, the Envoys might have a challenge on their hands."

Garrick chuckled. "If it's an alliance, it won't last long. But for now, it might be just what they need to shake things up."

The camera panned back to the key position, where Liam stood at the center of the phalanx. His eyes swept over the battlefield, the faint flicker of movement in the distance catching his eye.

"Here they come," he muttered, gripping his sword tightly. "Get ready, everyone. This is about to get messy."

The Envoys braced themselves as the alliance began its advance, the storm of battle about to break once more.

The crowd's fervor reached new heights as Garrick's words cut through the growing chaos of the battlefield, brimming with excitement. "Ladies and gentlemen, it seems the stakes have just been raised! We've got a game-changing announcement that could turn this entire match on its head!"

Lyra leaned closer to her microphone, her tone vibrant with curiosity. "Oh, this is going to be good. What's the twist, Garrick?"

The massive screens around the arena flickered, focusing on the mountain at the far edge of the battlefield. Its jagged peak shimmered faintly under the arena lights, a stark contrast to the carnage in the center of the arena.

Hidden speakers all over the battlefield roared to life.

"A special banner has been placed at the summit of the mountain," Garrick announced, his voice booming across the arena. "The first guild to claim it will earn 50 points! That's right, folks — 50 points! Enough to change the leaderboard entirely!"

The crowd roared, their collective cheers vibrating through the stands. The energy was electric, the tension palpable. Lyra's laughter rang out, tinged with awe. "Oh, this is going to get messy! The question is: who's going to break for it first?"

The announcement rippled through the battlefield like a shock wave, halting some combatants mid-strike. Even the advancing alliance paused, their eyes shifting toward the mountain as the new objective became clear.

In the heart of the central platform, Alexander quickly approached Liam. His expression was sharp, his tone urgent as he addressed the young leader. "Liam, listen closely. That banner is everything now. If we secure it, we'll take the lead and force the others to come to us for the rest of the match."

Liam's brow furrowed as he glanced toward the mountain, its peak just visible above the chaos. "But what about the key position? If we leave it, the alliance will overrun it."

"We've got enough to hold without you here," Alexander countered, placing a firm hand on Liam's shoulder. "This is bigger. If you go alone and move fast you can make it before the other guilds know what happened."

Liam nodded, determination setting his jaw. "Understood. I'll make it happen."

Bella's communicator buzzed with the news as she regrouped with her recruits near the wooded area. Turning to Nysara, she didn't waste a second. "This is it, Nysara. You're leading this charge."

Nysara's eyes widened slightly, and then a confident grin spread across her face. "You got it. What's the plan?"

"Your ingenuity is our best asset right now," Bella said, her tone decisive. "That mountain's terrain is going to be a nightmare for anyone without a plan. Use whatever method you can come up with to get there first, empty your cells if you have to, but be smart about it. Get there first and grab those points."

Nysara nodded, her mind already working through strategies. "I'll take Roen and a few others. We'll make it happen."

Bella stepped closer, lowering her voice. "No, you have to do this one on your own. This is your moment, Nysara. Show them what the Originators can do."

Nysara gave her a quick salute, her grin unshaken. "Don't worry, Bella. I've got this."

Ava watched the announcement with a calculating gleam in her eye. Her eyes turned to Alarion who stood nearby, his violin resting against his side. "Alarion, you know what to do."

He arched an eyebrow, a faint smile playing on his lips. "You want me to weave my way to the top?"

"That's exactly what I want," Ava replied, her words brimming with confidence. "The others will try to brute force their way up that mountain, but you can outmaneuver them. Illusions, misdirection, traps — use every trick you've got to keep them guessing."

Alarion nodded slowly, his fingers tapping the neck of his violin. "Sounds like fun. Any specific orders?"

"Just one," Ava said, her smirk widening. "Get there first. And don't let anyone see you coming."

"Consider it done," he said, and suddenly the illusion faded as Alarion was already stepping into the forest tuning his violin.

Olive's expression was calm but serious as she addressed Celeste. "This is your moment, Celeste. That banner could define this match, and I need you to get it for the Bringers."

Celeste nodded, her grip tightening on her staff. "I'm on it. But what about the Envoys and the alliance? They'll be coming too."

"That's exactly why it has to be you," Olive replied. "You've seen how the others move. You've studied their tactics. Use that to your advantage. Outthink them."

Celeste took a deep breath, her resolve hardening. "I won't let you down."

Olive's expression softened slightly. "You never have. Show them what it means to be a Bringer."

The arena seemed to hold its breath as the battlefield shifted focus. The central platform, the woods, and the high ground — all eyes turned toward the mountain now looming large on the horizon. The towering peak was more than just another objective — it was a game-changer.

From the heart of the Envoys' phalanx, Liam sprinted out alone, his shield strapped across his back and his sword glowing faintly at his side. His footsteps were swift and controlled as he darted across open terrain, keeping his movements deliberate but quick. Behind him, the disciplined formation he had held for so long didn't waver, its defenders locking shields and spears in tight rows to hold the alliance at bay.

In the wooded expanse, Nysara activated one of her custom gadgets, a propulsion device that sent her vaulting over low trees and dense underbrush. Her Rotating Incada cell buzzed faintly on her wrist as she adjusted its settings on the fly. Every leap brought her closer to the mountain, her grin widening with each cleared obstacle. The weight of Bella's words echoed in her mind.

A whisper of strings broke through the air as Alarion moved like a shadow through the trees. His illusions shimmered faintly in his wake, casting phantoms of movement that misled anyone attempting to follow him. His violin rested lightly in his hand, ready to summon a barrier or distraction at a moment's notice.

Celeste steadied her breathing, her staff glowing faintly as she prepared to ascend. Her movements were measured and efficient, her mind assessing every approach and potential threat. She was the last to move, but she moved with purpose.

The massive screens around the arena split into four views, each one following a lone competitor as they began their uphill battle.

From the commentary booth, Garrick's words carried the tension and excitement of the moment. "And just like that, the race for the banner is on! Look at this, folks — each guild is sending their brightest star to claim that mountain for glory!"

Lyra joined in, brimming with enthusiasm. "It's a bold move, Garrick. They're not sending teams, they're sending champions. This is going to be a clash of wits, strategy, and sheer determination."

The camera panned out, showing the mountain silhouetted against the setting sun. Around it, the battlefield churned with chaos as skirmishes continued — but the true focus was on the four figures cutting their way through the terrain, each taking a unique path.

Garrick's voice once again came over the loudspeakers. "Only one can claim it. Only one can rise to the summit. Who will it be? Stay with us, folks — this is just getting started!"

11

The Shattered Banner

The mountain loomed above, its peak shrouded in simulated clouds that swirled with a quiet menace. Below, the cheers of the crowd were little more than faint echoes, carried by the wind that whipped through the jagged terrain. Each step upward brought a new challenge, and for Liam, Nysara, Alarion, and Celeste, the climb became a test of will, wits, and grit.

Liam gritted his teeth, his focus narrowing on the crumbling ledge ahead. The path was barely wide enough for his boots, jagged stone pressing into the soles with every cautious step forward. Wind howled around him, a relentless force tugging at his frame, while loose gravel skittered into the abyss below.

The void yawned beside him, vast and unforgiving.

"Just jump. You can make it." His instincts whispered the command with familiar confidence. He was strong enough — one surge of power, one leap forward, and he'd be past this. Easier. Faster. The way he always pushed through obstacles.

He shifted his weight, preparing for the burst of momentum —

The stone crumbled beneath his foot.

A section of rock broke free, tumbling noiselessly into the mist below. Liam froze, his back pressing against the cliffside, heart hammering against his ribs. His breath caught in his throat as he watched the last bits of gravel disappear into the void, the depth below impossible to measure.

"Not this time."

The wind tore at his clothes, kicking dirt against his face. His body ached from the tension, muscles coiled and burned with the need for movement. But lunging forward wouldn't work here. This wasn't a training ground where a fall meant bruises and scoldings. The gap wouldn't forgive a mistake.

"What would Celeste do?"

The question cut through his frustration.

Liam could picture her calm, steady hands adjusting her footing with precision, her measured breathing as she tested each step. She wouldn't rush. Wouldn't force it.

"You're not here to overpower the mountain. Work with it."

He exhaled slowly, pressing a palm against the rough stone. Testing it. Feeling the texture, the weight beneath his fingers. It was solid, but worn, fragile in places. Moving with new care, he shifted his foot to the next hold, pressing more gently this time, letting his weight ease into it rather than force it down.

The rock held.

Another step.

He inched forward, breath shallow, muscles trembling with restraint. The void still loomed, wind still howled, but his focus stayed on the ground beneath him, the stone that hadn't crumbled.

One more step.

The ledge widened beneath his boots.

Solid ground.

Slowly, he turned to look at the narrow ledge he just crossed.

"Being careful isn't so bad." His speech was rough, but level as he straightened his stride.

Farther up the mountain, Nysara's heart pounded as the propulsion gadget on her wrist flared to life, launching her upward in a controlled burst. The hum of the device filled her ears, steady and reassuring, as she soared from ledge to ledge. The wind howled around her, tugging at her jacket, but she hardly noticed. The rhythm of the ascent felt natural, each jump calculated, precise.

Her fingers brushed a narrow ledge, boots skimming the rock before she engaged the next burst —

Click.

The sound wasn't right. A sputter. A weak pulse instead of the consistent hum.

Nysara's stomach dropped just before the propulsion cut out completely.

"No, no, no!" The words tore from her lips as gravity seized her, yanking her back. She twisted midair, lungs tightening, and flung her arms toward the rock. Jagged stone scraped against her palms as her fingers caught a narrow outcropping, jarring her shoulders painfully as she wrenched herself to a halt.

For a breathless moment, she dangled there, legs kicking, the mountain pressing its silence around her.

Her pulse hammered in her ears. She could hear the wind now, the soft crumble of dislodged gravel trickling down the cliffside far below.

"Don't look down. Don't look down."

Instead, her eyes snapped to her wrist where the propulsion gadget hung lifeless, the Incada cell flickering weakly inside its casing. Sparks arced along the edges, dimming to nothing.

"Great. Perfect timing," she hissed.

Awkwardly, she shifted her grip, wedging her shoulder against the rock face just enough to free her hand. She fumbled with the gadget, twisting open the side panel with numb fingers, her other arm straining to hold her weight. A gust of wind swept through the pass, nearly tearing the delicate device from her grip.

"Come on. Work."

The cell blinked weakly in response, its pale glow sputtering like a dying ember.

The wind howled louder. The cold crept into her fingers.

Her hands were shaking — too much. The tiny components slipped as she tried to realign them.

Her jaw clenched. "This would be easier if —"

If Liam were here.

The thought struck hard-and-fast.

"He wouldn't be stuck like this. He wouldn't need gadgets. He'd just muscle his way up, climb with raw strength like it was nothing."

Her fingers trembled again, the ache in her shoulders deepening.

A spark. The gadget let out a feeble whine, then died completely.

She held her breath. She thought of trying again, but something inside her snapped.

With a frustrated growl, she shoved the device into her pack and let it drop against her back. The cold ache of failure pressed against her chest.

"You're not Liam. And you don't have to be."

Her focus shifted upward, locking onto the next ledge.

The wind. The height. The ache in her arms. None of it mattered now.

With a deep breath, she reached for the stone above her, fingers digging into rough cracks as she shifted her weight. Her body strained with the effort — muscles burning, boots scraping for grip as she pulled herself higher.

It was slower. Harder. Messy.

But she climbed.

Every inch demanded effort. Every foothold a deliberate choice.

By the time her hands found solid ground, her body trembled with exhaustion. She dragged herself over the ledge, chest heaving as she collapsed onto her back, staring at the endless gray sky.

The wind howled. The mountain hadn't changed.

But she had.

Nysara flexed her fingers, raw and scraped, then sat up with a shaky breath. Dust streaked her palms, but the ache in her muscles was matched by something unfamiliar.

Pride.

"Guess I don't need tech all the time," she muttered, brushing off her hands as she rose, already scanning for the next ledge.

A steady gust of wind raked across another section of the mountain, howling like a living thing as it whipped along the narrow stone ridge. Alarion stood at the fork in the path, his breath visible in the chill air. To his left, a narrow trail vanished into thick mist, the swirling gray swallowing the stone after only a few feet. To his right, a wider path offered no cover, wind howling unchecked over the exposed rock, harsh enough to sting his skin.

He hesitated, gripping his violin case tighter against his chest. The wind tugged at his cloak, pulling against the clasp that held it together. He stared into the mist, watching how it pulsed and shifted with an almost unnatural rhythm. Was there solid ground beneath it, or a sheer drop waiting just out of sight?

He took a step toward the broader path.

The wind immediately surged, sending a loose spray of gravel skittering across the stone and into the void below. His stomach clenched as he caught sight of a small rock twisting through the air, tumbling endlessly into the pale nothingness beneath him.

His free hand curled into a fist.

"Not great," he muttered, flexing his fingers as he backed away from the wind's edge.

But the mist…

His gaze shifted back to it, the uncertain, swirling gray. His mind spun with possibilities — thin ledges, sudden drops, blind corners. He could feel the weight of indecision settling in, a pressure between his ribs he despised.

"What would Nysara say right now?" he whispered, barely audible over the wind.

The answer came easily, unbidden.

"Pick a path, Alarion. Commit. Stop overthinking everything for once."

The corner of his mouth twitched, but the bitter truth lingered. She was right. She often was.

He exhaled sharply, narrowing his eyes at the mist.

"The exposed path is too obvious," he reasoned aloud, voice steadying. "And that wind is getting stronger. Which means…"

His focus returned to the fog, heart pounding against his ribs.

"This isn't about knowing everything in advance," he muttered, clutching his violin tighter. "It's about trust."

His foot shifted forward, crunching on loose stone. The fog was absolute — swallowing the mountain whole just steps beyond where he stood. It reminded him of an empty stage, waiting for the music to give it shape.

He clenched his jaw. No more hesitating.

"Trust yourself. Move."

The mist swallowed him whole as he stepped forward.

Cool dampness clung to his skin immediately, the air muffling even the sound of his breathing. His steps slowed as the stone became slick beneath his boots, wet with dew. Each foothold felt treacherous, yet he pressed onward, straining to see beyond the endless gray.

The mountain was silent here.

The mist thickened. He couldn't tell if he was going uphill or down. The silence pressed heavier, the damp curling along his skin like something alive.

His heart pounded faster.

"You're losing control," the thought came, dark and cutting. "You can't see. If you make a mistake —"

But a thought cut through the panic.

"Nysara wouldn't stop here."

The words snapped through him like a chord struck too sharply, raw and clear.

"She wouldn't second-guess this. She'd push forward."

And so, he did.

Alarion forced himself onward, planting his feet with more certainty. One step. Then another. The next foothold was slick but held. The mist remained unyielding, but he no longer flinched from it.

Gradually, the gray thinned. A faint light shimmered ahead — the first break in the fog.

Suddenly, he was through it.

The mist peeled away, revealing solid ground just steps ahead. The ledge broadened, the stone more stable, and beyond it, the path continued upward toward the summit.

Relief flooded his chest. He exhaled, glancing back at the swirling fog behind him.

"Thanks for the advice, Nysara," he mumbled, brushing dust from his cloak. "You were right. Again."

Not far below the summit, Celeste planted her staff against the rocky ground, the cold wind tugging at her cloak as she stared up at the massive boulder blocking her path. The jagged obstacle was wedged so tightly into the pass that there was no way to climb over it, and the narrow ledge left no space to go around.

Her first instinct was to study it — search for a crack, a weakness, something she could manipulate. She traced her hand along the rough stone, searching for an answer. The surface was solid, unyielding.

"Great," she muttered, stepping back and rolling the tension from her shoulders. "So much for finesse."

Time was slipping away. She could still hear the distant rumble of the fighting below. Every second spent here put her further behind.

Her grip tightened on her staff. She could still sense the even pulse of Incada energy within the weapon, calm and waiting.

"No way through. No way around."

She exhaled quickly. "Fine. If you won't move, I'll make you move."

Setting her feet, she shifted into a low stance, both hands gripping the staff firmly. The Incada stone embedded at the center began to glow softly, responding to her focus.

The first strike hit with a resonant crack, a sharp burst of light rippling along the stone's surface. Dust flaked loose from the impact, but the boulder barely shifted.

She adjusted her grip, resetting.

"Again."

This time, her swing came heavier. Energy crackled along the length of the staff, arcing from the embedded stone. The blow struck lower, and a hairline fracture spiderwebbed outward with a deep groan.

The wind howled louder now, but Celeste's focus narrowed. The problem was simple. The rock wasn't breaking because she was holding back.

"Stop testing it. Break it."

A third strike, the hardest yet. The force reverberated through her arms as a jagged crack raced along the boulder's center. Chunks of stone splintered free, tumbling down the mountainside.

The boulder shifted — still intact but weakened.

"Almost," she muttered through clenched teeth.

Planting her staff in the ground, Celeste raised her hands, summoning the last surge of energy she could muster. With a focused thrust, she struck the core of the crack, the pulse of energy resonating through the stone like a bell.

With a deafening snap, the boulder split clean down the center. The pieces fell away, crashing into the ravine below as a cloud of dust billowed around her.

Celeste stayed still for a moment, catching her breath, the ache in her arms undeniable. The pass was clear now — blunt, messy, but effective.

She exhaled and brushed stone dust from her gloves, sparing one last glance at the shattered remains.

"Not my usual style," she muttered with a wry smile, shouldering her staff once more. "But it'll do."

The summit loomed ahead, a jagged crest of stone illuminated by the faint glow of the banner planted at its center. The shimmering cloth rippled in the wind, its bluish hues refracting light like a beacon of victory. One by one, the climbers emerged, each arrival marked by a blend of exhaustion and determination.

Liam was the first to reach the peak. He dragged himself over the final ledge and stood, his chest heaving as he steadied himself against the wind. The banner stood only a dozen paces away, and for a moment, he allowed himself a flicker of pride.

"Not bad," he muttered under his breath, rolling his shoulders to shake off the tension of the climb.

But before he could take a step, the sound of shifting rocks caught his attention. He turned sharply, his eyes narrowing as Nysara vaulted onto the summit with her usual flair. Her movements were fluid, even after the strain of the ascent, and she landed lightly on her feet, a wide grin plastered across her face.

"Of course, you'd be first," she said, her tone teasing as she adjusted the strap of her pack. "What'd you do, smash your way up here?"

"Not exactly," Liam replied, his tone measured. "Though I'd love to hear how you got here without blowing something up."

Nysara smirked, her eyes flicking to the banner. "Maybe I'll tell you — after I win."

Before either could make another move, a hauntingly sweet note drifted through the air, drawing their attention. Alarion stepped onto the summit, his violin tucked under one arm, his expression calm but watchful. The mist he'd passed through seemed to cling to his silhouette, giving him an almost spectral appearance.

"Well," he said, his voice smooth, "this is quite the reunion. I hope I'm not interrupting anything...heated."

"You're late," Nysara quipped, though her tone lacked malice. "Figured you'd have some illusion trick to skip the hard part."

Alarion gave a faint smile, plucking a string on his violin. A harmless shimmer of light danced briefly in the air between them. "Oh, I did. But where's the fun in arriving too soon?"

"Good," Liam said, his tone tightening. "Then you're just in time to lose."

The wind picked up as Celeste climbed into view, her staff resting against her shoulder. Dust clung to her armor, and her hair was plastered to her forehead, but her eyes gleamed with fierce determination. She scanned the scene, her eyes resting on each of them before landing on the banner.

"Look at this," she said, her words carrying a mix of amusement and irritation. "I didn't think I'd find all three of you just standing around. Do I need to remind you there's a banner to claim?"

Liam crossed his arms, his jaw tightening. "Funny, I was about to say the same thing to you."

Nysara rolled her eyes but couldn't suppress a grin. "Wow, Liam, taking it slow for once? Never thought I'd see the day."

Alarion chuckled softly, his fingers brushing the strings of his violin as he stepped closer. "If we're done with pleasantries, shall we?"

The four formed a loose circle around the banner, their movements cautious, their eyes flicking between one another.

Celeste planted her staff in the ground, her posture firm. "One of us takes it, or none of us do. Your call."

"Subtle," Nysara said, adjusting a gadget on her wrist. "But I've never been one for sharing."

Liam shifted his weight, his hand resting on the hilt of his sword. "Neither have I."

The fight erupted like a storm, each of the four surging toward the banner with singular determination. Liam's heavy boots sent loose rocks tumbling as he charged forward, his sword glinting in the sunlight. "Out of my way," he bellowed, swiping at an invisible Alarion with a single-minded focus.

"Bold of you to assume I'd let you pass," Alarion replied smoothly, his violin bow gliding over the strings. A shimmering force field materialized in Liam's path, crackling faintly with light.

Liam slammed into the barrier, teeth gritted, and shouted, "You can't just hide behind these tricks forever, Alarion!"

"Not hiding," Alarion quipped, stepping closer. "Strategizing."

From the corner of his eye, Liam saw Nysara darting around the edge of the chaos. Her movements were so quick they seemed to defy gravity, each step landing with uncanny precision.

"Typical Liam — going through walls instead of around them," Nysara teased, launching herself toward the banner in a graceful arc.

Her fingers grazed the fabric just as Celeste's staff slammed down in front of her, sending a shock wave rippling across the rocky terrain. Nysara twisted midair, landing nimbly on a nearby ledge.

"Hey!" she called, brushing dust off her jacket. "I had that!"

"Not with those reflexes," Celeste shot back, spinning her staff in a defensive arc as she advanced toward the banner. "Maybe if you spent less time tinkering, you'd actually grab something for once."

Nysara smirked, activating a small propulsion gadget on her wrist. "Let's see if you can keep up."

Before Celeste could respond, Alarion stepped into the fray, raising a hand. "Now, now, let's not get ahead of ourselves." He played a quick flourish on his violin, and three identical banners materialized, fluttering in the wind.

"Oh, come on!" Celeste growled, turning to face him. "Do you ever play fair?"

"Fair is so limiting," Alarion replied, his eyes glinting with amusement.

Liam, meanwhile, had shattered Alarion's initial force field and now barreled toward one of the illusory banners. He swiped at it with his sword, only for the image to dissolve into mist.

"Stop playing games!" he barked, spinning toward Alarion.

"Why stop when I'm winning?" Alarion said with a shrug, a faint smile tugging at his lips.

Nysara took advantage of the momentary distraction, darting low and fast toward the real banner. "Don't mind me," she called, her fingers outstretched.

A shimmering shield flared to life around the banner, stopping her just short. Alarion gave her a mock bow. "Mind you? Always."

"Great," Nysara muttered, fiddling with a small device. "Guess I'll just take this down myself."

Celeste rushed toward her, staff raised. "Not so fast."

Nysara jumped back, barely dodging the swing. "Careful, Celeste. You'll chip your precious staff."

"And you'll lose your precious gadgets," Celeste retorted, sweeping low and knocking a device from Nysara's hand.

While the two clashed, Liam surged forward again, his sheer strength scattering the remaining illusions. He locked eyes with Alarion.

"No more tricks," Liam growled, raising his sword.

"Who said anything about tricks?" Alarion countered, strumming a constant chord. A force field materialized under Liam's feet, tilting precariously and forcing him to steady himself.

"You've got to be kidding me!" Liam shouted, regaining his balance just as Celeste and Nysara converged near the banner.

The clash at the summit came to an abrupt halt as a low rumble reverberated through the mountain, the sound building in intensity until it became a roar. The ground shuddered violently, throwing all four competitors off balance.

"What's happening?" Nysara yelped, stumbling backward as loose stones skittered past her feet.

Before anyone could answer, an explosion tore through the air, the shock wave sending debris flying in every direction. Smoke and fire erupted from the arena far below, and a column of ash spiraled into the sky. The four fighters instinctively dropped to the ground, shielding themselves from the sudden chaos.

Liam was the first to scramble upright, his eyes snapping to the battlefield below. His chest tightened at the sight: smoke obscured much of the arena, but through the haze, he could make out figures moving in coordinated formations. They weren't recruits.

"What is that?" Liam growled, his hand tightening around the hilt of his sword.

Celeste's eyes widened as she squinted at the chaos below, her mind racing to make sense of the scene. Amid the black armor with glowing yellow accents of the invaders, a banner rose high above the fray — a jagged, black and yellow standard emblazoned with a symbol she recognized instantly.

"The Obsidian Shade," she whispered, the words carrying an edge of dread.

Nysara's head snapped toward her. "What did you just say?"

"The Obsidian Shade," Celeste repeated, louder this time. She pointed toward the banner, her hand trembling slightly. "That symbol — it's theirs. I've seen it before, back in the dungeon. It was their crest during the rebellion."

Alarion, who had been standing silently with his violin clutched tightly, turned to look at her, his expression grim. "You're sure?"

Celeste nodded. "Absolutely. The armor, the crest — it all matches."

Liam's jaw clenched as he scanned the battlefield again. Now that Celeste had pointed it out, the sight was unmistakable. The Obsidian Shade forces, perhaps a hundred strong, were moving with ruthless efficiency. It looked as if all the guilds had joined together at the key position and were holding for now, but they were surrounded, their defensive line thinning with every passing moment.

"They're overwhelming the guilds," Liam said, his voice taut with frustration. "We have to get down there."

Nysara shook her head, pointing toward the slopes of the mountain. "It's not that simple. Look."

They followed her gesture and saw smaller groups of Shade soldiers advancing up the mountain. Their movements were unnervingly quick, their blackened glowing yellow armor gleaming against the rocky terrain.

"They're coming for us too," Nysara added, her speech tight.

The four shared a tense glance, their earlier rivalries now seeming trivial in the face of the enemy below.

At the same time Liam, Nysara, Alarion, and Celeste were fighting on the mountain, The Clash at the key position was relentless. The Envoys held the platform in a tight phalanx, shields locked in perfect formation, the edges of their Incada infused steel glowing faintly. Their disciplined ranks formed an impenetrable barrier, deflecting each wave of the alliance's assault with measured precision.

Across from them, Olive braced her staff, golden light rippling along its length as she gestured for the Bringer recruits behind her to hold position. Sparks of energy danced across the battlefield as projectiles struck the Envoy shields, bursts of radiant force dissipating harmlessly against their wall of defense.

"They're holding too tight!" Olive called over her shoulder, chest heaving from exertion. "Focus on the shield edges! We just need a break in their line — "

A shimmering illusion surged into existence to her left as Ava materialized, The Weavers fanning out behind her in synchronized elegance. With a flick of her wrist, Ava sent a wave of energy across the platform, The phalanx wavered — just slightly — but the Envoys adapted too quickly.

"This isn't working," Ava muttered under her breath, sweeping strands of crimson hair from her face as her team set up a lattice of energy traps along the perimeter.

On the other side of the formation, Bella charged forward, pulse gauntlets crackling with raw Incada energy as she led the Originator strike. Her devices emitted a steady hum as she loosed a pulse shock into the enemy's line, forcing the shields back a half step. A small opening — too small.

Before she could press the gap, a figure surged forward from the Envoy side — Elise. Her shield caught Bella's next strike with a loud clang, deflecting the blast with practiced ease.

"Gonna have to try harder than that, Bella," Elise said through gritted teeth, raising her sword.

Bella's gauntlets flared, the pulse charging with a clipped whine. "Oh, don't worry. I'm just getting started." She struck again, the energy burst, colliding with Elise's shield, sending a ripple of blue light across its surface.

Elise staggered but didn't break. With a roar, she countered, slamming the rim of her shield into Bella's side and following with a precise sword strike aimed for Bella's gauntlet arm.

Bella barely managed to twist away, the Incada pulse crackling along the ground as she stumbled back. She clenched her jaw, recalibrating her gauntlets with a crackle of energy surging around her fists.

"Tough as ever, Elise," Bella smirked, narrowing her stance. "But even a stone wall cracks under enough pressure."

Elise's shield raised, unshaken. "Who said anything about building with stone?"

The duel raged, both locked in a personal battle as the larger fight pressed on around them.

Olive's head snapped around as the first explosion tore through the far side of the arena, a geyser of flames and stone erupting from the earth with violent force. The shock wave hit like a physical wall, throwing her backward.

Smoke. Ash. Screams.

The phalanx of shields faltered, many of the competitors now lying on the ground, confused, some hurt, but mostly ok.

More explosions followed, rippling in rapid succession around the arena's perimeter. The crackling discharge surged along the edges of the battlefield, shorting out the energy traps Ava's Weavers had placed and overloading Bella's pulse gauntlets with a loud pop.

Bella recoiled, clutching her gauntlets as they sputtered. "What was that?!"

Elise fell back, her shield raised, but her gaze wasn't on Bella anymore. It was on the thick black smoke rising from the arena's edges.

Then, through the haze, they emerged.

Figures clad in blackened armor with glowing yellow accents — their helmets crowned with sharp, angular visors that seemed to drink in the dimming light. They moved as a unit, precise and synchronized, pressing towards the key position with brutal efficiency.

A banner unfurled among them; black fabric slashed with a jagged yellow crest.

Olive's breath caught. The symbol was vaguely familiar.

"The Obsidian Shade..." she whispered.

Rhane staggered to her side, coughing as the smoke thickened. "What?"

"That banner," Olive said, voice tightening as she pointed to the unmistakable sigil. "I've seen it before. The dungeon is full of artifacts bearing it. Roland—" She thought "it could be them."

Realization dawned in Rhane's expression. "You're saying this —"

"— isn't part of the event," Olive finished grimly, heart pounding in her chest.

Across the chaos, Alexander raised his blade above his head, orders echoing above the confusion.

"Form up! Defensive line! All guilds — together!"

But even as the guilds rallied, Olive could feel the shift in the battle.

The tournament was over.

This was war.

The silence that hung over the summit was broken only by the faint crackle of distant fires and the dull rumble of collapsing stone. Smoke and ash choked the air, carried upward by the mountain winds. For the first time since the climb began, no one moved.

Nysara crouched beside a jagged rock, her hands fumbling with the damaged propulsion gadget on her wrist. The once-steady glow of its Incada cell now flickered weakly, its energy drained. She clenched her jaw, her usual nimble fingers betraying her as the mechanism refused to respond.

"I can't fix this fast enough," she muttered, barely audible. Her delivery lacked its usual confidence, the words thick with frustration and — though she'd never admit it — fear.

Alarion stepped away from the ledge, his usual grace replaced with a hesitancy that didn't suit him. He stared down at the battlefield, his expression unreadable.

"This isn't just an attack," he said, manner quiet but firm. "The Shade never did anything halfway. This...this is an attempt to take over."

Nysara's head shot up, brow furrowing. "You're saying they planned all this? Even the tournament?"

Alarion's eyes remained fixed on the chaos below. "They planned something. The timing, the numbers, the chaos — it all fits." His voice, normally tinged with wit, was grim.

Celeste stood with her staff gripped tightly in both hands, her knuckles white. Her breathing was controlled, but the tension in her shoulders betrayed her. She looked at the advancing soldiers below, then to the smaller groups climbing toward them.

"We were so focused on winning," she whispered, more to herself than anyone else. Her speech carried a bitterness, edged with regret. "No one saw this coming."

Liam planted himself in the center of the group, his sword resting heavily in his grip. His usual confidence had been replaced with a rare stillness, his eyes scanning each of them as if measuring their resolve.

"The tournament's over," he said, voice even and heavy with resolve. "This isn't a game anymore."

A deafening explosion ripped through the air from the arena below, cutting through the tense quiet like a blade. The ground trembled violently, and a plume of fire and smoke shot into the sky. The shock wave rattled loose stones, sending them skittering down the slope.

Nysara flinched, her wide eyes fixed on the defensive line struggling against the onslaught.

"If we don't move fast," she whispered, "there won't be anyone left to help."

Alarion's jaw tightened, his hand gripping the neck of his violin as though it were a lifeline. "Rushing in blind won't change that," he countered. "Look at them — the Shade's coordinated. We'd never make it down the mountain in time to turn the tide alone."

Nysara shot him a look. "So, what, we just sit here? Watch? If we do nothing, they're going to die."

"We're not equipped for this," Alarion insisted, gesturing toward their exhausted forms. "Half of us can barely stand. Charging in now —"

"— Is better than standing here while they burn!" Liam's yell cut through, heated. His knuckles whitened on his sword. "If there's even a chance we can help, we have to take it."

Celeste shook her head. "You think running in without a plan will save them? You'll get us all killed, Liam. We need to think."

Liam's glare snapped toward her. "We don't have time to think."

Alarion spread his arms. "And what do you suggest we do? Run straight into the front lines? Get cut down like untrained civilians?"

The argument thickened, tension tightening the air. No one seemed willing to give ground.

Then Celeste took a step forward, her staff planted firmly in the rocky soil. She spoke with quiet strength, the kind that didn't need volume to be heard.

"We're not ready for this." Her words were steady but soft, almost resigned. "But..." Her grip on the staff tightened. "...we don't have a choice."

The wind howled through the summit, carrying the scent of ash as her words hung between them.

Nysara broke the silence, words softer now. "We may not be able to stop the whole attack...but we can at least take the ones spread thin between us and the main force. Let's start with that."

Liam exhaled sharply, his focus shifting toward the smaller squads advancing toward their position. His posture straightened.

Alarion nodded slowly, though tension still remained in his expression. "Alright. But we do this smart. Together."

Celeste's eyes met his, her head inclining. "Agreed."

Liam set his stance, his sword raised. "Then we press forward, one fight at a time."

The four turned as one, no further words needed. The time for debate had passed.

The battle had just begun.

12

The Enemy Revealed

The first thing Roland felt was the cold. Stone beneath him. Damp. Unforgiving. His head throbbed with a deep ache, the kind that muddled memory and made the edges of thought swim. His pulse pounded behind his eyes.

How long had he been here?

His eyelids fluttered open, the pale, sickly yellow glow of Incadise lanterns pressing against his vision. He grimaced, the bitter scent curling in his lungs, oppressive and damp, so different from the warmth of Incada's steady light.

Chains rattled.

Roland shifted, the bite of iron against his wrists bringing the rest of his awareness back. Shackles, heavy and solid. No visible locks — just seamless black iron pinning him to the wall.

His staff was gone.

The absence was immediate. A void beneath his skin.

He strained to reach for it, but the connection was faint, smothered by distance — or interference.

The Sentinel Shard embedded in the staff had been with him for years. More than a weapon, it was a part of his soul.

But it wasn't here.

Panic scratched at his thoughts, but he forced it down.

Focus.

The Obsidian Shade had taken him. That much was clear. The lanterns, the cold stone, the taint of Incadise — symbols of defiance against everything The Everlight embodied. But there were no signs of battle scars here, no urgency.

Which meant they believed him contained.

His captors were fools.

The quiet was deafening, broken only by the constant drip...drip...of water from somewhere beyond the stone walls.

No. Not silence.

Voices.

Faint, but close.

He forced his breathing shallow and stilled.

Two guards. Just beyond the iron door.

"...don't care what the others say. You're the one who saw it — he didn't do anything. He just touched the thing and dropped."

"I told you. That staff — there's something wrong with it. Power in it that's not...right. We're lucky Valis didn't order it destroyed."

"Wouldn't matter if she tried. You saw how it resisted. He touched it and started seizing, the thing still didn't move. She had us push it to the vault with another box instead — safer that way."

The vault. Still in the arena.

Close.

Roland's heart quickened, clarity cutting through the fog of pain in sharp relief. His staff hadn't moved far. And more importantly —

They couldn't move it.

They didn't understand. Sentinel Shards were not held. They were bound. And even from here, weakened, exhausted —

Roland closed his eyes.

He reached.

The faint hum stirred within him, the Sentinel Shard's pulse faint but responding. He exhaled, drawing on the connection. The distance. The door. None of it mattered.

His staff belonged to him.

A ripple of energy stirred beneath his skin, the pulse of the Shard aligning with the rhythm of his heart. The guards' voices outside continued, oblivious.

"— shouldn't even be keeping him. We have the field secure. Why not just — "

A deep, resonant hum thrummed through the stone.

Now.

The door burst inward with a deafening crack.

The heavy wood shattered off its hinges as Roland's staff rocketed through, a blur of silver and polished wood. It struck the nearest guard full in the chest with crushing force, sending him sprawling to the floor in an instant, unconscious before he hit the ground.

Roland surged forward.

The chains binding his wrists snapped as the Staff responded fully to his call. The iron twisted and cracked, falling away in smoking fragments. His hand closed around the staff as it came to him — familiar, steady. Whole.

The second guard was outside the door.

"— What the —?!"

Roland moved.

The staff spun in his grip, low and controlled. He stepped into the corridor, silent but fast, sweeping the staff low across the guard's ankles. The man toppled with a choked grunt.

Before he could recover, Roland brought the staff down — just enough force to knock the wind from his lungs. The guard slumped, coughing, dazed.

Roland pressed the end of his staff against his chest.

"How long have I been down here?"

The guard struggled for breath, glaring in defiance.

"I won't — "

The staff pulsed, its Sentinel Shard thrumming as Roland's voice dropped.

"How long?"

A beat of hesitation. Then, through clenched teeth —

"About a day. The battle — still happening. Your guild — "

Roland's breath caught.

"A whole day."

His heart twisted. He hadn't just failed to protect them — he hadn't even been there.

He released the guard, leaving him gasping on the cold stone. Turning away, Roland adjusted his grip on the staff and exhaled, centering himself.

There's still time. They're still fighting. But not for long.

He broke into a run, the staff gleaming in his hand as he raced upward through the twisting tunnels, toward the light —

Toward the battlefield.

Toward the key point.

The arena screens flickered. The once-crisp displays breaking into fragmented images — clouds of smoke rolling across the battlefield, flashes of light as defensive barriers sparked. And the blurred forms of armored figures pressing toward the guild formations near the key point. The crowd's cheers had long since quieted, replaced by a restless clamor of confusion.

In the announcer's box, Garrick's words carried through the strained silence, calm but tight.

"Citizens of Ileydria, we are — ah — seeing some unexpected movement on the field. Defensive lines remain intact, but...something is clearly wrong here. Lyra, can you zoom in on the north quadrant view?"

Lyra's hands moved deftly across the console, adjusting the visuals. The image snapped into sharper focus — revealing dark-clad soldiers pressing in coordinated formations, armor accented with a sickly yellow glow. A jagged black banner rippled in the wind, the sigil upon it foreign and menacing.

"Garrick...that crest. It's not from any of the guilds," Lyra's response overlapped his, her normally measured tone wavering.

Garrick leaned closer, eyes narrowing as the figures advanced. "This is beyond tournament protocol. Guild leadership has formed a defensive perimeter, but..."

In the stands, the crowd's confusion quickly turned to alarm as the true nature of the attack became clear. Scattered throughout the audience, off-duty guild members and veterans rose from their seats, instinctively moving toward the arena floor to help their comrades below.

"The barriers!" someone shouted from the front rows. "Lower the barriers!"

But the translucent walls of blue light remained steadfast, humming with their usual steady energy. A group of Envoy veterans pressed against the barrier, their hands flat against the shimmering surface as they tried to find some way through or around it.

In the announcer's box, Lyra's hands moved frantically across the emergency control panel. "Garrick, the barrier controls — they're not responding. The system's locked down."

"What do you mean locked down?" Garrick asked, though his attention remained fixed on the chaos below.

"I mean the barriers won't lower," Lyra said, her voice rising with urgency. "The emergency override isn't working. The whole system's been compromised somehow."

A chime echoed from the console. Lyra pressed a hand to her earpiece, listening as the message relayed directly into her feed. Her posture stiffened.

"Garrick, we've just received a direct order from the Tournament Authority. All public broadcasts are to be suspended immediately until the situation is contained."

Garrick drew in a measured breath. For a moment, the weight of it all hung between them. Then, his manner returned to its professional calm, though tension pulled at the edges.

"Understood."

He turned back toward his microphone, addressing the crowd one final time before he cut the feed.

"To all watching across the kingdom — by order of the Tournament Authority, this broadcast will now be suspended while leadership works to resolve the situation. We remind you that guild leadership is present today — seasoned guardians of our realm who have long upheld the safety and unity of Ileydria. We urge you to remain calm and trust that this matter is in capable hands."

"Wait...Garrick, look there!" Lyra pointed abruptly at one of the inactive side monitors, still receiving a residual field feed.

Through the haze of smoke and flickering energy barriers, a single figure emerged from the lower tunnels. His silhouette was unmistakable. Cloak torn. Staff gripped tightly in hand. Moving with purpose.

Garrick's eyes widened. "That's...Roland."

Lyra's breath caught. "He was missing. How —?"

Garrick's tone lifted, "Ladies and Gentlemen I am as confident as ever that this will be resolved and we will be back on the air soon enough, standby."

Below them, more spectators had reached the barrier walls, some pounding against the energy fields with their fists, others calling out to the combatants who couldn't hear them over the din of battle. The barriers held firm, their protective glow now feeling more like a cage.

Lyra grabbed her microphone, her professional composure cracking as she addressed the crowd. "Ladies and gentlemen, due to technical difficulties with the barrier system, we are implementing an immediate evacuation of the arena. Please make your way calmly to the designated exits. Do not attempt to breach the protective barriers — they cannot be lowered at this time."

The broadcast cut out.

The main arena screens dimmed to black.

The room fell silent once more, save for the distant muffled sounds of movement outside the glass.

Lyra exhaled, her speech quieter now, but still heavy with concern. "Do you really think they can handle this, Garrick?"

He didn't answer right away, Looking out at the arena with a blank expression. Finally, he shook his head slightly but forced a halfhearted smile.

"They will. Roland, Alexander, Sunniva — they're even stronger than you know. They'll end it. They *have* to."

Lyra's brow furrowed, unconvinced.

Garrick leaned back, exhaling shakily before giving a weak chuckle. "Besides...better them than me, right? If I were out there, I'd be curled into a ball behind the nearest shield wall."

Lyra's glare cut through his forced humor. "*Garrick.* This is serious."

His smile faltered, but he shrugged, voice quieter. "If I don't laugh, I'm just...going to fall apart. You saw what I saw out there. That was war."

She nodded slowly, her gaze lingering on the arena.

Outside, the faint sound of battle echoed. And somewhere in the heart of it all, Roland was running with every ounce of strength in him.

The air above the key point pulsed with constant waves of blue energy as the next barrage struck the guild defenses. Barriers rippled across the formation, their soft light expanding on impact.

Yet the attacks kept coming.

Alexander's stance remained firm, his blade glowing with the same energy. He deflected an arrow marked with the sickly yellow glow of Incadise, the corrupted energy dispersing with a hiss as it met the barrier. But this enemy wouldn't be pushed back, the Shade pressed harder, forming a solid wall of their own defensive barriers, their twisted yellow light flickering but unbroken.

The Guilds were holding the line — but barely.

A pulse of pressure shook the air as Olive unleashed a surge from her staff, expanding a shimmering arc of Incada energy that rippled along the front. The energy swept away an incoming volley, scattering it harmlessly, but the effort showed in her stance.

Alexander exhaled, lowering his sword as the next wave stalled. "We're holding them back for now, but this can't hold forever. I know our guilds are strong, are they so strong that we can't push them back?"

Olive shook her head, glancing toward the Shade's front line, where jagged black shields crackled with the corrupted yellow glow of Incadise barriers. Her staff dimmed slightly as she adjusted her grip.

"It's not them," she replied tightly. "It's us. The Incada cells in our weapons — they're set up for the tournament."

Alexander's brow furrowed. "The calibrations? You're saying we *can't* break those barriers?"

"Not with the way our weapons are configured," she answered. "The Incada in the cells is tuned for impairment, not destruction. The pain is real enough, but the energy's been tuned back — enough to simulate combat, but not enough to tear through an Incadise barrier like those."

Alexander's grip tightened on his sword. "You're saying we *could* break them if —"

"No." Olive cut him off sharply, shaking her head. "Not safely. The way these cells are tuned, we can deflect, disable, and hold a defense, but the energy won't cut deep enough to shatter an active barrier like theirs. And we *can't* adjust them without dismantling the cores."

Alexander's eyes swept the battlefield again. The Shade line remained strong, the corrupted yellow pulses holding firm against every strike they sent back. His jaw tensed. "And if we *could* change the calibration — "

"We'd be fighting to kill." Olive's reply was softer now, but absolute. "That's not why we're here. These recruits aren't near ready to see a blood-soaked battlefield. We would lose half of them to shock."

Silence hung between them for a moment, broken only by the distant clash of barriers and the rhythmic sound of pulsing energy.

"The Shade knows it too; they had to have planned for this. It's the one time they could attack and not have to be concerned with all of our Sentinel Shard Weapons." Olive added, gesturing toward the front. The Bringers and Envoys were holding their formations, pressing back each Shade assault with calculated, precise defense.

"Our recruits aren't hesitating to attack out of fear, Alex" Olive continued. "They're holding back because they know or have quickly found out their weapons won't break through those Incadise barriers. Even if we could recalibrate our weapons, if we push through and obliterate them, we *lose* what makes us different from them."

Alexander nodded slowly, his expression grim but resolute. "We keep holding. Until we find another way."

Another blast of yellow energy struck the barrier, sending a pulse of sickly light crackling along its edges. Olive raised her staff again, the Incada gem flaring in response as the barrier reinforced. The blue light was soft but even, stable.

Yet the Shade's energy didn't weaken.

The corrupted yellow glow continued to press against the barrier — unyielding.

"Hold your line!" Olive's yell cut through the chaos, firm and unwavering as she raised her staff. A crackling burst of yellow energy surged toward the defensive ranks — she caught it midair, the Incada dispersing the impact with a shimmering barrier before the force could break through.

"Shields high! Together, not alone!" she called again, heart pounding as her eyes swept the battlefield.

The guild formations held, but just barely.

At the center of the line, Sunniva anchored the defense, her shield planted firmly, a glowing barrier flaring outward in a protective dome. Calm. Unshaken.

To the left, Cobus stood like a fortress, hammer sweeping wide as he deflected a trio of Shade attackers, his guildmates pressing closer behind him for cover.

But the right —

The right was faltering.

Elise held her ground, shield raised, her stance solid despite the relentless pressure from the Shade soldiers pressing toward her. Her line was thin but holding. Almost.

Then Olive saw them.

Two younger recruits near the edge of Elise's formation. Their shields too low. Their stances broken. One had stumbled, barely able to rise, while the other hovered over him, trying to cover him as he recovered.

But the Shade soldier closing in didn't hesitate. His weapon raised, the sickly yellow glow of Incadise pulsing along the blade.

Too fast. They wouldn't recover in time.

"Move!" She yelled.

Olive held her breath as she surged forward. The world narrowed to that moment — her boots striking stone, her staff a blur of blue light as she threw herself between the soldier's blade and the recruits.

Steel met energy with a loud *clang*.

The Incadise blade glanced off the glowing length of her staff, sparks rippling where blue met yellow.

But the Shade barely staggered.

The blade snapped back instantly. Olive couldn't adjust her grip in time, and he struck again.

The weapon sliced across her side, a shallow line of pain flaring as she staggered, breath catching in her throat. The wound wasn't deep, but it stole her balance — her staff dropping just enough to leave her unguarded.

The Shade loomed over her, blade raised again, the jagged edge catching the light.

Her fingers tightened on the staff. Too slow. She couldn't block in time.

"Not like this —"

The blade fell —

And suddenly *stopped*.

A blur of silver and polished wood collided with the soldier's weapon mid-swing, intercepting the strike with a deafening *crack*. Sparks of pale light flared as the corrupted energy fractured against pure, radiant silver.

The Shade barely had time to react before the same staff, guided with unwavering precision, spun back and struck him full in the chest. The force was devastating.

The air rippled and resonated outward. The soldier was hurled backward, skidding across the stone in a heap, his weapon clattering from his grasp.

Silence.

Roland stood where Olive had fallen, his cloak torn, face flush, but his grip on his staff was sure. The pale silver light of the shard pulsed gently, contrasting against the violent yellow glow of the weapons before him.

The Shade soldiers surrounding the key point faltered.

They stared, weapons half-lowered, their eyes shifting between Roland and the fallen soldier. For the first time since the attack began, the advance paused.

Fear.

They had felt it; the lines of Obsidian Shade Soldiers showed their first signs of concern.

High above the battle at the Key Position the wind screamed as it tore across the mountain's jagged face, carrying the scent of smoke and battle from below.

The descent began with controlled precision.

Liam's blade caught the first Shade soldier clean across the chest, the pulse of energy flaring blue as the impact knocked the opponent out cold. The soldier dropped with a grunt, weapon clattering to the stone.

To his right, Nysara moved like a storm — spinning low, her batons striking in tandem. Each blow sent a sharp crack through the air, the soldiers folding under the strikes. Despite the burning in her muscles and the ache from her injured shoulder, she kept moving, refusing to fall behind.

Alarion stayed to the rear, his bow drawn across the strings of his violin. With a single piercing note, a burst of shimmering force rippled across the ledge, staggering two Shade soldiers back into a heap. Their helmets hit the stone with a resounding clunk as they slumped unconscious.

Celeste pivoted into the next strike, her staff glowing with a blue pulse as she intercepted a spear thrust. She twisted the weapon in a perfect arc, sweeping her opponent's legs out from under them before planting the end of her staff against his chest with a burst of light. He went limp.

"We're clear!" Liam called, as the last Shade soldier crumpled.

A moment of stillness. The wind howled, carrying the distant rumble of the battlefield below.

"They weren't expecting us to break through so fast," Alarion muttered, lowering his bow and scanning the slope ahead. The mist had thinned here, revealing a narrow path leading lower.

Nysara wiped sweat from her brow, wincing as she adjusted her grip on her batons. Her propulsion gauntlet still hung lifeless at her wrist, the damage too severe to risk mid-fight repairs. She clenched her teeth, shaking off the ache from a hundred scrapes and bruises.

"They were too spread out," she added. "They're desperate to slow us, but it almost seems like they are sizing us up."

Liam nodded grimly. "Well, I'd say they've bit off more than they can chew."

A voice echoed from the mist oozing with sarcasm.

"Yeah, we sure did…"

They all turned as another figure emerged onto the ledge below.

Harro Vorne.

His blackened robes rippled in the wind, the faint yellow pulse of Incadise woven through the threads. The splintered staff across his back throbbed with corrupted energy, and his face — half-shadowed beneath his hood — wore a cold, measured scowl.

Three Shade soldiers flanked him, each with their faces covered by the distinct Obsidian Shade helmets.

"So, you're here to give us a real challenge?" Liam mocked, sword raised.

Harro ignored him. His focus fixed on Celeste.

"A Bringer," he said. "Of course."

Celeste met his stare, her grip strong on her staff, though her pulse quickened. "And you are?"

Harro's lips curled in something close to a sneer. "Someone who learned the truth about your precious order. The hypocrisy. The lies. Tell me, *Bringer* — have they started clipping your wings yet? Telling you how to hold back? How much power you're *allowed* to wield before it makes them uncomfortable?"

Celeste's jaw tightened, but she didn't rise to the words. She quoted a well-rehearsed phrase from the early pages of the Bringer's Handbook, "Power isn't meant to be wielded without purpose, and that purpose is to serve The Everlight."

"That's exactly what they want you to believe." Harro's eyes narrowed, the pulse of Incadise along his staff brightening slightly. "Control. Restraint. They call it balance, but it's just fear, isn't it? Fear of what you could *become*."

Liam's sword lowered an inch, confusion flickering across his face. "What are you even talking about?"

Harro's eyes snapped at him. "You wouldn't understand, Envoy. Your people never do."

A tense beat hung between them.

Then Harro gestured forward, and his soldiers lunged.

The fight exploded with violence.

Liam met the first attacker head-on, his sword clashing against a wickedly curved blade. Sparks flew as his blade repelled the corrupted strike. Suddenly Liam adjusted his grip and brought the hilt of his sword down on the Shade soldier's helmet sending him stumbling backward from the pain.

Alarion's bow whirred, sending a pulse of sonic energy rippling through the air. One of the Shade soldiers staggered but pressed through, blade slicing toward him — until a baton caught the man hard across the helmet, dropping him like a stone.

"Got your back!" Nysara called, but her voice was strained, breath ragged from the effort. She barely sidestepped the next strike, pain flaring in her shoulder as she deflected the blow.

Celeste's staff met Harro's in a bright collision of blue and yellow. She twisted low, sweeping for his leg, but he caught the strike with a grunt, barely shifting under the force.

"If you want to beat me, it won't be like that," Harro hissed. He countered and his strike came down hard, nearly knocking her from her feet. "You let them weaken you."

Celeste gritted her teeth, focusing on her breathing. She countered with a burst of energy from her staff, forcing him back a step.

"If I fought like you want me to, I'd be trying to kill you!" She shot back, Harro snarled and struck again.

Meanwhile, Nysara's luck ran out.

She ducked another Shade soldier's swing, but the pain in her shoulder slowed her reaction. The blade caught her across the thigh — shallow, but deep enough to buckle her leg.

She cried out, dropping to one knee.

"Nysara!"

Liam's roar echoed as he tore across the slope, in a crazed flurry somewhere between rage and concern, the last Shade soldier standing in his path didn't stand a chance. His blade hit with a crackling pulse, sending the attacker sprawling.

Alarion quickly slid to Nysara's side, bracing her weight with his arm. "You're alright," he murmured, "They won't get through this." With his off arm he positioned his violin, braced it with his jaw, grabbed his bow, and began to play a note. Suddenly, a dome of blue encased the two of them. Alarion called out to Liam who was now barreling towards them, "I've got her, go help Celeste!"

Liam shifted his weight and found himself just a few steps from where Celeste and Harro were still going blow for blow.

With all the commotion going on, Celeste shifted her focus toward Nysara and Alarion. Harro noticed her distraction and lunged for Celeste's unguarded side.

But Liam had already made up the ground.

As his staff made it to the halfway point in its wide arch toward Celeste's side Liam's sword intercepted it. The two weapons clashed and with a strong right step Liam forced his Staff upwards.

Celeste, now refocused on the fight, saw this opening and in a fluid motion sent the base of her staff right into Harro's core.

Harro faltered. His knees buckled, his weapon clattering from his hand.

The pain from the hit had locked his limbs, the surge of Incada energy leaving him reeling in so much pain he couldn't bring himself to move. Liam stepped closer, sword angled at Harro's throat.

"Don't worry," Liam said, voice dry, "That'll wear off...eventually."

Celeste was already at Nysara's side, helping Alarion brace her weight.

"Can you walk?"

Nysara winced but nodded. "With help. Yeah."

"Then let's move. The key point's just ahead."

They left Harro where he fell, assuming they could come back for him after the conflict below had been resolved.

The descent from the mountain blurred into a haze of exhaustion and pain. The wind tore at their cloaks, carrying the bitter tang of smoke and the distant clash of steel. Nysara leaned heavily on Alarion's shoulder, her wounded leg leaving a crimson trail down the worn stone path. Celeste stayed close, her staff ready, while Liam took the lead, his sword still drawn despite the brief calm.

The battlefield opened before them as they rounded the final ridge.

The defensive line at the key point held firm — a crescent of shimmering Incada barriers arcing from left to right, guild banners fluttering in defiance of the tragic attack.

Beyond the defensive line, the Obsidian Shade stood poised in disciplined formations. Weapons drawn. Unmoving. Watching.

Liam let out a breath. "We made it."

A loud whistle echoed from the right flank as Elise caught sight of them, her eyes narrowing on Nysara's injury. She signaled with a quick motion, and almost immediately, a Weaver in pale gray robes rushed toward them, a wooden flute already drawn from her satchel.

Alarion eased Nysara to the ground near the defensive line. The Weaver knelt, her eyes soft with concern as she pressed a gentle hand to Nysara's leg.

"Stay still," the healer explained, raising the flute to her lips. A delicate, familiar melody filled the air, the notes weaving together with the soft blue glow spreading from the instrument. The music shimmered along the wound, and the blood slowed its flow as the power took hold.

"The Song of Restoration," Alarion sighed, "why didn't I think of that."

Nysara exhaled shakily. "I'm fine. Really —"

"You're not," Celeste interrupted gently, kneeling beside her. "Let her work."

The tension in the air remained thick, but there was no movement from the Shade. Not yet.

And then Roland was there.

His cloak tattered. His staff glowing faintly.

He approached them cautiously, his eyes sweeping from Liam to Celeste, then resting on Nysara, worry shadowing his face.

"You're hurt." His speech was rough, but even.

Nysara smirked, wincing as the melody continued to weave through her leg. "Yeah, well, you should see the other guy."

Silence settled awkwardly.

Roland's hand tightened on his staff. His face was pale, the exhaustion clear now that the adrenaline had ebbed. Yet his eyes held a weight beyond physical strain.

"I owe you all an apology." His voice was quieter now, raw with something close to regret. "I should have seen the patterns."

Liam's brow furrowed. "Roland, what are you —?"

"The Shade," Roland cut in. "The patterns we noticed before the tournament — the disappearances, the sabotage. They weren't accidents. They were testing us. Preparing for this." The unmoving Shade soldiers were still standing in formation. "I should have seen this coming."

Celeste shook her head. "You couldn't have known."

Roland met her eyes, guilt still clouding his thoughts. "I *should* have. And now they're here." His grip tightened around the staff. "We need to find a way to end this. Before anyone else gets hurt."

A pulse of movement stirred across the Shade's ranks. A shift. Quiet, but undeniable.

They were waiting.

For something.

At the same time, not that far out the sound of boots echoed against stone.

A squad of Obsidian Shade soldiers moved swiftly through the narrow corridors of the broadcast tower, their dark armor making them appear as shadows against the pale walls.

A low voice, calm but forceful, echoed ahead. "Sweep the next floor. No resistance yet. Move."

Doors splintered beneath the force of their boots. Offices, storage rooms, all empty. The tower's staff had either fled or been evacuated when the broadcast cut. They were close now.

Closer to the voice that had tried to reassure the kingdom.

At last, they reached the broadcast booth.

The double doors, reinforced steel, stood defiant. One soldier stepped forward, placing a gloved hand against the metal. The Incadise in his gauntlet flared with a faint hiss — and the locks twisted with a shriek as corrupted energy pulsed through them.

The door burst open.

Garrick and Lyra flinched back from the sudden intrusion, the flare of yellow light reflecting off the console screens. Garrick instinctively moved in front of Lyra, though he was unarmed.

"Wh — what is this? You can't just —"

The largest of the soldiers stepped aside as a figure strode through the broken threshold.

She removed her helmet with measured calm, her pale features framed by dark hair bound in intricate braids. The angular black sigil of the Obsidian Shade was etched into the collar of her armor, the faint pulse of Incadise threads woven through the fabric.

Lady Kaeryn Valis.

Her eyes fixed on Garrick. Cold. Calculating.

"Can't?" Her voice was a whisper, yet it carried enough weight to still the entire room. "We already have."

Kaeryn stepped forward, her soldiers spreading behind her to block every possible exit. The room felt smaller, the shadows pressing in as the distorted yellow glow played along the walls.

"This booth has been silenced for long enough." Kaeryn's tone remained calm, yet there was a lethal edge beneath it. "I want the broadcast restored. Now."

Garrick swallowed hard. "We — we're under direct orders from the Tournament Authority. We can't —"

Kaeryn's lips curled into the faintest smile.

"Can't?"

In a single, fluid motion, she pulled a small Obsidian ring from her belt. The sigil embedded in it pulsed, the Incadise casting faint tendrils of light along her fingertips as she held it aloft.

"You mistake this for a request."

Garrick's eyes flicked from the ring to the soldiers. To Lyra.

Lyra's response was barely a whisper. "Garrick..."

He exhaled shakily. Then, with a hesitant motion, his hand hovered over the console. "Restoring the feed...just don't hurt anyone."

Kaeryn gave a satisfied nod as the screens flickered back to life. One by one, the massive arena displays powered on, their light spilling out into the stands. Throughout the battlefield previously hidden screens appeared in view of the competitors. Across the kingdom, the broadcast reconnected, sending the live feed from the announcer's booth to every corner of Ileydria.

Kaeryn stepped forward, the camera lens adjusting automatically to frame her image.

She looked into the camera. And spoke.

"People of Ileydria."

The world's noise faded beneath her voice, carried through every screen, every device still linked to the network.

"You have been lied to."

The words rang cold, echoing across the arena floor where guild forces and Shade soldiers alike turned toward the screens.

"For too long, your so-called protectors have fed you falsehoods. They speak of unity. Of peace. Yet look now — your champions struggle, unprepared, because they have chosen comfort over strength. Restraint over truth."

Her expression sharpened.

"The Obsidian Shade was never your enemy. We were the guardians of power — true power — before your kings allowed it to be buried beneath laws designed to keep you weak. Your guilds have shackled you, binding strength behind layers of control so fragile it crumbles the moment it is tested."

She paused, letting the silence weigh heavy.

"And why?"

Kaeryn lifted her ring, the Incadise glow intensifying.

"Because they fear what true strength looks like. What it can become."

Kaeryn's speech lowered, almost intimate.

"The truth of your history has been erased. The line of Belaran — once the rightful heirs of this kingdom — was not lost to time. It was taken. Silenced by those who could not bear to see power held by those who *earned* it."

She spread her hands.

"The Obsidian Shade exists not as a rebellion...but as a restoration. To bring this nation and its Guilds back to their proper pursuit of strength. And since the bloodline of Belaran has been severed —"

She let the words linger.

"— I will act in its stead."

The screen cut out.

Garrick found his voice, though it came out rougher than he intended. "The barriers — you locked them down. You're keeping people from helping."

Kaeryn's eyes shifted to him, cold and measured. "I prevented chaos. Your guild members would have flooded that battlefield, turning my controlled demonstration into a massacre."

"Controlled?" Lyra's reply was ripe with disbelief. "You mean you were afraid of a fair fight."

Kaeryn let out a soft laugh, the sound cutting through the tension like a blade. "Fair? Why would I fight fair when I can fight smart?"

Garrick stepped forward, his hands clenched. "You're a coward. You talk about strength, but you made sure you wouldn't fight us at full force."

"Coward?" Kaeryn's smile was razor thin. "I accomplished exactly what I came here to do with minimal losses. That's not cowardice — that's strategy."

She turned toward the exit, her soldiers already moving to flank the doorway.

"The broadcast served its purpose. The people have heard what they needed to hear." She paused at the threshold, not bothering to look back. "What happens next depends entirely on whether they're wise enough to listen."

As fast as they arrived, Lady Kaeryn and her elite force vanished, leaving Garrick and Lyra stunned.

For a short time, there was only silence. Then with a synchronized surge the Shade soldiers recommenced their attack on the main force, and the guild lines returned to their task of holding things together.

At the center of the formation, shielded behind layers of shimmering barriers, the guild leadership had gathered. Roland, Olive, Alexander, Hadassah, and Evander stood in a tight circle, voices low and urgent as they assessed the situation. Sunniva, and other leaders remained on the front lines, leading the defensive effort as the Shade's relentless assault showed no sign of slowing.

"Something's wrong." Olive said, her staff planted beside her as she scanned the battlefield. "We all saw Kaeryn's message. That was clearly the point of this attack — her speech, her declaration. So why are they still fighting?"

Alexander's brow furrowed, blade still in hand though at rest. "Because we're still standing. If they can break the line, it doesn't matter what message she gave. They'll have proven their strength through blood."

Olive shook her head. "No. Look at them. They're not even fighting like they were before. Their tactics are messy, erratic. They're attacking without any clear objective now. This isn't a strategy — it's desperation."

She exhaled, speech quieter but just as firm. "I think they're already lost. The Incadise...it's consumed them. Twisted their minds. They're attacking because they can't stop."

A heavy silence followed.

Alexander's expression remained hard. "It doesn't matter why. If the line breaks, we will lose lives. We need a solution. Now."

Roland stepped forward, his grip tightening on his staff.

"There's a way to end this," he said quietly. "I've seen the tunnels."

Alexander's focus snapped to him. "What tunnels?"

Roland spoke quickly, urgency in his voice. "When I was taken, I was searching through a network of tunnels below the arena. They run beneath the entire complex. That's how they've been moving forces without us seeing. If we can get into those tunnels and flank them from below, we can break their formation — split their barriers and disrupt their hold long enough to end this without casualties." As he spoke, he placed his hands together and slowly pulled them apart, the map of the tunnels appeared as a hologram just as it had before his capture.

Evander crossed his arms, nodding. "Flank them from behind while the line holds strong. It could work — but how do we get down there? If there's an entrance, we haven't seen it."

Roland's gaze shifted toward the ground beneath them. "We don't need an entrance. We make one."

Hadassah, who had remained silent, stepped forward. Her face was streaked with dirt, the satchel at her side marked with burn scars from the battle. But her eyes lit with understanding.

"I can do it."

Alexander arched his brow. "You're sure?"

She nodded, tapping the satchel at her hip. "The Originators collected Incada cells at the start of Guild Wars — had to stock up to fight all of you. Some of them cracked during the fighting, unstable but still usable. I can create a controlled breach straight through the biome floor and the stone beneath it. It'll be loud, but it'll work."

Alexander exhaled. "Do it."

Hadassah knelt without further discussion, unbuckling the satchel and arranging several glowing Incada cells in a careful pattern across the stone. The cells pulsed, syncopated and sharp, as she linked them with delicate strands of conductive wire.

"Everyone back."

The group stepped away as Hadassah placed her palm against the central cell. Energy surged through the formation, the glow intensifying as the crystals reached critical resonance —

BOOM!

A blast of radiant blue light consumed the center of the key point. The floor cracked wide with a harsh, shattering sound as stone splintered and gave way. Dust billowed up from the opening, the edges glowing with residual Incada energy as the dust settled.

The tunnels lay open beneath them.

Dark. Silent. Waiting.

Before anyone could speak, a voice cut through the smoke.

"We're going."

Nysara.

She stood at the edge of the breach, her propulsion gauntlet still slightly scorched but active, the faint blue pulse of her restored energy shimmering along its surface. Her batons hung ready at her sides.

Alexander blinked. "Nysara, you just —"

"I'm fine." Her words were steady. "We've been fighting together this entire time. If you're sending a flanking team, it should be us. We've got the experience of working together. We can do this."

Alarion nodded, adjusting his grip on his violin bow. "She's right. The four of us know how to fight as one. Send us."

Liam gave a half-smile, sword resting on his shoulder. "Besides, we already took out one of their leaders coming down the mountain. Might as well rack up a few more."

Roland exhaled. "Fine. You're with me."

Alexander glanced between them, hesitating only for a moment before nodding. "Evander, you take a team down the east tunnel. Hadassah, west. Roland, center. End this."

The four nodded in unison.

Hadassah's speech was softer now as she stepped back from the breach, her face serious.

"Go quickly."

Roland met her expression with a grim nod, then turned toward the others.

"This ends, now."

13

Breaking The Siege

The tunnels seemed to breathe with the pulse of distant battle. Roland led the group, his outstretched hand holding an Incada gem that was casting pale blue light along the rough stone, shadows stretching long behind them. The air felt heavier here — thick with dampness. Somewhere above, muffled and distorted, came the dull thunder of combat. The clash of barriers flaring. The echo of voices.

They were unable to help.

Yet.

Liam followed a step behind, his sword angled low, attention sweeping the narrow corridor. Alarion next, every step measured, his violin bow drawn against the strings. Celeste kept pace beside him, staff at the ready, the faint hum of Incada steady at her fingertips.

At the rear, Nysara pressed forward, her jaw tight, face pale but determined. She favored her left leg, the deep gash from the mountainside battle still fresh beneath her pants. Her propulsion gauntlet hummed louder than usual, a sign of the quick repairs she had done to at least make it functional. Her batons drawn, the worn edges scuffed from their descent.

The silence hung like a weight for too long.

Nysara exhaled quickly. "Can we get moving? We don't have time for sneaking"

Roland kept his focus ahead, delivery even. "We flank them. Not alert them."

Nysara's steps didn't slow. "They're still winning. Our people are holding that line while we're crawling through these tunnels."

"We stay the course." Roland's tone remained calm but resolute. "Our job is to split the line. We finish this. The right way."

She fell quiet, though tension rippled in her movements — shoulders coiled, batons clenched too tightly.

The tunnel narrowed further, the shadows pressing in. Faint moisture traced the stone, the air damp and cold. The only sound was the soft scuff of boots against the rock.

A fork in the path.

Three passages.

Roland slowed, raising his staff to illuminate the divide.

"The split," he muttered, eyes narrowing as he traced the branching tunnels. "Evander's team should be left. Hadassah — right."

"Middle's ours," Liam muttered, adjusting his grip on his sword. "Let's get this done."

Roland nodded, exhaling slowly. "Stay close. No distractions."

He stepped forward, leading them into the deeper dark.

The first Shade soldier struck from the shadows.

A glint of metal. A blur of movement.

Roland caught the attack mid-swing, his staff colliding with the corrupted blade in a pulse of silver light. Sparks rippled where the Incadise met the Sentinel Shard's power, the yellow energy fracturing beneath the pure glow as the Shade staggered back.

"Contact!" Roland called.

The tunnel erupted into motion.

Liam surged forward, intercepting a second Shade soldier who lunged from the side. His blade met the attacker's with a ringing clash, the energy from his Incada core flaring bright at the point of impact. Liam's focus was razor-sharp angled steps, deflecting each strike just enough to throw his opponent off balance before driving the hilt into their side. The soldier crumpled.

Another Shade rushed from a side alcove, blade raised — A pure note from Alarion's violin cut the air, the resonance splitting into a dissonant chord that rippled outward. The shade soldier staggered, clutching his head as the vibration pulsed through his head.

"Finish it!" Alarion called, already shifting his bow for the next strike.

Celeste was there before the echo had faded. Her staff spun, striking low, and as the soldier dropped to one knee, she extended her free hand. A ripple of shimmering blue light expanded from her palm just in time to intercept a dagger flung from further down the tunnel.

The blade struck the barrier, sparking harmlessly before clattering to the ground.

"Keep the pressure up guys!" Liam shouted, adjusting his stance.

The remaining Shade soldiers circled tighter, no longer pressing the attack but standing firm, weapons raised, as if daring them forward.

Nysara's breath hitched. "We don't have time for this."

Without waiting, she raised her gauntlet and launched herself forward.

The propulsion roared to life — briefly.

A sputtering crackle.

The pulse cut out mid-lunge.

Nysara hit the ground hard, rolling into a defensive crouch as her gauntlet hissed with sparks. She grimaced, the damaged casing flickering weakly before going dark.

A Shade soldier surged toward her.

She moved.

Batons out.

The first strike came high — she ducked, sweeping low and driving a baton hard into the soldier's knee. He buckled. She shifted, twisting the second baton into his ribs with a brisk crack of energy that sent him sprawling.

Then came the next. A heavier weapon, a hammer crackling with unstable Incadise energy. Nysara didn't retreat. She pivoted — batons crossing as the hammer swung wide. She caught the shaft, redirected the momentum, and spun it from his grasp before a precise strike to his temple dropped him hard.

Her breath was ragged but measured as the last of the Shade soldiers crumpled, unconscious.

The tunnel fell silent again.

Nysara stood slowly, cradling her gauntlet, the scorch marks blackening the plating.

"That's… twice today," she muttered under her breath.

Celeste stepped closer, offering a hand to steady her. "You didn't need it."

Nysara looked back at her, lips pressing into a tight line as if she was annoyed, "Says the one who broke it in the first place."

Celeste chuckled, "Not like I knew… all this… was on its way… I was just trying to win."

Roland scanned the tunnel ahead. Quiet. For now.

"Focus, they're weakening," he said, speech low. "We keep moving. Stay sharp. If we break through here, we can reach the surface before the others."

The tunnel narrowed as they pressed forward, damp earth giving way to stone fractured by impact. The distant clash of energy above was louder now — echoing through the ground itself in rhythmic pulses.

"We're close," Roland reassured, his voice calm but taut with focus.

The path ahead widened. Cracks laced the stone, jagged fractures where the earth had split. A sliver of light cut through the dust — one of the blast sites where the Shade had torn into the arena during their initial assault.

Roland gestured for the group to slow. Liam shifted forward, sword at the ready, his breath steadying as they approached the breach.

They surfaced.

The arena sprawled before them, vast and scarred. Smoke drifted in thin ribbons from the fractured stone, mingling with the pale shimmer of Incada energy still holding the defensive lines at the key point.

Sunniva, Cobus, and Elise still commanded the front, barriers flaring blue as they deflected another wave of corrupt strikes. The guild banners still held. The formations were solid.

But the Shade were still attacking.

The soldiers pressed relentlessly, their weapons crackling with sickly yellow light. Despite their lack of coordination, they advanced — desperate. No strategy, only persistence.

"They're losing formation," Celeste whispered, brow furrowing.

"No," Alarion corrected, his eyes narrowing as he read the battlefield. "They're unraveling — but they're still fighting."

Roland's focus sharpened. Why aren't they retreating?

Then he spotted the movement — far left, near the arena's collapsed outer wall.

Another breach in the arena floor from the attack. Hadassah emerged first, her team closely behind her.

To the right, Evander's squad surfaced in formation, their weapons raised in perfect coordination.

Three teams. Three flanking angles.

The Shade was surrounded.

The ground trembled beneath their feet as Roland led the charge across the fractured stone, the roar of battle swelling louder with every step.

From the left flank, Hadassah's group kept pace, bursts of blue light flaring as her gauntlet discharged. Evander's squad mirrored the advance on the right; shields interlocked in a practiced wedge formation.

Near the fractured stone arch marking the outer ring of the key point, two Shade soldiers turned, their weapons already raised in preparation for the next assault.

They saw the teams closing in.

The first soldier's eyes widened. "What — are they flanking us? Since when —?"

"Focus," snapped the other, his gauntleted hand tightening on the hilt of his sword. The corrupted glow of Incadise pulsed along its edge, flickering with unstable energy. "Don't break. If we hold formation, the barriers will —"

"They're coming from all sides." The first soldier's voice wavered as he watched Roland's staff flare with brilliant silver light, cutting through the smoke like a beacon. "They'll split us —"

"They won't, but even if they do, we've already accomplished our mission!" the second soldier hissed. His eyes snapped toward the center of the Shade ranks, where the corrupted barriers still flickered but held.

He raised his voice above the din, calling out: "Reform the line! Close ranks — now!"

A dozen Shade soldiers shifted, their boots striking stone in unison as they pivoted, turning their weapons to face the oncoming flanking squads. Their barriers surged back to life, half facing the key point, half facing the flanking teams.

Liam yelled, "They're trying to reform! Push harder — don't give them the chance!"

Roland didn't answer — he just surged forward; the distance was closing. The key point was just ahead.

And the Shade soldiers were running out of time.

Liam's blade was first, deflecting a halberd strike with a ringing clash. He twisted, dropping low as his sword swept the attacker's leg out from under him in a single fluid motion.

Celeste moved in tandem, her staff sweeping high as a pulse of Incada energy rippled outward, forming a protective barrier that caught a second strike aimed for Nysara's exposed side.

Alarion followed, a burst of harmonic energy echoing through the air. The notes struck clear and loud — enough to stagger three Shade soldiers who recoiled, clutching their heads as the energy disrupted their focus.

Roland drove the assault forward, his staff glowing as he met the nearest barrier head-on. The pale silver light of the Sentinel Shard flared — energy slicing through the corrupted yellow shield as though peeling it apart at its source.

The Shade line buckled.

But they didn't break.

The remaining soldiers shifted, attempting to form a desperate defensive circle, their barriers flickering but holding.

"They're still fighting," Celeste chirped, speech tight with disbelief.

Roland's grip tightened on his staff; his focus fixed on the trembling soldiers.

"No." His voice was quiet but sure. "They're trying not to break."

A surge of energy — Alarion's bow sang as a pulse of harmonic force swept through the air, sending two more Shade soldiers collapsing in a daze.

To his right, Celeste's staff connected with the ground, a flare of Incada surging upward in a wide arc. The blast shattered the nearest soldier's guard, his weapon clattering from his hand as he fell with a groan.

The remaining Shade soldiers faltered.

Some dropped their weapons entirely, hands raised in silent surrender. Others, their eyes wild with the sickly yellow sheen of Incadise corruption, fought on — lunging wildly, their movements more desperate than precise.

Roland met one head-on. The corrupted soldier's blade screamed toward him, but Roland's staff intercepted with a loud crack. With a controlled twist, he redirected the strike, the pulse of his staff rippling outward in a brilliant flare. The Shade fell hard, unconscious before he hit the stone.

And just like that — It was over.

The battlefield stilled, save for the distant hum of the remaining Incada barriers and the ragged breathing of recruits holding the defensive line.

Celeste exhaled, lowering her staff as she scanned the field. Her gaze caught on another recruit, clutching his shield to his chest as he knelt beside a wounded comrade. Blood smeared his cheek, his eyes wide, distant.

She moved before thinking.

Crossing the fractured stone, Celeste knelt beside the recruit. "You're safe," she said softly, her words gentle but certain. "The fight's over. Stay with me."

The recruit blinked, his breathing soft. "I — I thought they were going to —"

"They didn't." Celeste shifted her staff, pressing a pulse of Incada energy into her wounded companion's shoulder. The blue light flared, sealing the wound enough for a healer to manage the rest. "Help's coming. You did well."

She straightened, offering the recruit her hand. He took it, trembling but steady as she guided him back toward the defensive lines where the healers were already moving through the aftermath.

When she turned back, her eyes met Roland's across the field.

He stood near the center of the ruined arena, silent as the wind tugged at his tattered cloak. His staff was still faintly aglow, yet his face — his eyes —

Haunted.

Roland looked over the battlefield, taking in the fallen Shade soldiers, the fresh cracks in the stone, the wounded recruits being tended along the lines.

They had won.

But it had been too close.

Roland felt the ache deep in his chest. The Shade had nearly shattered the line. The recruits nearly slaughtered — and he hadn't seen it coming until it was almost too late.

He clenched his staff tighter, the shard's light flickering in response.

"Never again."

The sound of footsteps drew his attention. Liam, Alarion, and Nysara were approaching, battle-worn but standing tall.

Nysara's gauntlet was sparking slightly at the wrist — damaged again — but her face was tight with frustration.

"I —" she started, voice hoarse. "I should've been better. My gear —"

Alarion cut her off gently, placing a hand on her shoulder. "Nysara. Look around. We're standing because of you. Those guys never stood a chance against what you did in those tunnels."

Liam nodded, sheathing his sword with a tired grin. "Yeah, you took out half their force before any of us even broke a sweat."

Her expression softened. "...I almost lost."

"But you didn't." Roland's reply was quieter, measured as he stepped closer. "We win together. Always."

Before she could answer, a familiar voice rang out behind them.

"Now that was the finest piece of battle coordination I've seen in years!"

Olive, the acting Bringer commander strode toward them, grinning despite the grime streaking her robes. Her staff pulsed with a warm, steady blue glow, and the sheer relief in her manner was unmistakable.

She clapped Roland firmly on the shoulder. "That was incredible. All of you. This is what the guilds were meant to be — together."

Alexander wasn't far behind, his expression calmer but no less sincere.

"Strong leadership," he added, nodding toward Roland. "But it wasn't leadership alone. Unity won the day."

The battle was over.

The wind bit harshly against the mountainside, howling through the broken crags where shattered stone bore silent witness to the earlier battle above.

Harro Vorne lay motionless against the cold earth, the pain still radiating from where Celeste's staff had struck him full in the chest. His limbs were heavy, his breaths short. The numbness from the pulse of Incada energy still burning in his system.

He forced his fingers to curl, fighting the stiffness in his muscles.

"Get up...You're not done yet."

The ache in his chest dulled as sensation slowly returned. He pressed a hand to the stone, pushing himself up. His robes were torn, the dark weave scorched and tattered, but the pulse of Incadise along the edges remained — faint threads of yellow flickering in the fabric. Proof of his strength.

Strength they refused to understand.

Harro coughed, staggering upright as his balance returned. From this height, he could see the remnants of the battle below — the guild forces celebrating, the Shade surrendered, or out cold.

They had lost.

And yet — A thin, bitter smile twisted his lips.

"You still think this was about the arena… Don't you?"

His voice was hoarse, dry as he staggered forward, speaking aloud into the empty wind as if daring the mountain itself to listen.

"You're celebrating already, aren't you? Calling it a victory. Here come the speeches about the noble sacrifices…" He spat the words.

"You never even realized…You weren't the ones being tested."

His breath slowed as he braced a hand against his knees, forcing himself to stand fully. The sensation of pain was fading now, the aftershocks of the Incada pulse finally receding. His body was whole. Stronger than it should be.

That was the norm with the tournament weapons, simply simulated pain. Nothing more.

"Do you think we lost? Do you really think a hundred or so fighters collapsing in your precious arena was the end?"

He laughed, the sound echoing hollowly against the cliffs.

"This was never a battle. It was a stage."

His eyes shifted toward the announcer's box.

"They never asked why we didn't retreat," he muttered. "Why so many fought past the pain. Past reason."

The answer was obvious.

"Because we needed them to see."

The memory of Kaeryn's words echoed in his mind, as clear as when he had heard it through the arena's broadcast feed.

"You have been lied to."

She had spoken every word perfectly, just as planned.

"None of this was for you." Harro whispered. "It was for them. For the people. Let the kingdom see The Shade. Let them see the cracks in their protectors. Let them wonder if maybe — just maybe — she was right."

Another bitter chuckle escaped him, quieter this time.

"And now, the Shade fighters left behind will be captured. Hauled off in chains. You'll think they are done. But they'll be watching. Listening. Spreading our truth to anyone who will listen."

His hands clenched into fists.

"And the ones you believe Incadise consumed?" His lip curled. "It was real. Wasn't it? So, you'll try to heal them, recover their minds, you might even think you've cured them and let them loose. I wonder what they will do next?"

A gust of wind tore at his cloak, but Harro only stared downward. The real damage had already been done.

Kaeryn's words would echo in the hearts of the kingdom long after today.

And now — now he had to find her.

His grip tightened on his broken staff,

"I'm coming, my Lady," he whispered. Then he turned, retreating into the misted trails exiting the arena, leaving only silence where he had fallen.

Three months had passed since the attack on the tournament now being referred to as the resurgence.

Liam woke to the ache in his shoulders first. A deep, satisfying burn — a reminder of the joint training session the day before.

He blinked against the early morning light filtering through the narrow window of his quarters in the Envoy barracks, the pale glow of the Incada sconces set to their dimmest setting. The scent of polish and oiled leather lingered in the air; his uniform folded neatly on the stool beside his bunk.

"Bringers hit a lot harder than I give them credit for," he thought, letting out a chuckle.

Liam shifted, wincing as he rolled his neck, the tension from yesterday's session settling like iron bands across his back. Still, a faint grin pulled at his lips. He could already hear the early stirrings from the training yard below — clashing practice blades, shouted drills, the rhythm of practice in full swing.

It was different now. Everything was.

Three months since the resurgence. Three months since the attack of the Obsidian Shade.

The arena had been restored faster than Liam thought possible — its broken biomes and the eerie tunnels below repaired with layers of fresh Incada-weave reinforcing the structures. From the outside, it looked whole again.

But the city wasn't the same.

He'd seen it during his patrols. The tension in the air. The way crowds listened just a bit longer to the guild leaders' speeches. The way guards were stationed near public gatherings, their eyes watchful.

Rumors spread quietly, despite the council's best efforts. Stories of Shade activity popping up in the outer villages. Reports of strange symbols burned into buildings near Nerol.

And people listened to Kaeryn.

Liam exhaled, pushing himself up from the cot. His uniform felt heavier these days, even when it wasn't on his shoulders.

Outside, the city was healing — but not whole.

He tugged his boots on, shaking off the morning stiffness. No time for brooding. They were still standing. Still fighting.

And so was his team.

Celeste had been the hardest to read since the battle. She kept busy — throwing herself into volunteer work with the Bringers' training initiative, often staying late into the evening to mentor new recruits. She was stronger. Sharper. But quieter, too.

Nysara, at least, had been easier to keep track of. The Originators had her focused in a workshop since the battle ended, using her experience in the tunnels as a way to refine new portable propulsion prototypes. Liam had checked in a week ago and found her hunched over a half-disassembled gauntlet, sparks flying as she muttered something about recoil dampening ratios.

And Alarion — Liam couldn't help but grin. Alarion was everywhere.

Songs of Restoration during public gatherings. Ceremonies for the rebuilt sectors of the arena. A duet with the High Weaver Ava herself just last week. His music had become a symbol of recovery for the city. Liam knew it wasn't just the performances, though. Alarion didn't just play to entertain. He played to make people feel whole again.

The thought was heavy but reassuring. "The fight for Alarion won't be over until Ileydria is whole again."

Liam strapped on his belt, fingers brushing the hilt of his practice blade. Another day. Another step forward.

As he stepped out of his quarters he nearly stepped over the letter. He squinted down at the envelope lying on the floor just inside his door. No seal. No markings except his name, inked with deliberate precision.

Frowning, he bent to pick it up and broke the seal. The parchment was heavy, official, though the message inside was short.

"Liam Valoria, you are summoned to the royal palace at midday. Speak of this to no one. The matter is of the utmost importance."

Signed King Ryune.

Liam read it again.

And a third time, just to be sure.

"Okay...definitely not a prank."

He sat back down on the edge of his bed, running a hand through his hair as his mind started racing.

"The palace?" He thought.

Since the battle, he'd seen guild leadership a handful of times. Mostly Alexander giving loud, dramatic speeches about "the bravery of the tournament champions" while half the recruits cheered and the other half tried to avoid eye contact with Roland's unending serious stares.

But the King?

Midday. That gave him hours, but no answers.

Why keep it secret?

The city still bustled, but the usual hum of daily life felt...off. Guards had doubled at the guild halls, and more than once, he'd heard hushed whispers in the market about the Shade's message.

And yet, no one had seen Lady Kaeryn since the broadcast.

The palace was quieter than he expected, he had never been there but anticipated every day here to be like the grandiose fanfare that was the Guild ceremony on the day of his assessment test.

He adjusted his collar, trying not to fidget as the great double doors ahead loomed closer.

Whatever this was, it felt… heavier than the celebrations that had followed the battle.

A meeting with the king.

And no explanation why.

Liam swallowed, pressing his palm flat against the cool wooden door. It swung inward without resistance.

The chamber beyond was a stark contrast to the ornate corridors. Functional. Quiet. Stone walls reinforced with heavy pillars, the long table set beneath a single banner displaying the royal sigil intertwined with the guild crests. Incada lanterns hung evenly along the walls, their glow illuminating the faces already gathered.

Alexander. Ava. Roland. Bella.

And King Ryune himself, standing near the head of the table, hands folded behind his back.

But what caught Liam's attention first —

"About time!"

Liam blinked as Nysara grinned at him from her seat near the middle of the table, one leg kicked up lazily over the chair beside her clearly meant for him. "We were starting to think you got lost. Or maybe overslept. Again."

Alarion smirked from his place next to the vacant chair, arms crossed with his violin case slung at his side. "Could've at least brought breakfast."

Liam scoffed, but the tension in his chest eased just a little. "Right. Next time I'm summoned by the king, I'll be sure to bring you pastries."

"You'd better," Celeste added softly from where she stood on the far end of the table, her staff resting across her back. Her eyes were warm despite the teasing edge. As Liam settled into the seat left open between Nysara and Alarion, he realized —

It was the first time all four of them had been together since the battle.

King Ryune seemed to notice the shift, his expression softening. For a long, weighted moment, he studied the four of them before speaking.

"Reunited at last."

The words, though quiet, carried a weight that silenced the room.

"I wanted to see you together again — not simply as warriors, but as friends. You accomplished more that day than most could ever hope to achieve."

He paused.

"But I did not call you here merely to reminisce."

The king's hands folded behind his back, the soft glow of the light catching in the pale streaks of his silver hair.

"Three months have passed since the resurgence. Since Lady Kaeryn's message to the kingdom. And while your victory resulted in peace here… that peace is unraveling."

A shift of tension rippled through the room.

Alexander was the first to speak. "Sire, the arena has been secured. The Shade has been scattered. We've doubled guard shifts in the capital districts —"

"And yet," Ryune cut in gently, "disturbances persist. Reports of splinter groups operating in the border towns. Recruits disappearing. Symbols appearing on the doors of old guild halls. And, most troubling of all —"

He stepped back, gesturing toward the table. A shimmering projection flared to life in the center, the crest of Nerol, a northern province, glowing faintly.

"Rumors. That Kaeryn herself was seen near Nerol, rallying those who would listen to her cause."

Silence.

Liam exchanged a glance with Nysara, her face pale beneath the steady blue glow of the map.

It was Alarion who finally broke the silence, his manner even quieter than usual. "You think she's still recruiting. Even after… everything?"

Ryune nodded. "Her words were chosen carefully. Calculated to divide the hearts of our people. Some have begun to listen."

Roland spoke then, his voice carrying that same calm, measured authority it always had. "Then you're planning a countercampaign."

"Yes," Ryune confirmed. "But not with soldiers. Not with force alone. Which is why you are here."

The king turned to fully face the four of them.

"This mission requires not just skill, but trust. Tact. The ability to understand not only the danger we face, but the people drawn to it."

He gestured toward them as a whole.

"You four are living proof that unity between the guilds is our strongest weapon — stronger than any barrier the Shade can conjure. That is why you will take on this mission. Together."

Nysara blinked. "Wait… us? We're first-years."

"You were." Roland spoke up from the other side of the room, stepping forward. His eyes were focused on hers. "But no longer. You've proven yourselves in both battle and restraint. You are ready."

King Ryune nodded.

"You will seek out what the rumors are calling Shade Covens — neutralize their threat where possible, but without lethal force. If the people can be saved… bring them back to The Everlight. They are still Ileydrians. Still our people."

Celeste shifted, her speech low. "And if they can't?"

The king's expression hardened.

"Then you will ensure they can do no further harm by bringing them here to be jailed."

The words hung in the air. Heavy.

Liam swallowed hard but nodded. "And Kaeryn? What if she —"

"That," Ryune interrupted softly, "is the other reason I have chosen you."

The map projection shifted. A new image flared into focus — the ancient seal of House Valis, fragmented and distorted.

"Kaeryn claims to be a descendant of General Moryn Valis. If true, it would change everything we know about the events directly following Lord Balaran's demise."

Alexander's jaw tightened. "You need proof."

"Yes. And I trust they will find it."

The king stepped back, voice lowering with finality.

"You leave at dawn."

The palace doors closed behind them with a deep, resonant thud, the sound echoing briefly across the courtyard. The afternoon was calm, the pale glow of the Incada sconces lining the stone walls casting soft pools of light across the polished marble paths.

For a moment, none of them spoke.

The weight of the mission pressed heavily on their shoulders, heavier even than it had felt inside the king's chambers. Out here, in the cool evening air, the reality of it settled in — quiet, undeniable.

Liam was the first to break the silence. He exhaled, adjusting his belt before glancing around at the others with a halfhearted grin.

"So… no pressure, huh?"

Celeste shot him a flat look, though the corner of her mouth twitched. "Yes, Liam. Sent on a kingdom-wide mission with the fate of Ileydria hanging in the balance. Completely casual."

Nysara crossed her arms, a smile breaking on what was moments ago a strangely serious look. "We've got this, guys, and who would have thought just a short while back we would be setting out as The King's Elite Task Force!"

Liam Laughed, "Did you just make that up? Because I don't remember him calling us that."

"I mean we are pretty good…" Celeste jested back with a wink.

Silence stretched again. Only the soft rustle of the banners in the wind remained.

Alarion, standing slightly apart from the group, tilted his head back, focusing on the guild banners, all untouched. But for how long?

"This line we're walking…" His speech was softer, uncertain. "It's thin, isn't it? One step too far, and we risk becoming the thing we're trying to stop." He lowered his gaze, meeting theirs. "We all saw how they fought. The corruption. The fanaticism. How do we make sure we don't become the same?"

Celeste didn't answer right away. She let the silence settle, the weight of his words as real as the task ahead. When she finally spoke, it was quiet, measured.

"We don't seek power," she said. Her hand brushed the worn length of her staff, "We do what we do for the good of Ileydria and the will of The Everlight."

Nysara nodded slowly, "And we do it together."

Liam sighed, rolling his shoulders before giving a more genuine smile. "Well then. Guess we better not screw it up."

They all shared a quiet laugh, even Alarion, though his expression remained distant.

From the palace gates, the city stretched out below them — lights twinkling in the distance, the glowing skyline of buildings blocking out the afternoon sun, the marketplace quiet as shops began closing for the day. On the surface, everything seemed normal again.

But it wasn't.

The Obsidian Shade was still out there. Lady Kaeryn was still out there. And somewhere in the shadows, more of The Shade — misguided or worse — still believed they were right.

Celeste's grip tightened slightly on her staff.

They would make things right.

Together.

Glossary

Places

Aldintine - Southern settlement housing the main headquarters for the Bringers Guild, featuring a massive central spire as its primary landmark.

Bringer Dungeon - Underground storage facility beneath the guild complex where corrupted Obsidian Shade artifacts are contained behind protective barriers.

Combat Arena - Stone platform arena designed for precision one-on-one duels with clearly marked Incada boundary lines.

Duriel Arena - Grand tournament venue named after King Duriel, featuring towering columns and gilded carvings depicting the kingdom's restoration.

Grand Arena - Massive competition space with changeable terrain and biomes, capable of simulating forests, deserts, mountains, and other environments.

Ileydria - The kingdom founded by the Ildini people after their pact with The Everlight, ruled for over 1,000 years in peace.

Lestin - Western settlement near Ebonwood Forest, serving as the main headquarters for the Envoys Guild.

Nerol - Northeastern province where Obsidian Shade activity has been reported.

Storage Facility Three - Guild supply depot that was robbed, leading to the discovery of organized theft patterns.

Torvain - Western settlement near mountainous terrain, serving as the main headquarters for the Originators Guild.

Veyora - Northwestern settlement with forested surroundings, serving as the main headquarters for the Weavers Guild.

People & Groups

Alexander - General and leader of the Envoys Guild, known for his commanding presence and authoritative leadership.

Ava - Leader of the Weavers Guild, a household name across the kingdom renowned for her charm and artistic talent.

Bella - Mastermind and leader of the Originators Guild, brilliant and calculated with occasional quirky tendencies.

Bringers - One of the four great guilds, composed of scholars, strategists, and mystics who serve as spiritual guides and keepers of wisdom. Colors: violet/purple.

Envoys - One of the four great guilds, composed of soldiers, fighters, and athletes who protect the kingdom. Colors: golden/yellow.

The Everlight - Ancient divine/mystical force that guides the kingdom, source of wisdom and power, accessible through meditation and righteous action.

Ildini - The original people who encountered The Everlight and founded the kingdom of Ileydria. The royal bloodline and some advisors are the last living Ildini.

King Ryune - Current ruler of Ileydria, grandson of King Duriel, who began ruling at age 50 and is now 170+ years old. Divided the Sentinel Armor into 400 shards.

Lady Kaeryn Valis - Leader of the modern Obsidian Shade, claims to be descended from General Moryn Valis and seeks to restore "true power" to the kingdom.

Lord Belaran - Ancient Ildini leader who betrayed The Everlight, created the corrupted Incadise, and led the original Obsidian Shade before being defeated by King Duriel.

Obsidian Shade - Corrupted army originally led by Lord Belaran, recently reformed under Lady Kaeryn Valis using Incadise corruption.

Originators - One of the four great guilds, composed of innovators, inventors, and engineers who advance the kingdom's technology. Colors: slate blue.

Roland - Arch-Bringer and leader of the Bringers Guild, regal and philosophical figure who commands respect and serves as spiritual guide.

Weavers - One of the four great guilds, composed of artists, storytellers, and performers who inspire and support through creativity. Colors: crimson/red.

Items & Technology

Challengers of the Realm Tournament - Annual celebration and competition established by King Ryune to test unity, skills, and prevent complacency among the guilds.

Incada - Pure blue luminescent stone that serves as the kingdom's primary energy source. Mined throughout Ileydria and refined every seven years under Everlight guidance.

Incada Cells - Crystalline storage devices containing processed Incada energy, available in various sizes for different applications.

Incadise - Corrupted yellow form of Incada that grants immediate power but causes long-term mental deterioration and madness. Used by the Obsidian Shade.

Rotating Incada Cells - Nysara's revolutionary invention featuring dynamic energy cycling cores that potentially triple the capacity of standard cells.

Sentinel Armor - Original artifact worn by King Duriel to defeat Lord Belaran, later divided by King Ryune into 400 individual shards.

Sentinel Shards - 400 fragments of the original Sentinel Armor, each containing unique powers. Distributed among the most deserving guild members across all four guilds.

Concepts & Abilities

Assessment - Guild entrance examination that tests character under pressure rather than just skill, designed to push recruits to their breaking points.

Attunement - Process of bonding with a Sentinel Shard over weeks of gradual exposure; dangerous for untrained users.

Phalanx Formation - Shield wall tactical formation emphasizing unity and mutual protection, core to Envoy training.

Song of Restoration - Weaver healing technique using musical magic to treat wounds and injuries.

The Resurgence - Term used to describe the Obsidian Shade's attack on the tournament, marking their return after 1,000 years.

Locations Beyond the Capital

Ebonwood Forest - Large forested region west/southwest of the capital, near Lestin.

Gilded Desert - Western desert region where Torvain is located.

Hestin's Pass - Mountain pass in the far north, likely a strategic border crossing.

Ileydrian Wilds - Vast wilderness area in the southern part of the kingdom.

Uldrian - An eastern settlement known for its farmlands where most of the kingdom's crops are grown.

Map Of Ileydria:

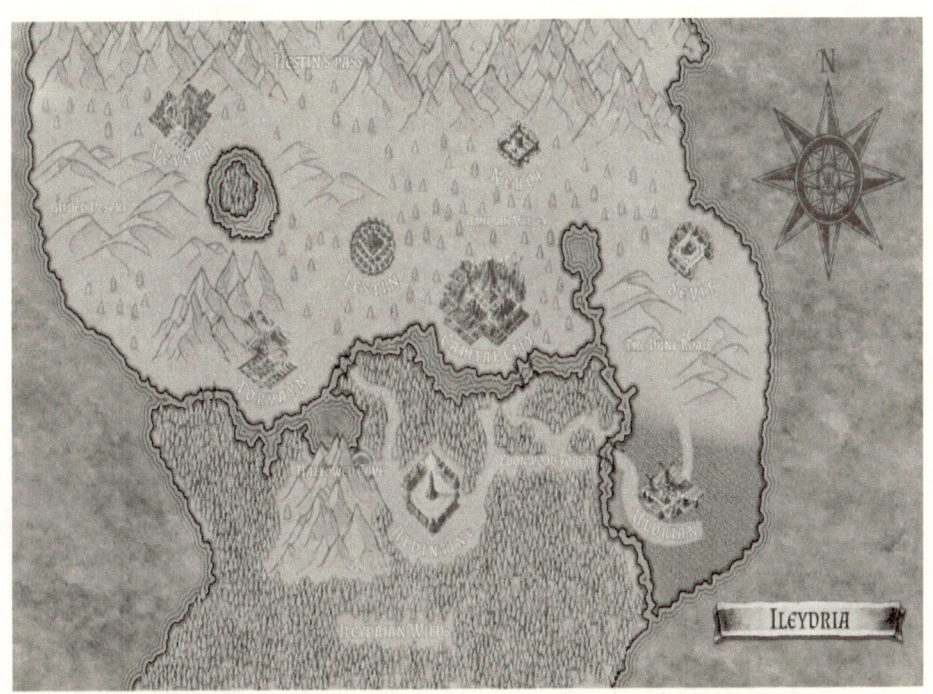

Ready to wield the power of Incada yourself?

Your journey through Ileydria doesn't end with the final page. Step into the arena as a Guild Commander in *Challengers of the Realm: The Trading Card Game*, where you'll build your own deck of Heroes, Tools, Banners, Instants, and Locations to face off against friends in strategic battles. Will you lead the disciplined Envoys, the innovative Originators, the inspiring Weavers, or the wise Bringers? Master the same energy system that powers Liam's sword, Nysara's gadgets, Alarion's illusions, and Celeste's barriers as you deploy recruits to key positions and unleash devastating combination attacks. With multiple formats including 1v1 Duels and epic four-player Guild Wars, every match becomes your own Challengers Tournament. The cards you hold contain the same Incada energy that flows through the pages you just read — now it's time to command it yourself.

Visit challengersoftherealm.com to begin your ascension.